# IN
# THE
# FRAME

IN THE FRAME

# IN THE FRAME

*A Rosedale Investigation*

# LYN FARRELL

**CAVEL
PRESS**

Kenmore, WA

# CAMEL PRESS

A Camel Press book published by Epicenter Press

Epicenter Press
6524 NE 181st St.
Suite 2
Kenmore, WA 98028

For more information go to:
www.Camelpress.com
www.Coffeetownpress.com
www.Epicenterpress.com
www.lynfarrell.com

Cover design by Scott Book
Interior design by Melissa Vail Coffman

In the Frame
Copyright © 2023 by Lyn Farrell

ISBN: 978-1-68492-037-2 (Trade Paper)
ISBN: 978-1-68492-038-9 (eBook)

Printed in the United States of America

**For Shauna**

*Who knows me well and loves me anyway.*
*Keep your face to the sunshine, Sweetheart,*
*& all your shadows will be behind you.*

Definition of Phrase "In the Frame"

*In police parlance, if a person is "in the frame"
they are suspected of a crime.*

# ACKNOWLEDGMENTS

I WISH TO ACKNOWLEDGE MY SON-IN-LAW, Dr. Robert Stuart, who provides the medical expertise for all my books. He's amazingly knowledgeable, having worked as a physician in Emergency Medicine for decades before becoming Chief Medical Officer for Aurora Health Care.

In addition, I want to thank the MSU Creative Writer's group who have been my supporters for years. My family, especially my daughters, Linda, Jacquie, Lisa and Shauna always read and comment insightfully on my books. This manuscript has been copy edited by Micah Walker, a young friend of our family, and a talented and tactful editor. Because I suffer from impatience and a slight case of ADD, one of the members of the MSU Group, Linda Nuttall, checked the final line edit. And Becky Weiser, Curator of the Hagen History Center provided information about the insurance and security of the art collections in Erie, Pennsylvania.

Lastly, I must commend the patience and support of my publisher and Executive Editor, Jennifer McCord and my publisher, Phil Garrett. I would not be a published author without them.

First recorded as published in 1838,
"Monday's Child" is a fortune-telling rhyme
that predicts a child's future, based on
the day of the week they were born.

"*Monday's child is fair of face,*

*Tuesday's child is full of grace,*

*Wednesday's child is full of woe,*

*Thursday's child has far to go,*

*Friday's child is loving and giving,*

*Saturday's child works hard for a living*

*But the child who is born on the Sabbath day*

*Is bonny and blithe and good and gay.*"

# ONE

Dark-eyed Billy Jo Bradley, the youngest member of the Rosedale Investigations team, was preparing to make a dramatic entrance. She lived in the upstairs apartment of the house that had been converted to the offices of Rosedale Investigations, a private investigator business. The CEO of the business, Detective PD Pascoe, had offered her a job as the computer analyst for the agency and a free apartment several years previously. PD and Billy Jo's grandfather, Aaron, were friends from their days as soldiers in Viet Nam. When Aaron lay dying, he made PD promise to take care of his granddaughter. He had honored his promise.

Billy Jo glanced out her window that overlooked the back yard. It was June and the bright pink and red peonies were at their peak. She turned to look at herself in her full-length mirror critically, noting the nicely tailored teal suit, black heels and nylons. The edging of a severe white blouse peeked out at the neckline and cuffs. She gathered up her long curly hair and tucked it into a wide silver barrette at the base of her neck. A tendril of dark hair curled forward on either side of her face. She quickly tucked them behind her ears. Although she rarely wore makeup, she touched her lips with a tinted lip gloss and added a shiny mascara to her eyelashes.

A quick glance at her cell phone told her she was already fifteen minutes late for the weekly case review going on in the conference room downstairs. Her phone buzzed and she saw a text from Sylvia Walcott. She said she would be there shortly and was bringing the painting. Billy Jo sent back a smiley face. Then she sat down on her bed, picked up her laptop computer and opened the power point presentation summarizing her argument to serve as point person on the investigation into the painting that belonged to Sylvia's grandmother.

It would take her another few minutes to review her presentation, but the team would just have to wait until it was exactly right. Her future in the private detective agency—and even beyond—depended on it.

IN THE MAIN FLOOR MEETING ROOM, PD PASCOE drummed his fingers on the conference table. "What the hell is keeping that girl?" he said, his voice sounding decidedly irritated. "She knows that we were going to discuss the painting this morning."

Detective PD Pascoe, the CEO of the Rosedale Investigations firm, wore a plain dark suit and thin tie that morning. Dory Clarkson, the agency's investigator, had teased him about his outfit earlier saying the suit was "a bit sad" and that it made him look like an FBI agent. In the world of local cops it was an outrageous insult. FBI agents were considered to be plodders whose disdain for local law enforcement was well known and deeply resented. *He really needed to unlock his wallet and buy a new suit*, she had told him.

"I'm sure Billy Jo will be down shortly," Dory said soothingly. An older African American woman, this morning she was wearing a black sarong dress with silver jewelry and pewter high heels. Dory had joined Rosedale Investigations upon her retirement from the Sheriff's office two years earlier, having worked there since she was seventeen.

PD gave an exasperated grunt. He expected the team to be prompt on case review days. "While we're waiting, you may as well give all of us an update on your stake-out, Dory," he said.

"Once Billy Jo arrives, we need to talk about our missing person's case, too," Wayne Nichols said.

Detective Wayne Nichols, also formerly of the Rosedale Sheriff's office, was casually dressed in slacks and a sport shirt. He had salt and pepper hair, high cheekbones and intense hazel eyes. His skin tone was reddish, reflecting his Native American ancestry. Now sixty, Wayne was well past the age at which people usually marry, but he and Lucy Ingram, M.D. were tying the knot at the end of the summer.

"Go ahead, Dory," PD said impatiently. "Don't want to waste the whole morning."

"As you know, I have been surveilling Mrs. Wade Armstrong for almost a week now. To remind you of the specifics, her husband came to us asking if we would investigate whether his wife Lydia was having an affair, an affair he suspected was with his *brother*."

"I recall that they had a pre-nup and if they divorced, she would get a minimal settlement. Wasn't there a wealthy father who was elderly? And hadn't he put pressure on the couple to produce an heir?" Wayne asked.

"That's right. Anyway, I was sitting in my car outside their expensive home last night around ten p.m. when the front door opened and I saw Lydia's slender figure silhouetted against the rectangle of light. She came down the sidewalk and walked right up to my car." Dory chuckled. "I opened the car window, prepared to come up with some dopey on-the-spot explanation of what I was doing there, but she immediately asked if I wanted to come inside and have a cup of coffee."

"Lordy, Pete," PD said. "What did you do?"

"What could I do? I said 'yes' and we went inside. Her husband was out-of-town on business and she introduced me to his brother, Phil. I figured I'd been presented with the ideal opportunity to observe the body language of the couple and could probably tell by their behavior whether the husband's suspicions were correct."

"What did you see?" Wayne asked.

"I didn't really have time to observe anything because Lydia told me right off the bat that she knew her husband suspected her of having an affair with Phil. I looked right at him and asked him directly if they were sleeping together. Her murmured something like, *I wish.* Then Lydia scooped a small box out of the trash. It was a pregnancy kit. She had just taken the test and learned it was positive. She was planning a small celebration with her husband when he got home."

"Did you leave then?" PD asked.

"No. I asked if I could speak with her alone and Phil left the room. The woman knew what I was going to ask and confessed she had been *prepared* to sleep with Phil in order to conceive, because her husband had a low sperm count."

"She told you that? God, the things women tell each other," PD said, shaking his head.

"To continue . . . she said the affair hadn't been necessary. The baby was Wade's and once her husband's father heard the news, he had promised to rewrite his will in the child's favor. If she hadn't produced a child by the time the old man died, her husband would have been disinherited and all the money would have gone to Phil."

"I wonder if she told you the truth, Dory. She could have been sleeping with her husband and his brother," Wayne said. Decades of work in law enforcement had given him a deeply suspicious mind.

"Agreed, but since both of them denied the relationship, I think our job here is done," Dory said.

"I agree. Send Mr. Armstrong your report and add another five thousand dollars to his bill, please. With such a good outcome, I doubt he'll even notice," PD said.

Dory rose and went over to the sideboard. The scent of good coffee permeated the room as she topped up everyone's cups. She smiled at her partners, thinking how well things had worked out for all of them.

In the years the four of them had worked together, the Rosedale Investigations team had become a family. PD had become Billy Jo's grandfather. When he tracked her down after her grandfather Aaron died, she was waiting table and in such dire staits that she was living in her car. Since joining Rosedale Investigations she had become a computer whiz, very adept at preparing backgrounds on their clients. She had often tried to take on more responsibility, but was blocked by PD as being too young and inexperienced.

Dory had become Billy Jo's surrogate mother—her actual mother having passed away from ovarian cancer several years earlier. Seeing them side-by-side, anyone would have been surprised to learn about their relationship as the two women looked about a different as was possible for two human beings to look. Billy Jo was Caucasian, weighed about a hundred pounds soaking wet, and preferred to dress in midriff-skimming tie-died tops and ripped blue jeans—when she wasn't wearing pajamas. Dory had a warm golden complexion and her hair was usually done in a complicated braided style. She was always fashionably dressed and although she should have lost forty pounds, she preferred to describe herself as "voluptuous and well-nourished." Dory nagged Billy Jo about her unprofessional outfits and lack of footwear. Billy Jo teased Dory about being a "fashion Nazi". They adored each other.

Detective Wayne Nichols had, to Billy Jo's surprise, become the doting father of the girl. When Wayne joined the agency, she feared he would be critical of her, as she was young and hadn't had any police training. In fact, the opposite had happened and Wayne was often her sole supporter when she offered to do more advanced investigations. At the time of his engagement to Lucy, Wayne confessed to his lovely fiancé that he had always wanted to be a father. Billy Jo had fulfilled that long-dormant hope.

"I HEAR BILLY JO COMING DOWN the hall now," Wayne said. The door to the conference room opened and the beautifully-dressed young woman walked in.

"Good morning, everyone," she said. The team looked at her in stunned silence. Despite Dory's nagging, she often came down to staff meetings barefoot and in pajamas. PD was open-mouthed. Wayne grinned and Dory applauded.

Wayne was the first to comment on Billy Jo's appearance saying, "Very nice outfit. May I ask the reason for your dressing so professionally this morning?"

"Yes, do tell," Dory said, grinning. "PD, shut your mouth. Stop gawping at the girl."

Billy Jo walked to the head of the table and set her laptop computer down. "I have a presentation to make this morning and a request. While we rarely have a formal lead investigator on our cases, I am asking for an exception. I want to serve as the point person doing the research on the painting inherited by Mrs. Georgia Walcott."

Just then a movement outside the conference room window caught her eye and she saw a young woman walking up the sidewalk. The girl was struggling to control a large square package in the summer wind. *Perfect timing*, Billy Jo thought.

"Please tell me you aren't persisting in wanting to investigate that damn painting. Doing historical art investigation is decidedly *not* in our wheelhouse," PD said.

He was right. She knew he was. Rosedale Investigations focused primarily on missing persons, documentation of infidelity and finding lost property, as well as collaborating with the Sheriff's office when they were faced with major crimes.

"I am," she said calmly. At that moment the team heard the front doorbell ring and Billy Jo left to answer the summons. She opened the door to a pretty young woman around her age, a blonde, dressed in a stylish red cloche hat, black trench coat and heels.

"I'm Sylvia. Can I come in?" She had a large flat package wrapped in brown paper and sealed with masking tape in her arms.

"Of course. Please do. Here, let me help you with that," Billy Jo said, reaching for the package. The other members of the team had left the conference room and assembled around Billy Jo's desk. They were all looking on curiously.

"It's the damn painting," PD whispered to Wayne who nodded.

THE PREVIOUS AUTUMN, AN ELDERLY WOMAN named Georgia Walcott had contacted the business. She had inherited an oil painting of children playing on the beach from a distant relative and wanted to know its provenance. None of the senior team thought Rosedale Investigations was the right entity to determine either the history of the painting or whether the painting had ever been stolen, which was Mrs. Walcott's major concern.

Billy Jo subsequently contacted the University's Art Department and referred Mrs. Walcott to a faculty member whose staff did professional art restoration. It took nine months, but the lakeside painting of three children had since been cleaned and fully restored. Mrs. Walcott then returned to Rosedale Investigations and asked if they would do the provenance. A vote was taken as to whether the business should take on the case. Billy Jo was outvoted three to one, despite presenting what she thought was a persuasive argument. It hadn't helped that Mrs. Walcott was an elderly widow on a small pension. PD said even if they took the case, it was unlikely to earn the business much money.

Sylvia Walcott, Mrs. Walcott's granddaughter who did estate valuations, had recently moved in with her grandmother, and was promised the painting as her inheritance. Billy Jo and Sylvia had corresponded by email and text. When Sylvia offered to bring the painting to their premises, Billy Jo (unbeknownst to her employer) had approved the visit.

"Shall I remove the wrapping?" Sylvia asked and Billy Jo nodded. The room grew silent except for the sounds of masking tape being pulled off and brown wrapping paper unfolded. Up to that moment, Billy Jo's only sight of the painting had been in miniature pictures taken on Sylvia's cell phone. They certainly had not done it justice. The painting compelled the viewer. The bright breezy day, the three barefoot children dressed in bathing suits and playing in the white capped waves virtually sprang to life. Billy Jo could almost smell the summer air and feel the wind on her face. She wanted to walk into that long-ago blissful childhood, the likes of which she had never experienced.

"Do you like it? Sylvia asked.

*Like it?* A stunned Billy Jo could only nod and swallow. Dory walked forward to see the point of contention more closely. Looking at it for a long moment, she turned back to her male partners and said, "I want to change my vote."

After Sylvia left, having provided the business a payment of $3000 toward the research, if they would agree to do the provenance, Billy Jo took the team through her presentation. An hour later they were still deadlocked. The vote was now two to two, but she could tell from PD's expression that he was starting to give in. While Dory reiterated some of her points, Billy Jo quickly texted the instructor of her "Art and the Law" class (she was enrolled in the criminal justice program at the University of Tennessee). He approved her researching the painting and writing up her findings as her capstone project in the class. She told the team about his approval, failing to suppress a grin.

Since starting the class, Billy Jo had spent hours searching the National Stolen Art database. One of the visiting lecturers told the students that some of the most valuable paintings in history, often stolen from museums, were now in private and likely criminal hands. Thinking of becoming an art theft investigator, Billy Jo saw herself surrounded by a swirl of dark-suited handsome young FBI agents who were stunned by her in-depth knowledge of the art world. In her fantasy, all the young men wanted to date her. She refused them all with a gracious wave of her wrist, adorned with an antique diamond bangle, a gift from a grateful client.

"Okay, okay, but we need to move on now," PD said sounding irked.

"Hold on a minute, PD. Has Billy Jo received your permission to take the lead on the investigation into the artwork?" Wayne asked.

"Two weeks," PD said, looking harassed and running his hands through his thinning white hair. "I'm only approving you working on this for the next two weeks, and if an active case needs a computer background during that time, you will attend to your regular work before looking into this ridiculous waste of time."

"Thank you, thank you, thank you," Billy Jo rose from her chair and reached out to hug him. He shook her off. Shortly thereafter, the two men left the building.

"Did our colleagues look a bit nervous to you?" Dory asked as the door slammed shut behind them.

"Wayne did. PD just looked irritable, as usual. He has been a real Crabby Patty lately. Where were they going anyway?"

"Over to the hospital to get vaccinated. At least PD is, don't know about Wayne."

"I have the file Sylvia received on the work done by the University's Art department. Let's go thru it," Billy Jo said.

She set the file down on the conference table and pulled out the report. The research document included a detailed description of the painting listing the dimensions, (38" X 42") the materials used, (oil on canvas) the framing, (wooden gold-leaf frame over stretcher bars) and a verbal description. The artist had painted the number '20' in the bottom right-hand corner above his signature.

For a moment Billy Jo was confused, thinking the work might have been done in 2020. *No*, she realized, *the artist meant 1920, not 2020.* The painting was more than a century old. The artwork had been done by Jeremy Iverson-Jones and had an estimated value of $50,000. The report quoted Mrs. Walcott as saying the title for the painting was Wednesday's Child.

The words struck a faint chord in Billy Jo's memory. "Dory, do you remember an old nursery rhyme with those words? The one that starts, '*Monday's child was fair of face, Tuesday's child was full of grace, Wednesday's child was . . .*'. Sorry, I can't remember the rest. What was Wednesday's child?" Billy Jo asked.

"Wednesday's child was full of woe," Dory said and the two women frowned at each other as silence captured the room and a dark cloud seemed to move over the sun-streaked children playing so innocently in the waves.

# TWO

WAYNE PARKED HIS TRUCK AND HE AND PD joined the long line of patients (many with walking frames or seated in wheelchairs) in a queue leading to a tent outside Rosedale General where COVID 19 vaccinations were being given to first responders and the elderly. There had been rumors that doses of the vaccine had been given to family members the previous day, while first responders had been turned away. Lucy Ingham, M.D., Wayne's fiancé, was incandescent with rage when she heard the news. She volunteered to supervise the injection staff and promised the hospital administration that it wouldn't happen again.

PD recognized a young man walking from patient to patient with a clipboard. It was Nick Overton who worked for the health department doing contact tracing. He had arrived at PD's cabin the previous year and when he learned he was a retired detective, was entranced. He pestered PD for stories about his cases, which he was tickled to relate.

"Hey, Nick, how's it going?" PD called. The kid waved and held up a finger. He would be with them shortly. "I'm going to ask him where my name is on the list. Maybe he can move me up."

"We need to talk about the missing person's case," Wayne said. "Because of the time it took to deal with the painting, we never got around to it this morning."

"Right. The missing woman's name is Abigail Forester. She's a childless widow in her

early sixties. Hang on a minute. Here comes Nick."

"Hi, Detective Pascoe," the young man said. "How's the sprained ankle?"

"All healed up. This is my partner, Wayne Nichols. He's a retired detective from the Sheriff's office in Rosedale."

"Good to meet you, Nick," Wayne said shaking hands with the boy.

Wondering whether his fiancé was working in the injection tent, Wayne's breathing quickened. Lucy was insistent that he had to get vaccinated but he had stalled. He didn't doubt the efficacy of the vaccine, but shots made him pass out. He'd been told it was called a vasovagal reaction and quite common, but it embarrassed Wayne deeply. Real men didn't faint, especially murder detectives, known in the force as the bravest of the lot. He'd kept that little fact a secret from Lucy.

"What can I do for you two?" Nick asked. He looked fresh-faced and perky, despite the long line of patients and the difficulty of understanding their names and addresses. The masks made conversation difficult and many seniors couldn't hear well either.

"Could you check to see where I am on the list," PD said. "My full name is Patrick Devlin Pascoe."

"Let me see." Nick ran his finger down the list of names and stopped near the bottom. "Right, found you. Sorry, we're really behind today. Some computer glitch doubled the patients and failed to request more staff. It's a mob scene in the tent."

"By chance is Dr. Lucy Ingram from the ER Department inside?" Wayne asked.

"She sure is. Raised a ruckus about the vaccines being given to family members at the end of the day yesterday, when some medical students and nurses hadn't been vaccinated. She put all first responders at the head of the line this morning. I can move both of you up a bit."

"Thanks, but I think I'll wait here," Wayne said, feeling a bit apprehensive. He stepped out of the line, having spotted a large oak tree on the hospital grounds that shaded a park bench where he could take a seat. He had some thinking to do. He'd planned a special surprise for Lucy at their wedding which was taking place at the end of the summer, but was having difficulty getting it done.

Lucy's father, now deceased, had been a well-known surgeon and her mother was a nurse, who stopped working professionally after her two daughters were born. The marriage deteriorated when her father fell in love with his surgical assistant. He wanted a divorce and her mother refused. According to Lucy, who was very young at the time, the parents had many bitter arguments. Once she walked into their bedroom and saw her father giving her mother an injection. There was something terrified in her white-faced mother's expression that had stayed with her ever since. She returned home from school a month later to find her mother dying. She watched in horror as her mother took her final struggling breaths. Her premature death had been the impetus for Lucy becoming a physician. No one would die on her watch—not if she could possibly prevent it.

Lucy's younger sister, Anne Ingram, left home at seventeen and drifted into the drug world. When Wayne learned the family history, he promised himself he'd find Anne one day and help her get treatment for drug dependency. He hoped to have her attend their wedding, but hadn't gotten very far in his search. Glancing at the line of patients waiting for their shots, Wayne saw that PD, accompanied by Nick, was now entering the tent.

It was a beautiful sunny June day with a temperature in the high 70's. A chirping noise attracted his attention. It was a female Indigo Bunting who was building a nest in the hydrangeas planted on either side of the bench. He smiled at the hard-working bird and asked, "I'm not having much luck finding Lucy's sister. What do you think I should do next?" The bird, alarmed by the one-sided conversation, flew off.

When Wayne looked at the tent again, PD was already emerging with a bandage on his upper arm. To his dismay, Lucy, was with him. She was walking determinedly toward him with a 'take no prisoners' expression on her pretty face. Although Wayne mounted a spirited resistance, Lucy prevailed and led him into the big vaccination tent. She was about to inject his arm with the vaccine when she noticed him looking wide-eyed and unsteady. "Look up. Right now!" she said. "PD, prop up our friend here. He's about to land on the floor."

"No, I'm not," Wayne protested, but he looked at the ceiling in the tent anyway, and before he could protest further, the shot was in his arm.

"Now that wasn't so bad, was it?" Lucy asked, teasingly. "I'm actually known for giving pretty painless shots. Both of you will have to have a second shot in three weeks. Stop rolling your eyes," she laughed. As the men exited the tent, they were provided with vaccine cards and dates for their second doses.

"Let's go to the Donut Den and get some coffee," PD said. "Unless you feel the need of something stronger."

"Coffee is fine. Just need to sit down," Wayne said gruffly. They drove to the local coffee shop, got seated in a booth and ordered. "Remind me what we know so far about our missing lady, Mrs. Forester," he said when the coffee arrived.

"Okay. Abigail Forester was initially reported missing to the Sheriff's Office by her nephew Jonathon Forester. That was two weeks ago. The sheriff had her phone records and financials checked. Her calls were all local as were her purchases, including a new vehicle. Detective Rob Fuller went to the car dealership and met with the car salesman. He remembered Mrs. Forester, who traded in her old car for a blue Subaru Forester, a demonstrator with about 5,000 miles on it. She had her dog with her, a large black-and-tan Bernese Mountain dog. The salesman said the dog was very protective of its owner and wouldn't let him pet it. She told the man she was being pestered by her nephew to change her will and had decided to stay with a friend for a while to decide what to do," PD said.

"Did Detective Fuller check out her friend?"

"Yes. Her best friend's name is Nancy Webb. She lives over on Grant Street. Mrs. Forester wasn't at the Webb residence when Detective Fuller visited, but he was told she was expected back shortly. After that, Sheriff Bradley told Jonathon there was no evidence a crime had been committed and he wasn't going to look further into the matter. That was when Jonathon and his wife Christine contacted us. We turned the case down at first, given what the sheriff's office found, but they were persistent and promised a serious retainer, so we said we'd look into the matter," PD said.

"I'd like to speak to Jonathon Forester again. Detective Rob never actually saw the woman at Nancy Webb's house and something doesn't feel quite right here. Her nephew could be involved in her disappearance," Wayne said.

PD nodded, they paid for their coffees and departed.

# THREE

Back at Rosedale Investigations, Billy Jo was starting work on the provenance for *Wednesday's Child*. She had located the URL for the International Foundation for Art Research that contained a "Guide to Provenance." Packed with directions, the document was twenty-five pages long and hard-going. The Guide cautioned that looking for an art object's provenance required creativity, persistence, attention to detail and the ability to think outside the box. Billy Jo thought she had those traits, but realized with a sinking sensation that the task required skills well beyond hers.

People who did this kind of work were experts. Many had trained in well-known institutions in the U.S. and abroad and had decades of experience. They were connoisseurs and apparently "connoisseurship" was a skill acquired over the years as an expert became steeped in the work of a particular artist. Feeling daunted by the task she was undertaking, Billy Jo recalled the first time she went zip-lining. She had been standing on a platform looking down into a gully a hundred feet below—her heart pounding. As she had done that day, Billy Jo felt she was about to step off into nothing but air.

"You asked for this," she reminded herself and looked again at the recommended first step in the Guide. Thanks to the faculty member from the University, Dr. Brock Hayward, who supervised the restoration, the painting had been carefully vetted, except for one striking omission. The Guide said it was important to look on the front and *back* of paintings for inscriptions, dates or other information. She needed to see the back of *Wednesday's Child*. Although it would probably be a dead end, Billy Jo took a deep breath and dialed Sylvia Walcott's phone number.

Billy Jo rang the doorbell of the small red-brick ranch house where Mrs. Walcott and her granddaughter, Sylvia, lived. It was a warm day and the scent of Mrs. Walcott's pink damask roses perfumed the summer air. The door was opened moments later.

"Hi, Billy Jo. Come on in. I want to introduce you to my grandmother, Georgia," Sylvia said.

The front door opened directly into a small living area. Like the homes of many elderly people, it was filled with knickknacks—souvenirs of days in the past when the family took vacations and purchased the items. The furniture, a dark brown couch upholstered in a nubby vintage fabric and two matching chairs, were encased in see-thru plastic covers. A tall grandfather clock rang the hours as Mrs. Walcott, using a metal walking frame, entered the room. She was at least eighty-years-old, had gray hair pulled back into a tight bun, silver framed glasses and a pink crocheted shawl around her shoulders. She was wearing what looked like a nightgown. Billy Jo approved.

"Gramma, this is Miss Bradley who works for Rosedale Investigations. That's the firm looking into your painting. At least I hope they are," Sylvia said, smiling.

"Yes, we have agreed to do some research on the painting," Billy Jo said. "And I'm pleased to meet you, Mrs. Walcott."

"Please have a seat. You and Gramma can get to know each other while I get us some tea," Sylvia said as Mrs. Walcott lowered herself awkwardly into a wooden rocking chair—the only piece of furniture not covered in plastic.

Billy Jo looked at the painting, proudly hung over the room's tiny fake fireplace. Even in the dim lighting of the small room, the artwork practically danced off the walls. The water was a translucent mosaic comprised of multiple shades of blue, aquamarine and green with tiny sparks of white. In the shadowy room, one could practically see the water move. Billy Jo wondered how the artist had achieved that effect. He was obviously a master of his craft.

"Miss Bradley is it? How can I help?" Mrs. Walcott asked.

"I have some questions for you. Is that okay?"

"Of course," she said, as Sylvia entered the room carrying a tray with a silver tea set. In the midst of a sea of tacky 1950's décor, the tea set struck a fine opulent note. Sylvia poured the steaming tea into their cups and handed around a china plate filled with store-bought cookies.

"What did you want to ask me, young woman?"

"You inherited the painting from a Mrs. Chase Wilson, right? Do you know where she got it?"

"Yes. I was told she purchased the painting at a garage sale."

*A garage sale.* Billy Jo's heart sank. Unless there was something on the back of the painting, there would be no telling who owned the artwork before Mrs. Chase Wilson. "How did you come to inherit the work?" she asked.

"Although I was only a distant relative, I was next in line when Mrs. Wilson passed. She was determined that the painting stay in the family."

"I wonder if we could take the painting down so I could see the back."

"No problem," Sylvia said and walked over to the wall where the painting was hung.

"You be careful now," Mrs. Walcott said sharply, as Sylvia lifted the piece gently off its hook. She set it down on the shabby brown carpet and rotated it so Billy Jo could see the back of the piece.

"I'd like to take some photos, okay?" Billy Jo asked and both Mrs. Walcott and Georgia nodded. She knelt down and tilted the painting away from her, quickly snapping photos on her cell phone. Her heart beat faster. Taped to the back of the painting was an envelope.

"There's an envelope here. Have you opened this to see what's inside yet?" Billy Jo asked.

"No, but we can. Here you are, Gramma," Sylvia said as she gently tugged the envelope loose and handed it to her grandmother.

"I need my letter opener," Mrs. Walcott said. Sylvia nodded, walked over to a roll-top desk piled high with letters and bills, pulled out a silver opener and gave it to her.

"Sylvia, can you open the drapes in here? I can't see a dratted thing." As the light came into the room in wide bands and dust motes rose in the air, the old lady pursed her lips and removed two pieces of paper from inside the envelope. They were crispy and yellowed with age.

"Can you read the writing?" Billy Jo asked.

"Yes. There are two documents here. One is a death certificate and the second is a handwritten note. The note says, 'I painted this work for Dr. Cedric Brookover. It's of his children, Sarah, John and Emily. I only hope they can forgive me. I am so profoundly wretched that I can't go on.'"

The room was silent for a few shocked moments before Billy Jo asked, "Whose death certificate is it?"

Sylvia took the piece of paper from her grandmother's gnarled fingers. "It's for Jeremy Iverson-Jones, the artist. Goodness, he was only forty when he died."

"What was the cause of death?" Billy Jo asked quietly.

"Suicide," Sylvia said. She was standing behind her grandmother, looking over her shoulder. Mrs. Walcott had gone as white-faced as the knitted antimacassar on the headrest of her rocking chair.

Billy Jo left the residence shortly thereafter. Although deeply troubled by the contents of the envelope, she knew her research had just taken a giant leap forward. She had the name of the family who commissioned the work, the artist's name and his death certificate. From those two documents, she also knew the city where the artist lived and worked. It was a good start and for the first time, she felt a stirring of optimism about the provenance quest.

# FOUR

BILLY JO WAS BUSY PREPARING BACKGROUNDS on Mrs. Abigail Forester, her nephew Jonathon and his wife Christine, when the couple arrived at Rosedale Investigations that afternoon. Dory answered the door and took them to the conference room where Wayne and PD were waiting.

"We have some information for you about your aunt," Wayne said after the couple took their seats.

"Good. We've been worried about her. It's been several weeks now since we've seen her," Christine Forester said. She was dressed in designer jeans, expensive-looking shoes and a light melon-colored sweater. Her hair was perfectly cut and she looked like she had just emerged from the beauty salon. Wayne noticed Dory looking jealously at the woman's purse and shoes.

"What we've discovered is that your aunt has been hiding from you," PD said and his dark eyes narrowed.

"That's complete crap," Jonathon said, shaking his head. He was a good-looking man with smooth cheekbones, light brown hair and a cleft chin. He took his sunglasses off and perched them on top of his head. "What makes you say that? And where do you think she would be hiding?"

"We believe she's still in Rosedale, probably with a friend. She purchased a new car and told the car salesman that her family was pestering her to change her will. Is that true? Have you been putting pressure on her?" Wayne asked, looking at them intently.

Christine cast a questioning glance at her husband who shook his head.

"We're worried she could have been kidnapped," he said.

"Extremely unlikely. Her purchases and phone calls have all been local," PD said.

"And people who have been kidnapped rarely take their dogs with them," Wayne said sarcastically. "Especially big dogs like the Bernese."

"You aren't giving up, are you?" Christine asked.

"No. We still plan to contact all her known associates. Did your aunt attend church?" Dory asked.

"Yes, she's a regular at St. Martha's," Jonathon told them.

"We will meet with her priest then," Dory said, and although she knew whatever Mrs. Forester told the priest in confession would never be revealed, sometimes there were other matters that came to light.

"We're going to give you one more week before we find someone else to look into this matter. Right now we're leaving. I have another appointment," Jonathon said shortly and taking his wife by the hand, led her from the conference room. Christine looked over her shoulder apologetically.

BILLY JO ENTERED THE CONFERENCE ROOM AFTER THE COUPLE LEFT.

"What background information have you got so far?" PD asked.

"First, I found that Mrs. Abigail Forester, our missing lady, has no criminal record, no children and her husband died several years ago of a heart attack leaving her quite well off. He was a businessman who owned his own company. Jonathon Forester is apparently her only relative. He's her husband's sister's son."

"What did you find on him?" Wayne asked.

"Unlike Abigail, Jonathon is not so squeaky clean. He was first in trouble with the law when he was sixteen. He swiped a car and went joy-riding. It was his cousin's vehicle and his father intervened. The case was dropped and the record expunged."

"How the heck did you get an expunged record revealed?" Dory asked, frowning.

"I do have my moments," Billy Jo grinned. "To continue, when Jonathon was eighteen, he helped himself to some of his grandmother's antique diamond jewelry and tried to fence it locally. The jeweler got suspicious and called the cops. Grandma refused to press charges, said Jonathon was remorseful, and once again nothing was done. He's currently a failed real estate developer, has borrowed heavily and isn't employed. Their home was recently repossessed to pay off most of his debts and they have moved in with his Aunt Abigail. Christine doesn't work outside the home and has four credit cards that are maxed out."

"Her clothes, purse and haircut are expensive. I'd say she's pretty high maintenance," Dory said.

"I suggest we go over to Abigail Forester's house while her nephew and wife are at their appointment. She might have a maid or another service person who would know something. And we need to check with her friend, Nancy Webb, too," Wayne said.

"It's a long shot, but I'll talk to the priest," Dory said.

Seeing the men gathering up empty coffee cups, Billy Jo decided to seize the moment. "Before you all leave, can I tell you what I found out so far about the painting?"

"There's no time for that now," PD said sounding irritated. "I told you regular cases take precedence. And don't give me that doe-eyed pleading look."

Billy Jo blinked back tears as the men left the office.

"You can tell me what you found," Dory said, patting her on the shoulder.

"PD is just a big meanie butt," Billy Jo said. "He's never going to make me a partner in the firm and I don't think he appreciates me at all."

"You know you have to buy into the practice to be a partner. Wayne and I each put in $25,000."

"He could waive that fee if he wanted to," Billy Jo said stubbornly.

"Regardless, I know PD appreciates you. He's just an old grouch lately. I think something personal might be going on with him. So, tell me about the painting," Dory said.

"I suppose you think I was too hard on Billy Jo," PD said gruffly as the men got into Wayne' truck.

"She's just a kid, PD. I am of the opinion that she's not sure what she wants to do with her life," Wayne said as he started the vehicle and pulled out of the driveway.

"As long as I am paying her a salary and giving her a place to live, she needs to work on what I assign her," he said gruffly.

"I actually think digging up the provenance for the painting is a bit like a cold case investigation. You might be surprised with what she learns."

"Just wish she'd do it on her own time," PD said with a grimace. "Turn right at the light. Grant Street is the next left. You can let me off at Nancy Webb's place while you go to Abigail Forester's house."

"I'll pick you up in half an hour," Wayne said as PD got out of the car.

Pulling into the nearby Red Maples subdivision, Wayne reached the address for Abigail Forester's home. A truck with the logo of a local landscaping business was parked in the driveway. He walked over to the man in a white coverall who was spraying the lawn. It was starred with dandelions. Lucy had mentioned their lawn needed "broad leaf weed control." Wayne asked her what the heck that was. "Dandelions," she had said.

"Excuse me. Could I ask you some questions?" Wayne asked, and the man set down his sprayer.

"Sure thing. I'm Sam Weddell, I own Pure Nature Lawn Company. I'd shake hands with you but don't want to get chemicals on people."

"Thanks for taking the time to talk with me. My name's Wayne Nichols, I'm a detective looking into the disappearance of Mrs. Abigail Forester. How long since you're seen her?"

"She's disappeared? That's odd. I was here last week and went to the front door to give her my bill. Abigail usually gives me a check, but a man opened the door, said she was out and that he'd give her my bill. He didn't ask me in or open the door very wide. I wouldn't want to get the man in trouble, but I got a funny feeling about him."

*Me too,* Wayne thought. "So you haven't seen her in the last couple of weeks?"

"Nope. Sure hope nothing bad has happened to her. She's a nice lady. Does all her own gardening and appreciates my work. Sorry, I have to get back to this spraying. The dandelions have been relentless this year."

"No problem, Sam. Thanks for your help. By the way, our lawn needs dandelion control too. I'll have my fiancé call you. If you think of anything else that would help us locate Mrs. Forester, here's my card. Call any time. If I don't answer, leave a message. I check them routinely."

# FIVE

After peering into Abigail Forester's dusty garage windows and seeing that it was empty, Wayne walked up the steps to the painted porch of the raised two-story home and rang the doorbell. A young woman answered the door. She had a lovely face, strawberry blond curls, and a snub nose sprinkled with freckles. Although she was probably thirty pounds overweight, somehow it just added to her appeal.

"How can I help you?" she asked, smiling flirtatiously and twisting a curl of her shiny hair around her finger.

"I'm Wayne Nichols, a detective looking for your employer, Mrs. Abigail Forester."

"Come on in. I'll put the kettle on. I'm Camille Raines, the housekeeper," she said cheerfully. Her curls bounced as she walked ahead of him.

He followed her down the huge hall that divided the house in two. It was an architectural style of home known as a "central passage house." On the right were mahogany double doors open to a paneled office with floor-to-ceiling bookcases. On the left was a living room with leather club chairs, a baby grand piano, and an intricately patterned area rug. A large floral arrangement of white Calla lilies and purple bell-shaped flowers adorned the ornate glass coffee table. Lucy had mentioned that she'd like Calla lilies in her bridal bouquet and showed him pictures of the elegant blooms. Otherwise, he wouldn't have known what the flowers were called.

Camille chattered away, turned down a side hall and entered the kitchen. It was original to the house, had sixteen-foot ceilings, metal cabinets painted yellow, and a large china hutch filled to the brim with crystal stemware. The housekeeper gestured to a dining booth on the far side of the room. The tabletop was red Formica; a black leather bench provided seating.

"Take a pew, Detective," she said and grinned.

Camille busied herself with the teapot and after checking if he wanted sugar or lemon, brought over two cups. "What can I tell you?" she asked taking a seat across from him.

"As I said, I'm looking for Mrs. Abigail Forester. Do you know where she is?"

Camille looked at him obliquely, showing the dimples in both cheeks. "Oh, I just might," she said, grinning.

"I understand the Sheriff's Detective came by the house last week and asked about her. If you knew her whereabouts at that time, you were required by law to tell Detective Fuller what you knew," he said gruffly.

"That silly boy never took the time to talk to me. Just to Jonathon and Christine. And I'm the one *in the know* around here." She looked like she could hardly suppress her amusement.

"This is a serious matter, Miss Raines. Where is Mrs. Forester?" Wayne asked, looking at her and narrowing his eyes, although in truth he found himself on the verge of laughter. The woman's cheer was infectious. She seemed to find life delightfully entertaining—despite the serious topic.

"Not sure I should tell you. You are working for Jonathon aren't you?"

"When I look for a missing person, all I want to do is confirm that they are alive and well. And if she doesn't want to live here, she doesn't have to," Wayne said.

Camille nodded. "Here's what happened. Abigail and Jonathon had an argument before she left. He was pestering her for money and I happened to be near the office door at the time. It was simply impossible not to overhear. Don't want you to think I make a habit of it."

"Go on," Wayne said, suppressing a grin and privately thanking God for snoopy housekeepers.

"I heard her say, 'I'm not giving you another dime, Jonathon.' When he stormed out of the office he practically knocked me over."

"When Mrs. Forester said she wouldn't give him any money, did you by chance hear what he said?" Wayne asked.

"I could hardly help hearing as he was walking past me when he fired his parting shot. He said, 'I'm going to have all the money when you are gone anyway. Why not loosen the purse-strings now when I need it?'"

Wayne wondered if it was true that Mrs. Forester's estate was willed to Jonathon and whether his words constituted a physical threat. "What happened then?" he asked.

"I went into the office to see if Abigail was okay. She told me that she had decided to stay with her friend Nancy Webb for a bit. She planned to make some changes to her will, but until she made a final decision, would be incommunicado. I offered to keep Sally, her Bernese Mountain dog while she was gone but she took the dog with her. I'm buddies with the dog and am known as the local dog whisperer." she said.

"Is she with her friend Nancy now?"

"Unless she decided to seduce Fr. Dominic at the church and claim sanctuary," Camille said smiling and batting her long eyelashes surrounding China-blue eyes.

Wayne rolled his eyes and tried valiantly to sound official as he asked, "Miss Raines, do you know where Mrs. Forester is at this time?"

With the air of a conjurer about to pull a rabbit out of his hat, Camille said, "I happen to have a *find my phone* app and permission to see her location." She stood up and walked to the linoleum-covered kitchen counter and picked up her phone.

"May I see?" Wayne asked and when she handed him her phone, he saw the address of Mrs. Nancy Webb on Grant Street. "Thank you very much. I'll let you know when she's located."

"Good luck, Handsome," Camille said archly, with a wink.

Wayne, shaking his head and quashing his amusement with difficulty, departed. Driving over to Grant Street, he called PD. "What did you find out?" he asked.

"Mrs. Webb hadn't seen her friend in two weeks," PD said.

"She's lying. I just spoke with her housekeeper and she has a find my phone app. It shows Mrs. Forester is at Mrs. Webb's house at present. How did you miss this, PD?"

"Beats the hell out of me," he said.

PD WAS STANDING ON THE SIDEWALK WHEN WAYNE PULLED INTO the Webb's driveway.

"Let's split up. I'll check the garage for her new car. If she was carjacked and kidnapped, the car wouldn't be here. And, I'll poke around to see if there are any garden sheds or outbuildings where she could be hiding," PD said.

"Okay, and I'll confront Nancy Webb about the penalty for lying to a cop," Wayne said, although he knew perfectly well he wasn't a cop any longer and hadn't been since he'd left the sheriff's office. Having been in law enforcement so long, however, he still felt like a cop.

"It's possible Mrs. Forester left her cell phone here and she is somewhere else," PD said.

"True. I'll check it out," Wayne said, walked to the front door and rang the bell. A tall slender woman with silver hair who looked to be in her early sixties, answered the door.

"Good afternoon. I'm Detective Wayne Nichols. Are you Nancy Webb?"

"I am," she said.

"I understand you told both the Sheriff's Detective and my partner, Detective Pascoe, that Mrs. Forester wasn't here. May I come in?"

Nancy Webb looked reluctant, but stepped slightly to one side and Wayne brushed past her. "Do you know Mrs. Forester's housekeeper, Camille?"

Mrs. Webb nodded.

"Her phone app shows Abigail Forester at this address," Wayne's eyes narrowed as he looked down at the woman. At that moment, a huge dog came bounding into the room. Nancy grabbed the dog's collar, trying to keep it from jumping on Wayne. She wasn't very successful at controlling the animal and Wayne backed up respectfully. The dog was growling.

While Nancy was calming the dog, Wayne quickly dialed Abigail's phone number. He could hear it ringing in the rear of the house.

"She forgot her phone when she left, Detective," Nancy said desperately, but it failed to ring true. He felt her tug on his shirt sleeve, but kept walking. The dog followed them, nails clicking on the floor as they headed to the kitchen.

At that moment, PD burst into the kitchen through the back door. "Mrs. Forester's car is in the garage and I see that her dog is here. I'm calling the cops to bring you to the station and interrogate to you about her possible murder, Mrs. Webb."

"That might be quite a stretch since Abigail Forester is alive and well," Nancy Webb said sarcastically. She sounded vexed.

"Back down, PD," Wayne said in a frustrated tone. "Mrs. Webb, please have Abigail come to the kitchen, now."

Without another word, Nancy Webb left the kitchen and shortly reappeared with Mrs. Forester. Although PD had received a photo of the woman from Jonathon, she was more vital and attractive in person, slim with curly brown hair and looking younger than her actual age.

"I assume you are Mrs. Abigail Forester," PD said.

"I am. You found me, but there's no law saying I have to live at my house," she said with a stubborn tilt to her chin.

"You're absolutely correct, Mrs. Forester," Wayne turned to Nancy. "Mrs. Webb, I apologize for my partner's accusation. It was totally unfounded. We'll be leaving now," he said and taking PD firmly by the upper arm, they departed the house.

As they walked out the front door and down the porch steps, Wayne said, "PD, what the devil is going on with you? Not picking up on her lying and then accusing a woman in her sixties of murder with absolutely no evidence, no means, and no motive. Poor woman was really peeved with you and rightly so."

PD gave Wayne a sidelong glance, looking apologetic, and got into the truck.

As they drove down the tree-lined streets of Rosedale, Wayne said, "On another matter, when we get back to the office, you need to apologize to Billy Jo and listen to what she's found out about the painting."

"Fine. I will. As far as what's going on with me, it's difficult for me to talk about," PD inhaled shakily. "I just discovered that I have a son."

There was a long shocked silence before Wayne said, "Got to say I never saw one that coming. No wonder you haven't been yourself. When can you meet him?"

"I can't," PD said.

"Why on earth not? He's your son, man," Wayne said, frowning.

"Because the way I learned I had a son was a call from the Rosedale Funeral home. He's deceased and they were looking for someone to pick up his ashes."

Glancing quickly at PD's downcast expression, Wayne drove the rest of the way to Rosedale Investigations in dumbfounded silence.

# SIX

A S THE TWO PARTNERS WALKED UP THE SIDEWALK of Rosedale Investigations bordered by pink tea roses, Wayne asked PD if he planned to share the information about his son with Dory and Billy Jo. "It might help you to talk about it," he said and PD nodded.

The women were having lunch at the picnic table in the backyard of Rosedale Investigations. The sun was out, the temperature had risen and the vanilla-like scent of the blossoming Viburnum shrubs lay sweetly on the humid air.

"What's going on, guys?" Dory asked.

"We found Mrs. Forester. She is at her friend Nancy Webb's house. You can send Jonathon a bill," PD said.

"And PD has something to say to you, Billy Jo," Wayne added.

"I'm sorry I was short-tempered this morning. What did you want to tell me about the painting?"

"With all due respect, Partner, that is a pretty pathetic excuse for an apology," Dory said, frowning. "You agreed Billy Jo had two weeks to look into the matter, and then you prevented her from giving you an update. She doesn't feel you appreciate her contributions."

PD took a deep breath. "You're right. I am sorry, Billy Jo. I didn't mean to sideline you."

"Well, you did," Billy Jo said, sounding pitiful. Then taking a deep breath she said, "So far, I've found out the name of the artist, the name of the man he painted the work for, Dr. Cedric Brookover, and when the artist died. There was an envelope pasted to the back of the canvas with the suicide note from the artist and his death certificate. From the documents, I learned the picture was painted in Erie, Pennsylvania."

"That's pretty amazing for only part of a day's work, isn't it, PD?" Wayne said holding his partner's eyes.

PD nodded. "Did you find out how old the painting is?"

"Yes, it's over a hundred years old."

"What's your next step?" Wayne asked.

"Mrs. Walcott said that Mrs. Chase Wilson, the woman she inherited the artwork from, purchased the painting at a garage sale. Since garage sale items don't usually migrate very far, I hope the old Brookover residence and Mrs. Chase Wilson's house are near each other. If I'm correct, there may still be people living in the area who knew both the families."

"I think the key is finding out who Dr. Cedric Brookover willed the painting to upon his passing. If he was wealthy enough to commission a portrait of his children, he probably had a will," PD said.

"Thanks, really helpful thought."

"PD has something else to share with both of you," Wayne said as both men sat down at the picnic table.

"A couple of days ago, I got a call from the local funeral parlor here in town," PD stopped. He swallowed, breathing hard. "Apparently I have, or had, a son. He's deceased. They have his ashes and want me to pick them up and dispose of them."

Both women looked shocked.

"That's awfully sad, PD. I'm so, so sorry," Billy Jo said and took his hand.

"That's a hell of a way to find out you had an offspring. I wonder why you were never informed about your son's existence during his lifetime. And, how did the funeral parlor learn you were his father, when you didn't even know he existed?" Dory asked.

"I have no idea," PD said.

"Who was the boy's mother?" Wayne asked.

"His mother was a lovely woman named Amy Weaver. I met her just before I was sent to Viet Nam. We spent a glorious couple of weeks together but once I was in Hanoi, I never got a card or a letter. I wrote her many times, but assumed she didn't want to hear from me again since the letters were returned. When the war was over and I came back to town, I tried to find her, but learned she had died in a car accident. I never even considered that I might have made the poor woman pregnant," PD said, looking shamefaced.

"Well, if your son died recently, somebody raised him and my guess is that Amy Weaver had parents or siblings who stepped in," Wayne said.

"What was your son's name?" Billy Jo asked.

"He was given my last name, and his first name was Ryan. The cause of death was pancreatic cancer. He was fifty when he died."

"If he was that old, he may have married and had children. Did you think about that?" Dory asked.

It was quite clear from PD's stunned look that he hadn't.

LATE THAT AFTERNOON WAYNE GOT A PHONE CALL. He was standing by Billy Jo's desk when the call came in.

"It's Detective Rob Fuller calling from the Sheriff's Office," he told the team who were nearby. "Hi Rob. What's happening?" He paused a moment before saying, "I know someone who can help. Her name's Camille Raines. I'll get her and we'll leave right now."

He hung up the call and turning to Dory and PD said, "Abigail Forester was driving to Nashville and ended up in a car crash. She's been seriously injured. The dog is in the car with her and won't let the EMT's get her out. I think her housekeeper, Camille Raines, can help. She told me that she is a dog whisperer. They want us at the site ASAP."

"Keep us up to date," Dory said and Billy Jo nodded. The men left the office, got into PD's car and set out.

"Was the accident on SR 6?" PD asked.

"Yes, just south of Interstate 840. An ambulance has been called, but the car flipped on its side and the air bag deployed. I hope Camille can get the dog out of the car so the medics can work on her. I'm calling her."

As they drove past green lawns and summer trees on either side of the road, they heard the sound of the call being answered.

"Mrs. Forester's residence, Camille speaking."

"Camille, this is Detective Nichols. Abigail Forester has been in an accident. She needs medical assistance and the dog won't let the paramedics remove her from the car. The Sheriff called a local vet who's ready to tranquilize the animal, but he's afraid if he sedates the dog, it will collapse and its weight will crush her. I'm coming to get you."

"That big dummy, I'll get her out of the car," Camille said, and even in this dire situation Wayne could hear her *joie de vivre*.

He ended the call as PD entered the Red Maples neighborhood and turned down Albert Avenue towards the Forester residence. Camille was standing at the curb, waving. She had forgotten to remove her white bib apron.

Climbing into the back seat of the car, she said, "I'm buckled up. Step on it, Detective."

"Do you have an idea of how to shift the dog?" Wayne asked as PD pulled out of the subdivision.

"I do. In order to control a large dog, one must become totally irresistible to the beast," she said, smiling mysteriously, and looking pretty irresistible herself.

"Did you know you're still wearing your apron?"

"This apron has a front pocket and I grabbed a handful of Sally's favorite treats," Camille told him.

WHEN THEY REACHED THE SCENE OF THE ACCIDENT, it was crowded with police vehicles, an ambulance and a two firetrucks. A female deputy was standing at the road waving the slowing cars away.

Wayne pointed out Deputy George Phelps who was stringing yellow crime scene tape from the highway to where the car came to a stop—at the edge of a ravine. "Looks like Sheriff Bradley is going to launch an investigation into this one," he said.

"Hope the woman makes it," PD said.

Wayne clenched his jaw and nodded. He opened the rear door of the car for Camille and gave her a hand getting out of the vehicle. She looked a bit shell-shocked as she took in the scene. They crossed a watery ditch and entered a daisy-starred fallow field. Sheriff Ben Bradley was speaking to the EMT's near the ambulance. The veterinarian, wearing a white coat with a stethoscope around his neck, was standing beside them. The sheriff broke off his conversation when they walked up.

"Thanks for coming. You must be Camille Raines," Sheriff Bradley said, holding out a hand to shake hers. "We got the car door open on the driver's side and braced the other side. We hope that will keep it from slipping down into the ravine. Do you think you can get the dog out, Camille? This is Dr. Rodriguez," he said gesturing to the veterinarian.

"Nice to meet you. I'm reluctant to tranquilize the dog for fear she will fall on the woman and cause her lungs to collapse. Her breathing is pretty shallow already," he said.

"No worries. I'll lure the dog out," she said and walked closer to the car. The raised open door of the vehicle looked like the blue wing of a small airplane in the hot afternoon sun. But looking inside the car,

Camille blanched and Wayne moved closer, putting out a hand, ready to catch her if she fainted.

Then she regained her composure, took a breath and gave a low melodic whistle. The big dog raised her head. "Come here, Sally. I have *cookies* for you," she said sweetly and whistled the little melody again. The dog stood up, putting her paws on either side of the injured woman who was not moving.

"Come on out now, Sally. I have your *favorite* treats," Camille crooned and the dog bounded abruptly out of the vehicle, landing on the ground.

The paramedics, who had been poised close by, moved in swiftly. One of the EMTs started gently lifting Mrs. Forester from the car onto a wheeled stretcher while the other medic pumped an oxygen bag continuously to ventilate the patient.

Then the car shifted slightly, making a metal-on-metal sound and the paramedics jumped back looking fearful. Wayne could see wisps of gray smoke coming out from under the hood and smelled gasoline.

"Everyone but the paramedics get back, right now!" Sheriff Bradley yelled and Deputy George started herding some rubber-necked spectators away.

PD was urging Camille to leave the scene. She had snapped a leash on the dog, but the big animal sat down and simply refused to budge. Despite handing out treats and tugging on the leash, moving the dog was like getting a small house to walk. The dog was refusing to leave her injured mistress.

The two paramedics were almost running as they rapidly transported the patient on the stretcher toward the ambulance when the car shifted again, making a horrible screeching metallic sound. Focused on getting Mrs. Forester into the ambulance, the paramedics didn't even look back as the car started to slide . . . ever-so-slowly down the hill.

"Everybody down!" Sheriff Bradley yelled as the paramedics started the ambulance and turned on the siren.

The ambulance was driving out of the field when Abigail's car began to slide inexorably faster and faster until it smashed into a towering burr oak tree at the bottom of the ravine. The tree split in half with a loud crack. The firemen jumped into action, dragging hoses to the edge of the declivity as the car burst into a gigantic ball of fire. The heat was searingly intense, the smell of oil and gas caused everybody to cough and gag. The sky was filled with black smoke and metallic particles that rained down as the firefighters desperately fought to subdue the blaze. The dog raised her head in the air and gave a long guttural moan.

Wayne walked over to the Sheriff. They were both coughing. "Are you okay?" he asked. The Sheriff nodded. "I noticed you had George stringing crime scene tape out to the road."

"I saw some skid marks, indicating the presence of a second vehicle," he said. "It's possible someone forced the woman off the road."

"You might want to go to the ER and have your breathing checked," Wayne said.

As the emergency vehicles started leaving the scene, it took the combined efforts of the two detectives and the 'dog whisperer' to manhandle the protesting animal into the back seat of PD's car.

"Do you think Abigail's going to make it?" Camille asked in a tremulous voice as they pulled away from the field and onto the road.

"I'm sure they will do all they can, but it was a pretty bad accident," PD said.

"And it looks like someone may have run her off the road," Wayne said.

"Which means if the poor woman dies, it's a case of murder."

Hearing this, the normally light-hearted Camille started to cry.

# SEVEN

D ORY HAD BEEN GETTING TEXTS FROM WAYNE about the accident
ever since they arrived at the scene, but the last one said there was
too much happening for him to update them again. He told them to listen to the police radio and both women had been glued to it since. The
voice on the static-filled line said, "Firetrucks needed. Accident off the
ring road to Nashville on Route 6, south of Interstate 840. Ambulance en
route. Proceed with caution. Potential danger at site."

Billy Jo's phone rang and she pushed the button to accept the call. "It's
Wayne," she said putting the call on speaker, but all they could hear in the
background was the Sheriff yelling, "Get down!" and then the horrifying
whoosh of an inferno before the call cut off. "My god, the car must have
caught on fire," Billy Jo said, her eyes were huge.

A short time later the crackling police radio reported 'fire fighters on
scene' and both of them took a deep breath of relief.

"I'm calling Wayne back," Dory said.

"We're okay, Dory," he said when he answered.

"Did they get Mrs. Forester into the ambulance?"

"Just barely, but I don't know if she's going to make it. The paramedics
were prevented from getting to her until Camille got the dog out of the
car. I saw them bagging her continually as she was being loaded onto the
stretcher."

"The police band didn't report a casualty."

"She was still alive when they got her into the ambulance. PD is
coughing and so is Camille. They were both far enough away from the
explosion that I'm sure there's no lasting damage, but they should probably be checked," Wayne said. "We're going to the ER."

Dory wished him luck before clicking off the phone and saying. "The car caught on fire, but they are okay. They got Mrs. Forester into the ambulance. She's on her way to Rosedale General," she told Billy Jo.

"Whew, that's a relief."

"I'll contact Jonathon and Christine and tell them about their aunt. They will want to go to the hospital. I'll go with them. Sometimes one learns a lot from what people say when family members are in critical condition. I don't completely trust those two. What are you going to do?"

"Doing some reports for clients to keep PD pacified and getting ready for my appointment with Professor Hayward at the University tomorrow morning. I wasn't getting any more ideas of how to proceed with the provenance for the painting until I stopped by the music store after work yesterday and bought the CD of Verdi's *Rigoletto*. You know how I listen to opera when I'm stuck for ideas. Anyway, I listened to the aria called, "La donna é mobile" and it gave me a brainstorm."

"Go on," Dory said, bemused by Billy Jo's choice of music and the girl's firm belief that opera helped her solve problems.

"I'm going to ask Dr. Hayward how he knew the title of the painting. There was nothing written in the documents attached to the back of the painting that provided the title, so Mrs. Walcott must have gotten it from the Chase Wilson family. And I want to see if there's any connection between the painting and the University here."

"Good ideas. Are you feeling better about PD after his rather half-hearted apology?" Dory asked.

"Once I learned about his son, I decided I was being bratty and piti-ful, feeling sorry for myself while PD was struggling."

"I'll go catch up with Wayne and PD at the ER." Dory paused seeing Billy Jo's face. "Don't worry. I'll text you an update as soon as I know anything." Then narrowing her eyes, she asked, "What are you planning to wear to your meeting with the professor tomorrow?"

"Oh, I have something in mind," Billy Jo said, airily.

"I know you don't feel people should judge you by how you are dressed, Kiddo, but it's a fact of life. So dressing in the professional style is best. And absolutely no flip-flops."

Billy Jo rolled her eyes, whispering, "Fashion Nazi," under her breath. Dory chuckled.

HAVING BEEN DISCHARGED FROM THE ER, Wayne, PD and Camille left for the office. Wayne was relieved not to have run into Lucy. She would not have been pleased that he had been so close to the explosion. He had tried to explain that his life seemed to lead him inexorably into danger. It wasn't his fault, he told her.

"I won't marry a dead man walking," she said and reminded him of his promise not to investigate murders or enter dangerous situations again. He'd had a hard time living up to that pledge.

"What do you want to do now, PD?" Wayne asked quietly. Camille was nearly asleep in the back seat, exhausted by seeing her friend in such dire straits.

"I'm going back to the site of the accident to take one more look and then I need to go to the funeral home and find out how they connected me with Ryan Pascoe," PD said.

"All right. Can you drop the two of us at Rosedale Investigations? Camille told Sheriff Bradley that Mrs. Forester was on her way to see her lawyer and was planning to change her will. I wonder who the recipient of her original will is, and if she knows what changes Mrs. Forester planned to make. My truck is there so I can drive her home afterwards."

PD nodded and drove slowly through the quiet shaded streets of the small town toward their place of business.

ARRIVING AT ROSEDALE INVESTIGATIONS, CAMILLE WAS roused and lured Sally out of the car with more treats. She tied her up on the porch. Wayne got the dog some water and ushered the woman inside the office.

"Can I get you something to drink?" he asked her. "I could make tea or coffee. And we have sodas and water."

She selected tea and they took their beverages down the hall to the conference room. "I'm very sorry to tell you that I called the hospital just now and found out that Mrs. Forester died en route to Rosedale General." Wayne stopped talking as Camille absorbed in the awful fact that her friend was gone forever. She shuddered and shook her head in sorrow, her eyes bright with unshed tears.

"I'm so sorry for your loss and regret asking you questions at this time, Camille, but could you tell me about Mrs. Forester's current will?"

Camille rubbed her eyes and took a sip of her tea. Her hands were shaking and she cleared her throat, suppressing her tears with difficulty. "Several years ago, Abigail told me she was leaving me her house, provided I would take care of her dog if she died first." She looked at him with watery eyes. "I told her not to be silly. I couldn't even afford the taxes on the place. She wasn't going to die early, and I'd keep Sally regardless, out of loyalty to her."

Handing her a tissue, Wayne said, "You said she was going to Nashville to meet with her lawyer because she planned to change her will. Do you know if you were still listed as inheriting her house?"

"My guess is that Jonathon and Christine are her beneficiaries now. They're her only blood relatives."

"You told me he was pestering her to give him some money," Wayne said.

"I know they are struggling financially," Camille said quietly.

*Maybe he decided to speed up the process of inheriting by forcing her off the road and causing her death*, Wayne thought. With Mrs. Forester now deceased, Wayne assumed the sheriff would want to interrogate Jonathon Forester ASAP. He hoped to listen in on the interview and sent a quick text to the sheriff asking when Jonathon was being questioned.

*"Come tomorrow at 11:00 if you want to observe,"* came the quick answer.

"Do you want me to take you home now, Camille?" Wayne asked. Looking at her, he felt profound pity for the woman whose cheerful exuberance had been crushed by the death of her friend.

She nodded and the two of them untied Sally from the porch and loaded her into Wayne's truck. Camille directed him to her place, a mobile home park on the outskirts of Rosedale. The trailers were connected to utilities in two parallel lines on either side of a large old house, no doubt the residence of the management. Her place was more welcoming than most with a petunia-filled porch, a red hummingbird feeder shaped like a strawberry and a single lawn chair.

"Since Abigail never made it to her lawyer's office, I could be wrong but I'm going to guess her home now belongs to you. You might call her attorney and, if you are a beneficiary, he will give you the specifics," Wayne said as he parked the truck.

"Okay," she said morosely and with a big black dejected dog trailing behind her, Camille walked to her house. Climbing the few porch steps to her front door, she turned back and waved to Wayne who found himself moved by her plight. He hoped she had inherited the house and if so, planned to help her eject the slimy Jonathon from the premises personally. He turned the truck around and headed back to the Sheriff's office in Rosedale. He wanted to talk with the sheriff before he interviewed Jonathon Forester. He needed to know that Camille might be at risk.

# EIGHT

Billy Jo reached the Tennessee State University campus later than she had planned the following morning, due to the time it took to dress appropriately and put on make-up. *Irritating how much time it takes to look this good*, she thought. Her appointment was for nine o'clock but she had trouble finding a parking place that wasn't reserved. Finally spotting a space with a parking meter, she pulled out the office credit card. She was walking rapidly toward Morrill Hall, a stone-clad building where the Art Department was housed, when her phone rang. She didn't recognize the number but pushed the accept button and said, "Hello."

"Dr. Hayward calling. I'm aware we have a meeting, but I'm running late and hope I can answer your questions on the phone. You said you needed more information about the painting we researched. I'm not sure what I can tell you, other than what was in the report we did for Mrs. Walcott."

"I saw in your report that Mrs. Walcott told you the title for the painting was *Wednesday's Child*. Do you know where she got the title?" Billy Jo asked.

There was a significant pause before Dr. Hayward said, "For that, there is someone else you need to speak with. He's very elderly now, ninety-two I believe. His name is William Dorne and he is a docent for the University's Art Museum. The Museum staff can give you his contact information if he's not on duty today." He sounded anxious to cut her questions short.

"Thanks, I will follow up with him," she said and then remembering the question she had come up with after listening to opera asked, "Is there any connection between the painting and the University here?"

"Good guess. Toward the end of Dr. Brookover's life, he was unable to decide who should receive the painting and brought it to the chair of our Art Department here. His name was Dr. George Dorne and William Dorne is his son. Dr. Dorne wanted the painting for the Art Museum, but the deal fell through. Sorry, but I need to go. I have another commitment."

"Well, thank you for your time, Dr. Hayward. I'll follow-up with Mr. William Dorne," Billy Jo said, bothered by why the professor had dodged a face-to-face meeting and seemed uncomfortable talking about the title of the painting. Then she remembered quoting the nursery rhyme to Dory and how dark the room had gone—as clouds moved in to cover the sky.

BILLY JO WALKED BACK TO HER CaR AND DROVE to the Art Museum located on the outskirts of the campus. It had been designed by a prize-winning architect and was shaped like the Opera House in Sydney, Australia. But unlike that curved iconic structure, this one had been made of triangular interlocking silver plates that resembled fish scales. Luckily, there were free visitor parking spaces. She parked her car and went inside the building that had a cavernous echoing lobby. A girl in the ticket booth told her that Mr. Dorne was on the schedule to serve as docent that day.

"He'll be here in about half an hour to officially open the galleries. We open at ten. William is such an old dear. Always behaves like a Southern gentleman. Feel free to browse the collections. Dr. Hayward called and said not to charge you for a ticket."

Moving through the semi-darkened galleries, Billy Jo looked in vain for another painting by Jeremy Iverson-Jones but saw none. When her phone buzzed with an incoming text, she read a depressing message from Wayne.

"*Mrs. Forester was driving to an appointment with her lawyer when she had the accident. She was DOA on arrival to Rosedale General.*"

DOA. Billy Jo shuddered, knowing the acronym meant *dead on arrival*. Their case had just gone from being a search for a missing person . . . to a potential murder investigation.

"ARE YOU TELLING ME THAT RYAN PASCOE'S WIFE refused to dispose of his ashes?" PD asked the funeral home attendant. The attendant, whose name tag read Curtis, was a shiny-haired young man. He was dressed in a black suit, white shirt and a bolo tie.

"That's what I was told, sir. The ex-wife said he had no other family. Her name is Gladys Bonner. She and Mr. Pascoe had been divorced for years and she didn't want any further responsibility for him. I think she was afraid she'd get stuck with the cost of a funeral," he said with a rueful look.

"Why did you look for me when his wife said he had no family?" PD asked.

"Because I thought she was lying," Curtis said. "They had both been living in Kentucky, but she called us here in Tennessee to pick up the body. It seemed weird, so I ordered his birth certificate from Vital Records. It listed his mother as a woman named Amy Weaver with a Rosedale address. I tried to call her, but on further digging found she died only two months after Ryan was born," he stopped talking then, noticing PD's grim expression.

"Are you okay, sir?" he asked.

"Yes, it's just bad news," PD said. "Go on."

"I looked to see who Amy had listed as the father on the birth certificate and it was a Patrick Devlin Pascoe. I recognized your name and found your place of business."

PD really didn't want to be related to a dead son he had never known, but he couldn't fault Curtis' instincts. Given the mother was his former girlfriend, there now seemed little doubt he had been the father. "I must compliment you on your investigative skills," he said dryly.

"I'm glad you aren't upset," Curtis said. "My boss didn't know about all my digging around."

"What happens now?" PD asked, dreading the next steps in this gruesome task.

"I will need to see your identification and if you are willing to take possession, I will release the ashes of Ryan Pascoe to you today."

"What should I do with them?" PD asked.

"Most people either put the ashes in the Little Harpeth River, or purchase a burial plot and have them interred. Sometimes families take the ashes to a place outdoors that was special to the person and scatter them there. However, I assume since you didn't know about Ryan's existence, you will want to do the easiest thing which is the river."

PD hesitated, not wanting to make a decision he might later regret. "I think I'll try to find out a little more about my . . . son . . . before I take that step," he said. He was thinking he would contact the ex-wife. She sounded bitter and resentful, but he was pretty good at getting information out of people. *And she must have loved the man once,* he thought.

After showing Curtis his i.d. and signing some papers, PD left the funeral home carrying a pressed-board container about the size of a shoe box containing the ashes of his late son. It seemed a sad, dreary finish to an untold story. Then he remembered Dory saying that Ryan might have had a child. That would be the first question he would put to Gladys.

There could be life in the story yet.

# NINE

BILLY JO HEARD WHISTLING COMING FROM AROUND A CORNER. It was a cheerful rendition of the song called, "I Can See Clearly Now." Then the person broke off his whistling and burst into lyrical song. The words rang out and Mr. William Dorne, the man who possessed a near-operatic tenor, walked into the gallery. He stopped singing instantly when he spotted her and doffed his hat, showing wisps of white hair on a balding pink head. He held out his hand saying, "I got a call from Professor Hayward. He said you were in search of some information about a painting by Iverson-Jones. Correct?"

"Yes, and thank you for seeing me," Billy Jo said and shook hands with the old gentleman, liking him instantly. He was only about as tall as she was and dressed in the height of fashion from years gone by. A white seersucker suit, a striped blue and white shirt, a wide tie with bluebirds on it, and a Panama hat completed his outfit. Looking at the nattily dressed gentleman, she was glad she had worn a Dory-approved blameless little black skirt, white blouse and low-heeled shoes.

"Let's go back to the coffee room," Mr. Dorne said and led the way through a labyrinth of darkened galleries. He switched on lights as they walked, setting alight the jewel-tones of original oil paintings hanging on dove gray walls—until they reached a door labeled Staff Only.

"Come in and have a seat. Do you want tea or coffee?"

"No, thank you. I'm doing the provenance for a century-old painting by Iverson-Jones. The owner, a Mrs. Walcott, contacted my employer, Rosedale Investigations, and requested our services. Professor Hayward said you could help. What can you tell me about the painting?" she asked.

"It's a long story, going back all the way to my youth. My father, Dr. George Dorne, was Chairman of the Art Department when the painting was offered to the University by Dr. Cedric Brookover. However, the transaction didn't go through."

"Why was that, do you know?"

"I think it was because of something my father learned during his conversations with Dr. Brookover. My parents talked about it with me later. The conversation stayed with me ever since because the word was so powerful."

"What word?" Billy Jo asked.

"Dr. Brookover told my parents that the painting was cursed."

"Cursed? That was the word he used? Cursed?" Billy Jo shivered. "That's horrid. Do you think the artist selected the title 'Wednesday's Child' because of the curse?"

Mr. Dorne frowned and said, "That's not the title. It's called *Children by the Lakeshore.*"

"Hmmm. Perhaps there are two titles then, because the woman I'm researching the painting for said it was called *Wednesday's Child*. That wording comes from an old nursery rhyme that predicts a child's future by the day of the week they were born. What else do you know?" Billy Jo asked.

"Dr. Brookover said he wished he'd never commissioned the piece— it was the last bright moment in his and his children's lives. Apparently, some pretty dire things happened after the painting was delivered. He didn't want more bad luck to be visited upon his children, if they inherited the work. My father learned that Brookover's wife, Wendy, died shortly after the painting was finished," Mr. Dorne said and a sorrowful expression crossed his kindly face. "It troubled my mother because she was young and healthy."

"How did she die? Was it an accident?"

"What else could it be?" Mr. Dorne asked as he shrugged his shoulders, and Billy Jo paused a moment to appreciate his naiveté. She had been working with detectives so long that darker possibilities came readily to mind.

"It's a terrible thought, Mr. Dorne, but it's possible Mrs. Brookover was killed. And the first suspect in a spousal death, as you probably know, is always the husband."

"Young woman, for such a cute and perky girl, you have a seriously gloomy mind," Mr. Dorne said. He frowned, looking at her incredulously.

"It comes from working with murder detectives," she told him wondering if dealing with crime on a day-to-day basis was making her jaded.

"I gather you don't know what happened between when Dr. Brookover owned the painting and Mrs. Walcott inheriting it. It's going to be quite a process to track the owners over the years," William Dorne said.

"I know," Billy Jo said and reached over to pat the shoulder of the sweet little man who had never considered the possibility that a woman could be killed by her husband . . . or a curse.

"Could you let me know what you find? I'd like to know what happens at the end of this century-old story," Mr. Dorne said.

"I promise to do so. You have such a lovely tenor voice. Have you ever considered auditioning for our local opera company?" Billy Jo asked.

"I had been giving it some thought and believe I will follow up on your suggestion. I have a question for you. Are you going to tell your employer about the curse?" he asked.

"I'll have to think a long time about that," Billy Jo said and departed.

WAYNE NICHOLS WAS SEATED IN THE VIEWING CUBICLE adjacent to the interview room at the sheriff's office. He was looking through the one-way view mirror at Jonathon Forester. The large man looked antsy and drummed his fingers on the table. When the sheriff and Detective Rob Fuller entered the room, Wayne clicked on the speaker so he could hear the interview. Sheriff Bradley sat down across from Jonathon at the table. As was the usual custom for on-site observers, Detective Rob stood in the back corner of the room.

"I wanted to offer my condolences on the death of your Aunt Abigail," the sheriff said. "I'm sorry to have to ask you to come in today, but I have some questions."

"Her funeral is going to be soon and arrangements need to be made. I have no intention of staying here very long," Jonathon said.

Given the placatory tone of the sheriff's questions, Wayne was a bit surprised at hearing the suspect's belligerence. His body language looked aggressive as well. The man's fists were opening and closing in his lap.

"I hope this won't take long. First, where were you from 1:00 p.m. to 3:00 p.m. the day your aunt was driving to Nashville?"

"I was cleaning out my aunt's garage. It hadn't been cleaned since Uncle Anthony died and it was full of junk."

"Can anyone confirm your whereabouts during that time?" Sheriff Bradley asked. He looked calm and his voice was uninflected, but Wayne knew his interrogation style. The sheriff always started out with a supportive tone, but could switch rapidly to a confrontational style—if the person started lying.

"My wife wasn't home and neither was the maid." Two little frown lines appeared between his eyebrows. "Why is this important? There can't be any question of what caused her death. She had an accident and the EMT's didn't get to her quickly enough to save her life. She died in the ambulance on the way to the hospital. I'm thinking about filing a lawsuit based on the delay in treatment, actually."

*The numbskull never disappoints*, Wayne thought. Totally predictable, he's always got his eye on the money.

"It seems your aunt may have been deliberately hit from behind by another vehicle," the sheriff said. He was still speaking quietly, but his tone had deepened.

"What?" Jonathon looked stunned. "Are you saying someone intentionally forced her off the road?"

"It's possible. We've sent the pictures of the tire and skid marks to the state lab. There were some paint chips on the rear bumper of your aunt's vehicle."

"I thought her car caught on fire," Jonathon said.

"It was only partially burned. The lab will get back to us in a couple of days with the make and year of the car that hit her."

Wayne knew those reports weren't always that precise, and even if the lab could give them the make and the year of the car, there were always hundreds, even thousands of vehicles with the same make, year and paint color. He had to give it to the sheriff, though. He was getting through. Jonathon had started to sweat. He reached into his pocket for a tissue, but finding none, wiped his forehead with the back of his hand.

"Well, it wasn't me who ran into her. I was cleaning the garage. You have to believe me, Sheriff."

"Actually I don't," the sheriff said flatly and Jonathon's eyes widened.

"I told you, I was cleaning out her garage when she left to go see her lawyer."

"So you knew she was seeing her lawyer?" the sheriff asked, his voice had turned silky smooth, the soft timbre of a predator calling quietly to a quivering prey.

"Yes, Aunt Abigail told me she was going to change her will. I asked her if I was going to inherit, and she said I would just have to wait and see," Jonathon said. "She knew I had some debts that needed to be paid. Despite her not telling me what she planned, I thought she was probably going to help. That's what has happened in the past. She would say she wouldn't give me any money and then a few days later, she would."

"I assume you know that if you were in *any way* connected to the accident that caused her death, you can't benefit from her will," Sheriff Bradley said and Jonathon swallowed. He asked if he could have a drink of water.

The interview didn't last much longer. Jonathon reiterated that he and his wife were making plans for the funeral and he had to leave. The sheriff said he might need to talk to him again, after the report on the bumper's paint chips and the road's skid marks came in.

"I assume you will make yourself available," the sheriff said coolly. Jonathon blinked, but nodded.

Making sure Jonathon didn't see him, Wayne exited out the back door of the observation room and waylaid the sheriff. "Good work rattling the little shit," he said.

"I did my best, but I have a feeling he's telling the truth," Sheriff Bradley said. "Want to get lunch?"

Wayne did and the two of them left the office for their local tavern.

# TEN

WAYNE WAS RETURNING TO ROSEDALE INVESTIGATIONS when his cell phone rang. He saw the pretty dimpled face of Camille Raines on his screen. "Hi Camille," he said.

"Hello, Detective," the woman's voice was quiet. She hadn't regained her ebullient personality yet, but seemed under control. "I just heard from Abigail's attorney. He hadn't known about her death and I had to tell him she passed," she stopped talking for a moment and cleared her throat. Wayne could tell she had been crying. "I asked if he could tell me about her will and he said he could, since I was one of the beneficiaries. I can hardly believe it, but you were right. Abigail left me her house and all its contents. Years ago, she told me that she was going to, but I thought she had changed her mind."

"That's wonderful, Camille. I'm pleased for you."

"The lawyer said Abigail also left me an additional monetary bequest that will cover the cost of paying the taxes and upkeep on the house."

"Terrific news. What about Jonathon and Christine? Did she leave them anything?" He slowed down as he turned into the neighborhood where Rosedale Investigations was located.

"He wouldn't tell me that, but said when I died, the house and any remaining income from Abigail would go to them or their descendants."

Wayne felt a shiver cross his broad shoulders. It already looked like Abigail's death had been engineered and now Camille could be in danger. He wondered if she should have police protection. He decided to ask the sheriff if he would have Deputy George drive by every day until the threat was neutralized.

"Did the attorney say when you could move into the house?"

"I can't move in until after the first of July. I'm pleased about that as it will give me time to sell my mobile home and pack up my clothes and personal possessions."

"I agree," Wayne said, as he pulled into the driveway of the business. Having several weeks before Camille could move into the house would also give the sheriff time to find the evidence to identify Abigail's assailant. Although Sheriff Bradley thought Jonathon was telling the truth about cleaning the garage when the accident occurred, Wayne was not so sure. He didn't trust the miserly little creep. "I assume Jonathon and Christine will move out by then," he said.

"I talked to Jonathon and told him about the will. I said I planned to move into the house next month and asked when he and Christine would be leaving. He said he wasn't planning to go anywhere," Camille's voice sounded discouraged.

*Oh he did, did he?* Wayne thought. "Would you like me to speak with him?"

"I certainly would. Could you do that?"

"It would be my pleasure," Wayne said. "Until you are safely moved in, I want you to call me immediately if Jonathon bothers you. In the meantime, I suggest you stop by the Forester house every day or so to keep an eye on your property. You don't want him to decide that some of the valuables in the house belong to him."

"I was thinking I should give them some money from Abigail's estate. I feel guilty that she cut them out," Camille said.

"Please don't do that until the investigation into Abigail's death is concluded. The sheriff is looking into whether someone deliberately ran Mrs. Forester off the road."

"Oh dear. I will hold off then, and thank you, Detective," she said.

"Don't you think it's time you called me Wayne?" he asked and could hear Camille's soft chuckle as she agreed.

BILLY JO WAS AT HER DESK AT ROSEDALE INVESTIGATIONS searching databases on her computer. She'd found the date of Dr. Cedric Brookover's death. He had died from a heart attack at seventy-three years of age. Nothing suspicious there. She'd even managed, using what Dory called her "seriously underhanded techniques," to access his will. All his assets were divided equally between his two surviving children. One of his daughters had died three years after her mother. The painting was not listed among his bequeathed possessions.

*Now what?* She asked herself, leaning back in her office chair to think.

There were three avenues she could pursue. First, she could gather more information on the artist himself. She opened a new document and typed Jeremy Iverson-Jones' name at the top. She'd found his birth certificate and saw he'd been born on a Monday, so *Wednesday's Child* wasn't titled for him. Plus, he committed suicide shortly after finishing the lovely iridescent work. In seeking to document the steps the painting took from the Brookover family to Mrs. Walcott, looking into the artist was a dead end.

Deleting the artist's name, she typed Wendy Brookover's name. It might be more productive to look into her. However, Mr. Dorne told her she had also died early. Researching her life wouldn't help either, since the painting still belonged to Dr. Cedric Brookover for decades after his wife passed away. She was about to delete Wendy Brookover's name when she decided she would check the day of the week she'd been born. It could take a bit of time to chase down her birth certificate, but could be worth it.

Finally, there was Mrs. Helen Chase Wilson. She had apparently acquired the painting from a garage sale and those were usually conducted within neighborhoods. She had obtained her address from Sylvia and once she located the original address for Dr. Cedric Brookover, it would be helpful to talk to the neighbors to see if anyone remembered a valuable painting being included in a sale many years ago.

*It would be far more productive to talk to people directly,* she thought. She wondered if PD would okay her making a road trip to Pennsylvania. If he approved her idea, she would ask her boyfriend, Mark, to go with her. A trip would be fun for both of them. Considering ways to get her boss to acquiesce, she went into the kitchen to make herself a cappuccino. She was returning to her desk when PD and Wayne entered the building. One quick glance at their faces swept away her plan to broach the idea.

"CONFERENCE ROOM EVERYBODY," WAYNE CALLED OUT, but it was a far cry from his usual jovial voice. Dory came out of her office and joined them. The team got seated and Billy Jo passed around the coffee carafe.

"I understand Abigail Forester was DOA when she arrived at the hospital," Dory said. "I was sorry to hear it. Was it an accident? I checked with Deputy George and he said there were skid marks on the road."

"What causes those marks?" Billy Jo asked.

"Skid marks are caused when a braked car slides on the surface of the pavement and in this case might mean that somebody forced Mrs. Forester's car off the road. Such patterns are becoming more accepted as forensic evidence. The sheriff sent off samples of paint from Mrs. Forester's rear bumper to the state lab. They will be able to tell the year and make of the car that struck her," PD said.

"I observed the interview the sheriff did with Jonathon Forester who maintained that he was cleaning out Abigail's garage when the accident happened. His wife was supposedly at the hairdressers. Camille Raines called me on my way in this morning. She inherited the Forester house, all its contents and a fair bit of Abigail's money. When she dies, however, Jonathon and Christine get the house and whatever money remains," Wayne informed the team.

"That makes me nervous," Dory said, giving Wayne a level look. "Do you want me to verify Christine's whereabouts when the accident happened?"

"Yes. In fact, please check where she was the entire morning," Wayne said. "Changing the subject, what's happening with the painting, Billy Jo?"

"I found out that the painting remained in the possession of Dr. Cedric Brookover, the man who commissioned the work, until his death in 1967. Tracing the chain of ownership between the date Dr. Brookover died and when Mrs. Walcott got the painting is going to be a challenge, but at least I'm only looking at around fifty years now, not a whole century." She took a deep breath and added, "I did have one thought, PD. I wondered if you would approve me driving to Pennsylvania to talk to people there. Obviously, I'll do all I can on the computer, but a visit is probably my best bet to figure out what happened to the painting after Dr. Brookover died."

PD hesitated, but after a quick glance at Dory (who was the CFO for the company) said, "Rosedale Investigations will cover gas, lodging and meals at the usual office rates. Since it takes a day to drive there and a day to drive back, you can go for four days, *provided* we don't find ourselves cooperating with the sheriff's office in a murder investigation before then."

"Thank you," Billy Jo said quietly but felt a corkscrew twist in her core, fearing it would turn out that Mrs. Forester had been murdered.

She decided she'd leave as soon as possible—before the sheriff's office got the report back from the state lab. Changing the subject, she asked, "Have you learned anything else about your son, PD?"

"Contacting the ex-wife today," he said shortly.

"Since we've now moved from the two cases under investigation to more personal matters, I have a question for you, Wayne. Have you got a date and more importantly a venue for your wedding yet?" Dory asked.

"Yes, it's going to be at seven p.m. on Saturday of Labor Day weekend and we will be married at the Episcopal Church in Rosedale. Lucy is sending out 'Save the Date' cards this week. We're still deciding on a place for the reception."

Everyone smiled and Billy Jo congratulated him.

"Okay, here are the assignments, people. Dory, we need you to track Christine Forester's movements the whole morning of Forester's accident. Wayne, I'd like you to talk to the sheriff's office about what role they want us to play if Mrs. Forester's death turns out to be murder," PD paused. "Billy Jo, before you leave, I want you to find out whether there is any family, no matter how distant, related to Mrs. Forester."

"The sheriff's office already checked and found nobody," she said, her voice sounding plaintive. But looking at the granite-like expression on PD's face she added, "I will double check."

"That will do it. We're adjourned," PD said.

TELLING THE TEAM THE DATE OF his UPCOMING WEDDING had increased the pressure Wayne felt to find Lucy's sister. His plan was to track down one of his old CI's who operated as an informant about the drug scene. On his way out, he stopped at Billy Jo's desk and looked intently at her. He had a feeling she had been withholding something about the painting.

She looked up at him saying, "Can I help you, Detective?"

"Like tell me the entire story about the painting, perhaps?" Wayne said, keeping his eyes tightly locked on hers.

Billy Jo took a deep breath and lowering her voice to a whisper said, "I didn't tell you everything because the painting is cursed."

"Cursed?"

"Yes and I don't want PD to know, so please keep it to yourself. He thinks this investigation is insane already and telling him about the curse would likely have him stop me looking into it altogether. I told you the offer to give the painting to the University fell through, but not the reason. The *reason* the Chair of the Art Department turned the painting down was his fear about the curse."

Wayne's eyebrows rose for a second before he frowned and said. "You need to tell Dory," and left the building.

# ELEVEN

A T FIVE O'CLOCK THAT EVENING, BILLY JO WALKED UPSTAIRS to her apartment and called her boyfriend, Mark. He was in Michigan, taking an advanced course on computer security for police departments. As a condition of the course, attendees were required to leave their phones in their hotel rooms. It was part of an exercise to see what they could find without their phones or laptops. He didn't answer and she left a message.

"Mark, it's me. I have gotten permission to take a trip to Erie, Pennsylvania. I'd like you to join me. I am leaving in the morning. It's a nine-hour drive and I'm staying at the Bayfront hotel. I know today is the last day on your course, so hopefully you can come. It's only about a four-hour drive from Detroit. I've been doing some research on a painting and think you will find it intriguing. I miss you." She paused before adding, "See you soon."

Just then her stomach growled and she stopped thinking about her boyfriend and gave some consideration to dinner. There was nothing in her little mini-refrigerator in her apartment and only fruit and donuts in the fridge downstairs. She called Dory.

"So the painting is cursed?" Dory said and Billy Jo laughed right out loud. Obviously, Dory and Wayne had already talked.

"It is," she said, amused.

"Well, well, well. That is indeed interesting. I called Evangeline Bon Temps, our local expert in the occult, and she said for an object to be considered cursed, a person owning it has to die. There are famous curses, like the curse of the tomb of Tutankhamen and several large diamonds have a reputation for being cursed," Dory said. "This is very cool, Billy Jo."

"I really don't want PD to know, so please keep it to yourself. He already thinks I'm a light-weight in the business. If he finds out the painting is cursed, he will pull me off the case. On another note, I wondered if you wanted to cook tonight by chance. There's nothing to eat here and I'm starving."

"Provided you tell me *everything* you learned from your visit to the University, I could be persuaded to cook. Stop at the grocery store and pick up some yellow and green peppers and a red onion. I can do shish-kabobs on the grill. Get one of the bags of salad, too."

"On my way," Billy Jo said and feeling a sense of relief that she could share her concerns with Dory, set out happily for the grocery store.

TWO HOURS LATER THE TWO WOMEN WERE FINISHING DINNER when Dory said, "Okay, fess up, Kiddo. I want the whole story of *Wednesday's Child.*"

"After that delicious dinner, I owe you. When I talked with Professor Hayward, he was weird about the painting," she paused frowning. "The only helpful thing he told me was that I should talk with a Mr. William Dorne."

"I assume you found him," Dory said.

"I did. He is in his nineties, but still works as a Docent for the Art Museum on campus. His father was the Chair of the Art Department when Dr. Cedric Brookover offered to give the painting to the Museum in the 1950's."

"You said the deal didn't go through," Dory said.

"Well, it was the *reason* the deal didn't go through that I left out. That's when Dr. Dorne learned about the curse. He declined the gift and Dr. Brookover returned to Pennsylvania with the painting."

"Obviously, Dr. Dorne took the curse seriously," Dory said thoughtfully.

"I assume so. Something else odd turned up in my visit with William Dorne. He calls the painting, *Children by the Lakeshore* and had never heard the title, *Wednesday's Child.* All I can figure is that there are two titles for the painting. Apparently, some bad things happened to the family after the artist delivered the artwork to the Brookovers," Billy Jo said.

"Like what?" Dory asked.

"For one thing, Mrs. Brookover died shortly thereafter. The artist subsequently committed suicide and a couple of years after that one of Brookover's daughter's died. She was only twelve."

"How are you going to find out what happened between Dr. Brookover's demise and when Mrs. Walcott inherited?"

"What I know so far is that Mrs. Walcott inherited the painting from a woman named Helen Chase Wilson who found the painting in a garage sale."

"And now you are going to Pennsylvania where I assume you hope to find some descendents of the Brookovers or the Chase Wilson family who know something that will fill in the gaps. That seems like an appropriate next step, but I am confused about why you seem to be focused on the title. It really has nothing to do with the provenance, does it?" Dory asked.

"No, you're right, but for some reason I can't let it go," Billy Jo hesitated before adding, "The painting has entered my heart, Dory. It's like the cold murder cases Wayne and PD talk about, the ones they didn't solve and continue to haunt them. Such a lovely evocative painting should never have been saddled with that terrible label. And, I don't believe in curses anyway," Billy Jo said.

"You don't? I do. And you should! You said the painting had crept into your heart. Years ago, I had the same reaction when I fell in love with an opal necklace." Dory got up from her kitchen table and picked up a bottle of red wine. She added some to her glass, and topped up Billy Jo's, before sitting back down at the table. It was getting dark outside and the warmth of the kitchen seemed an island of coziness lit by flickering candles.

"Go on about the necklace," Billy Jo said.

"It was antique, made in the 1920's, a gold chain with a large central opal and small strips of gold hanging from the chain that were tipped with smaller opals. I had the store put it aside for me and saved for months to afford it. The day before I went to pick it up, I did some research into opals and found out they are considered unlucky. Nothing deterred me. I had to own it."

"Do you still have it? I'd love to see it," Billy Jo said.

"Hang on," she said. "Let me tell you the whole story. The day I got the necklace, I was on my way home when I drove over a piece of sharp metal in the road. It caused a flat tire. It was pouring down rain outside and that was before we had cell phones. I had to change the tire myself and, as you know, I'm never dressed for such emergencies."

"As well I know," Billy Jo said and grinned.

"Anyway, I got the jack and the spare tire from the trunk, and set the jack in position. I levered the car up until the back of the vehicle rose off the ground and the tire would spin freely. Cars were racing past and I was drenched. I tried to flag down some help, but since chivalry was totally dead that day, nobody stopped. I decided to get back into my car and warm up before replacing the flat tire with a spare. That was when a car hit me from behind knocking my car off the jack. To make a long story short, I got a broken vertebrae in my neck and had to have surgery."

"Well, I don't see how you could blame the necklace for that," Billy Jo said, as she sipped her wine.

"Perhaps not, but the day I got home after the surgery, I fell into a clump of poison ivy in my back yard and got a horrible case. It was so bad I had to be hospitalized again and had no sooner gotten it under control than I broke an ankle. Enough was enough! The Universe was speaking to me. Despite its fragile, almost ethereal beauty, the damn necklace was cursed. I took it back to the store. They were unsurprised and told me a previous buyer had also returned it."

"I'm not sure whether this story makes me feel better or worse," Billy Jo said frowning.

"The reason I told you the story was to warn you. This quest you are on could be dangerous. A curse is nothing to wave casually aside. Promise me, Billy Jo," she looked at her seriously and the girl nodded. "By the way, have you come up with a name for this case?"

Billy Jo nodded. "I call it the In the Frame."

"I get it. It's because the paintings are framed and we have had several suspects in the frame for Mrs. Forester's murder", Dory said. "Please be careful."

"I will. I'm leaving early tomorrow morning. I called Mark and asked him to meet me there."

"Ah, young love. Having our dragon-tattooed Mark stay with you definitely makes me feel better, but try not to spend all your time in bed with Hot Stuff."

"Dory! You are bad," Billy Jo said, shocked.

"And you are weak for that boy," Dory said.

"Not as weak as you are for yours," Billy Jo responded, referring to Dory's on-again, off-again relationship with her boyfriend, Al. They both laughed.

Billy Jo pulled onto the highway at seven o'clock the next morning. She had done some research about the city the night before, learning it was Pennsylvania's access point to Lake Erie and the location of Penn State Erie, known as Behrend College. Presque Isle State Park on the peninsula was a popular recreation area. The city had an art museum, a history society, a planetarium, and a zoo. Other than the history society, she wouldn't have time for the other attractions of the city, except possibly to hike Presque Isle with Mark.

The place she had targeted as her starting point was the Erie History Society. They would be the most likely to know about the painting. The Society was located in a beautiful old Romanesque stone building, once the home of a lumber baron. Built in 1891, it had intricate wood carvings, multiple stained-glass windows, a solarium and a third-floor ballroom. The mansion was listed on the National Historic Register. Since Dr. Brookover was a noted academic, he might have even served on the Board of the History Society before his demise.

The Bayside hotel had a lovely infinity edge pool and was located right on Lake Erie. After a nine-hour drive, it would be a treat to have a swim. According to her GPS, she would arrive at the hotel at 6:30. Mark had texted her, cheered with the getaway. He expected to be there by 8:00. She could hardly wait to see him.

In her excitement, she had forgotten the fact that PD's two-week deadline for completion of the provenance on the paintings was fast approaching or that she hadn't found any relatives for Mrs. Forester. Those oversights would return to haunt her in the days ahead.

# TWELVE

DORY ARRIVED AT WORK EARLY THE FOLLOWING MORNING and went into the kitchen to make coffee. PD came out of his office to ask if she'd seen Billy Jo's report on any family members she'd found for the late Abigail Forester.

"Not that I saw. You can text her and ask," Dory said. "She already left on her trip. I'm off to meet with Father Dominic, Abigail's priest, this morning. He's conducting her funeral and may have something helpful to tell us. Just dotting some i's and crossing some t's."

"Where's Wayne?"

"He was headed to her autopsy. Sheriff Bradley was meeting him there. Since Wayne isn't an officer of the law now, the pathologist won't release any information to him, only to the sheriff. The post-mortem is being done by a new female colleague of Dr. Estes. Did you know our old curmudgeon of a pathologist is actually retiring? I thought I'd never see the day. The hospital has hired this young woman to shadow him for a few months before taking over. I pity the poor thing because Dr. Estes is a demanding task-master, especially in cases of presumed or actual murder."

"When I was a young detective just starting out some forty years ago, he was already old and irascible. I made the mistake of being late to an autopsy once and he practically bit my head off. What's the woman's name?"

"Dr. Katherine Lange, I believe."

"Thanks for the coffee, Dory. I'll text Billy Jo about the relatives of the Foresters. My instinct is that the driver of the car that smacked into Abigail Forester is a yet-undiscovered family member. And further that her murder is all about her money."

"Is it officially a murder case, then?" Dory asked.

"Not until the report on the skid marks come back, but as far as I am concerned there's no question." PD walked back to his office and texted Billy Jo, asking for her report. Although she was usually prompt in responding, he didn't receive a reply. He waited an hour and texted her again. Irritatingly, he received no answer.

WAYNE REACHED ROSEDALE GENERAL WHERE DR. ESTES did autopsies by 6:30 a.m. Although many families refused to have autopsies done these days, the pathologist was committed to doing a post-mortem on all suspicious deaths in Rose County. Wayne admired his thoroughness but knew the man barely tolerated him. *Coffee might help*, he thought and stopped in the hospital cafeteria on the first floor to get two coffees, one for him and one for Dr. Estes. Luckily the barista knew exactly how the pathologist liked his brew.

He was leaning against the basement wall when a young woman came walking quickly down the corridor. She was slim with reddish brown hair in a ponytail and glasses that hung from a cord around her neck. The woman was clad in a full-length white lab coat—the length of which indicated she was a member of the hospital staff and not a medical student. By tradition, they wore shorter coats.

"Good morning," she greeted him. "I'm Dr. Katherine Lange, the new assistant pathologist for Rosedale General and Coroner for Rose County."

She spoke with what he recognized as an Australian accent. Hoping he would get on better with Dr. Lange than he had with Dr. Estes, he set one of the coffees down and held out his hand to shake hers saying, "I'm Detective Wayne Nichols. Is Dr. Estes on his way?"

Her voice was cool when she said, "It's *former* Detective Nichols, I believe. I've been briefed. Is Sheriff Bradley joining us?"

"He is," Wayne said, chastened.

Dr. Lange checked her clipboard and said, "Dr. Estes is busy with other matters. He and I did the preliminary work yesterday with the help of the Morgue's Diener." Dr. Lange gestured to a white-clad assistant who had joined them. His name tag read Charlie Dep.

Wayne nodded to Charlie. They had met previously. When he initially asked Charlie about his title, he was told the word 'Diener' was German for *corpse servant*, an ancient occupation meaning the person who carried the dead.

The three of them walked into the chilly dissection room with its stainless-steel tables and white neck rests. Wayne stood at the side of the room, still holding the two coffees, as Dr. Lange clicked a remote that opened one of the long drawers holding the body of Abigail Forester. With Charlie's help, she expertly transferred the body onto the steel table.

Wayne was relieved to see that the woman on the table was covered with a white sheet. He had never bolted from an autopsy, or thrown up during a post-mortem in his entire career, but having the body covered definitely helped.

They heard a sharp rap on the door and Sheriff Bradley entered the Mortuary. He was in uniform.

"Nice of you to join us," Dr. Lange said coolly.

"Is Dr. Estes going to be with us this morning?" Sheriff Bradley asked.

"He is not," she said and pulled the sheet off the body with a flick of her wrist. Wayne grimaced. The body was already cut wide open and he could see the woman's organs clearly. He forced himself not to look away, but it was difficult.

"As you see, I've already begun. I don't like wasting the time of law enforcement," Dr. Lange said crisply.

"Thank you," the sheriff said quietly. He cast a quick open-eyed look at Wayne.

"Since you are here, Sheriff, I will present my findings on what I've done so far. I will fax you my complete written report later today. It is up to you whether you share written reports with *former* Detectives.

"Please proceed," Sheriff Bradley said.

"Mrs. Abigail Forester was sixty-two years of age and in moderately good health. There was no sign of alcoholism or drug use in her liver, nor did the toxicology report show any such substances in her blood. She was not a smoker and her lungs were clear. Her stomach contents revealed that she had eaten scrambled eggs and toast for breakfast. However, I regret to say that she had late-stage Non-Hodgkin's lymphoma." She paused and looked directly at the two men. The diagnosis hung in the air, a bitter presentiment of the battle Mrs. Forester would have faced, had she lived.

"I wonder if she knew about her cancer," Wayne said quietly.

"She did," Katherine Lange said. "The name of her primary care physician was on her medical record. I called him and he gave me the name of her oncologist. The oncologist had already informed her of the diagnosis," Dr. Lange paused.

Wayne and Sheriff Bradley glanced at each other briefly.

"What was her prognosis?" Wayne asked, knowing the young pathologist would have checked. She might only be an assistant, but this skinny little woman was a force to be reckoned with.

"Unfortunately, the lymphoma was well advanced. I personally would never make a *guess* about such a prognosis, but her oncologist told her she had about six months to live." Her mouth tightened.

"Somebody just tried to kill a dying woman," Wayne said

"And succeeded," Sheriff Bradley said.

# THIRTEEN

INVESTIGATOR DORY CLARKSON CHOSE A NAVY BLUE DRESS with long sleeves and a high neckline for her visit with Fr. Dominic, Abigail Forester's priest. Matching navy low-heeled shoes, a simple silver chain with a cross and silver post earrings completed her ensemble. Leaving her home, she drove to St. Martha's Cathedral. It was a large sanctuary with two wings. The façade of the building showcased a circular stained-glass window. She parked her car and walked toward the intricately carved wooden door. The temperature outside was soaring as it always did by the end of June.

It was mid-morning on a weekday and she wasn't sure the Cathedral would be open, but the door swung open easily and she entered the narthex and proceeded into the main part of the sanctuary appreciating the air conditioning. The interior had a peaked ceiling and thirty or forty rows of pews. The sides of the nave were decorated with paintings depicting the stages of the cross. *Such a gloomy religious tradition*, Dory thought.

She walked down the central aisle toward the altar. Beyond the pews at the front of the sanctuary, were broad curving steps leading up into the area for the choir and the altar. The stained-glass window on the façade, depicting Mary holding baby Jesus in her arms, was the lovely showpiece for the church.

Dory was a believer, but not a Catholic. Nevertheless, in keeping with the respect she invariably felt in any house of worship, she genuflected briefly and entered a pew. She bowed her head and waited in the empty silent church for the emotional release she normally experienced in places for worship. Her whole body began to relax and she felt her shoulders come down. She hadn't realized how stressed she's been. Ever since Wayne's call saying that the report on the skid marks had come back and she learned Mrs. Abigail Forester had been forced off the road, she'd been feeling anxious.

She took a deep breath, closed her eyes, sought a calm space and entered the bliss of silence. To help her relax, Dory often envisioned walking her dog in fields of wildflowers. She had just summoned the field to mind when loud musical notes coming from the organ shattered her concentration. She opened her eyes to see who was practicing. An older woman with permed gray hair was pounding away at the massive church organ.

*So much for emotional release and tranquility*, Dory thought. She had never found organ music conducive to meditation. At that point, a priest in a long black soutane, with a slice of a white dog collar at his neckline, entered the altar area. He knelt before the altar for a moment and then stood and noticed her. He was completely bald, tall and slim with dark shining eyes the color of mulberries.

"Father Dominic?" Dory said. "May I speak with you?"

"Confession isn't until six today," the priest said.

"My name is Dory Clarkson and I'm not here for confession. I'm from Rosedale Investigations and have some questions for you about Abigail Forester."

"Come to my office," he said and led the way back down the central aisle and turned into the north transept. They passed a small chapel dedicated to the Virgin Mary before coming upon a row of modern offices. Fr. Dominic walked past his secretary who said a pleasant hello. She was busy folding multi-colored newsletters.

Walking behind the priest in his perfectly tailored soutane, Dory was hit by a memory from her earliest childhood. For so many years, due to the dire poverty of her family, she wore only homemade clothes. Her grandmother had made her outfits from old garments obtained from other family members that were torn apart and sewn into clothing for her. The mean kids in school called her "Patches". She was one of only a handful of African American children in the school as it was, and her ratty clothes made her an easy target for their teasing.

The day she got her first paycheck from working at the sheriff's office, Dory went immediately to the department store in town and bought a skirt and blouse that actually matched. That day, she could hardly stop looking at herself in the mirror. Ever since then, Dory had spent much of her income on her wardrobe. She would never look like that poor black child in curly pigtails again.

Fr. Dominic opened the door to his private office and said, "Please come in." He gestured to a chair in front of his large oak desk. "Mrs. Forester's funeral is in three days. It will be held here followed by a church supper in the basement. All are invited to attend."

"Thank you, Father. I will be present, as will my partners at Rosedale Investigations. I don't know if you are aware, but it seems virtually certain that Abigail Forester was murdered. We are collaborating with the sheriff in investigating this terrible crime."

The priest looked stunned and crossed himself.

"Here is my private investigator ID," Dory said showing it to the priest. "I am well aware that all confessions, even those of a deceased person, are sacrosanct, and that you won't reveal what was said. I am not asking you for confidential information, but we would appreciate any help you could give us."

"That's terrible news. Poor woman. I will pray fervently for her soul. How can I help?"

"We know that Abigail was on her way to an appointment with her attorney to re-write her will when she was run off the road by someone which caused her death. I wonder if she discussed any changes she planned to make with you? That information could lead us to her killer. I assure you that cooperating with the authorities and helping to bring her killer to justice is protected under the Good Samaritan law."

"She did speak with me about her legal appointment in a private counselling session, separate from confession. Abigail had a strong sense of family duty and planned on leaving a life insurance policy to her nephew, Jonathon, but resented the undo pressure he was putting on her to inherit her entire estate. She recently learned she had cancer and was coming to the end of her life. That was the reason she was changing her will. We prayed together and I offered to have the congregation pray for her as well."

"Beyond the insurance policy for Jonathon, did she tell you anything further regarding the new will?" Dory asked.

"Yes. She was trying to locate a family member she had lost contact with many years ago. She felt terribly guilty that she had failed this person. If she could find him before she ran out of time, the remainder of her estate, beyond a large bequest to her friend Camille Raines, would go to him."

"Go on," Dory said, writing the details in her small notebook.

"I asked her if she wanted a blessing for her journey. She did and thanked me. I only wish I had urged her to take confession then. It's on my conscience that she died without the relief of extreme unction," the priest's mobile mouth quivered and he bit his lower lip. It was obvious he had cared about the woman.

"Did she give you the person's name by chance? The one she felt so guilty about?" Dory asked hopefully.

"She did. It was her brother's only son. Abigail's brother, Oscar, was the black sheep of the family. He died of alcoholism and she felt terrible about not helping his son, Steve, with support for his college education."

Driving back to the office, following the astoundingly productive meeting with Father Dominic, Dory dialed PD. He had been the person who had the idea that Abigail's death had to do with a family member . . . and her money. It looked like he had been right.

WAYNE WAS SITTING AT THE KITCHEN ISLAND WORKING on his lap-top that evening. Hearing the sound of garage door opening, he quickly closed the computer and stood up to greet Lucy. He'd closed the lid just in time. His fiancé had a tendency to be far too observant about anything that might lead him into danger. He didn't want her to see that he had been checking the police database for the West Meade area of Nashville. The crime rate in that area was 300% higher than in more affluent areas of the city and included murder, rape, robbery and assault. It was also a hang-out for druggies.

He kissed Lucy hello and she mentioned that she was on-call. Since Wayne had private plans for later than night, he hoped she would be called to return to work. He got lucky. She was paged around ten p.m.

"Going in to the hospital?" he asked, trying not to look relieved.

"Should only be there an hour or two," she said, looking around for her purse and lab coat. "See you later," she called as she walked out to the garage.

After making sure Lucy had left the neighborhood, Wayne grabbed his keys and drove his truck to the West Meade neighborhood. The area had once been one of the more affluent regions in the city and at least one old mansion remained on the historic places list. Lately, however, the area had gone downhill and was now a hot spot for drugs. His confidential informant, Larry the Lush, had called him several days earlier saying the neighborhood would be worth checking out for Lucy's sister. It was a tiny pinpoint of hope in a quest that had taken him almost a year.

He stopped at a fast-food place and was carrying a large white paper bag stuffed with hamburgers when he reached his target area. He strode the mostly deserted street calling out, "Anybody hungry?" He repeated the question periodically.

A few minutes later, a tiny, emaciated woman dashed out from an open door in a boarded-up building and grabbed for the white bag. The moon had risen and he could see her devastated face. She was dressed in rags and had no teeth. They had been eaten away by her meth addiction. Wayne kept a tight hold on his paper bag saying, "Hang on a minute. I want some information first. You can have the food once I find who I'm looking for."

The woman kept tugging at the bag. He looked down at her sadly. She seemed almost feral, reduced to being a non-human by drugs.

"I'm not a snitch," she said over and over as if repeating a mantra, something she had been taught to say. Her hands scrabbled at the bag and tore open a corner of it.

Wayne lifted her skeletal arm gently and said, "I'm looking for Anne, a young red-haired woman."

The woman blinked and seemed to recognize the name. "You a cop?"

"Used to be, but not now. And I don't care about illegal drugs. If you will take me to her, you can have the whole bag of food. I'm her . . . brother-in-law. I won't hurt her."

A sly look flashed across the woman's face and to his surprise she took his hand and led him down the darkened street. Some young men in the distance were standing in a cluster. They were wearing hoodies and looked furtive. On either side of the street he saw refurbished buildings and signs reading 'retail space to rent'. It was a sign of a resurgence and meant the druggies would soon vacate. If Anne was around here, he had to find her soon.

The woman pulled him forward and Wayne followed, hoping she wasn't leading him into an ambush. He kept a close eye on the gang of hoodies. Between one hand on the white paper bag and one hand held by the little woman, he wouldn't be able to reach his gun if attacked. Then his guide stopped short and pointed across the street to a building with a large scaffolding in front of it. A faint misty rain was falling. It made the scaffolding shiny and the buildings look faint and insubstantial. He recalled his foster mother telling him about the different types of rain in the mythology of Native Americans. Male rain was hard and pounding. This was a gentle "female" rain.

At first, he couldn't see what his guide was pointing at, but then he did. Sitting on the stoop of the building, mostly hidden behind the scaffolding, was a person asleep or in a drug trance. He couldn't see her face and wasn't sure he would recognize her anyway. Only one street light was working but through the hazy rainfall, he saw a glint of red hair.

"There," his guide pointed and pulled the bag of food from his hand. She ran away and he watched her go, feeling sad for the destroyed vestige of a woman. The white bag was the only thing that identified her moving silhouette as she darted down the murky street. Several dark-clad figures closed in around her. He knew they would take the food and she wouldn't get any. He regretted not helping her, but it wasn't his fight. He had his own quest to pursue.

Crossing the road quickly, he knelt down, wincing in pain due to his knee that needed replacing, to see the figure on the doorstep. She tipped her face up to see who was there and her eyes opened wide in fear. Despite the dark night, he was pretty sure he recognized her from the photographs Lucy had shown him. "Anne, I'm your sister Lucy's fiancé. I'm here to help."

A desperate acquisitive look made her eyes narrow, but she stood up shakily. "Lucy?" she asked and Wayne nodded. He reached for her bone-thin arm and she stood up to go with him.

Rosedale General hospital operated a drug detox facility on the northern edge of town. He would take her there. *Thank God, Lucy didn't come into contact with druggies unless they overdosed and came into the ER*, he thought. There wasn't much time to get Anne clean and in shape to attend the wedding. It was going to be close.

# FOURTEEN

Mark Schneider, Billy Jo's boyfriend, who was known to the Rosedale Investigations team as Dragon Boy (due to a large multi-colored dragon tattooed on his back), arrived at the hotel at 8:10 p.m. He stopped at the marble-topped front desk and asked the clerk to call Billy Jo's room. She didn't answer, so he left a message saying he had arrived. Hoping to see her appear in the lobby, he wandered around a bit before spotting the shining infinity pool fronting the ruffled blue expanse of Lake Erie. He walked outside. A cool wind had come up and there was only one person sitting on the pool deck. She had her back to him, but he could see the edge of a red bikini bottom, a corner of a straw sunhat and cherry-colored toenail polish on bare toes. He smiled. It was his girlfriend, Billy Jo.

Without alerting her to his presence, he went back inside to the bar and bought two strawberry daiquiris. Heading back to the pool, he stopped behind her chair and said, "Sorry to disturb you, Miss, but a scary-looking desperado in the bar insisted on sending you a drink."

She whirled around and saw him, stood up with a delighted shriek and kissed him hello. It was such an enthusiastic, prolonged kiss, he had a hard time not dropping the drinks.

"This was such a great idea," Mark said, sitting down on an adjacent deck chair and handing her a daiquiri. "We've never been on a trip before."

"We've never spent the night together either, not a whole night," she said, raising her glass in his direction and winking.

"And just why has that been?" Mark said, grinning.

"You know why. After the night Wayne went ballistic when he caught you with your zipper part-way down and me tightening the belt on my bathrobe, I decided there would never be a repeat of that episode."

"He did have a hard time seeing his girl with a disreputable computer programmer with only *loving* on his mind," Mark said and chuckled.

They toasted each other, sitting in side-by-side chaise lounges, sipped their drinks and watched the last of the sunset's purple clouds trail across the horizon.

"You said you've been investigating a painting?"

"I sure am. I'll tell you the whole story." She proceeded to give Mark the background, ending with her plan for the following day. After breakfast, they would hike the three-mile Presque Isle trail while they waited for the Historical Society to open. Then they would go to the place and Billy Jo would ascertain what background they might have on the Brookover family, as well the artist. Mark was assigned to see if the Society owned any other paintings by Jeremy Iverson-Jones. She handed him her cell phone with its picture of *Wednesday's Child*. Even in such a small format, Mark was impressed.

"I notice you have several missed calls from Dory and PD," he said.

"I know. PD asked me to look into Mrs. Abigail Forester's relatives. She's the major case we're investigating. The Sheriff's Office already checked and found nobody. I thought it was a waste of my time and didn't do it. That's what PD is calling about, but so far I've avoided responding. What?" she asked, looking at Mark's critical expression.

"You need to try to work on it, or you'll be facing the wrath of PD when you return."

"Okay, okay. I've got my laptop. I'll see what I can find later."

"Better text him," Mark said and Billy rolled her eyes but did so.

THE FOLLOWING MORNING THE COUPLE RETURNED from their hike, showered and changed before heading over to the Historical Society. They got there at ten a.m. The building was very impressive with a smooth lawn edged with boxwood and several ancient trees. The exterior was clad in irregular square pinkish stones. The left wing was topped with a rounded turret and the right side had a three-story chimney. A stone cupola covered the driveway leading to the front door.

Once inside, Billy Jo was captivated by three tall multi-paned stained-glass windows with lovely intricate designs. The colors of the glass were soft yellows, blues and golds. The sun came through the windows lighting the interior of the building and splashing color on the walls. The main floor had wooden walls, a coffered ceiling and a grand staircase that rose to the second level. They called out, but there was no response. The beautifully restored old place was silent as the history it contained.

The couple walked quietly from the entryway to the main floor salon. Glancing around the room, Billy Jo was surprised to see that it was completely empty—except for a single large easel positioned in the center of the room.

On that easel stood a painting. It was *Wednesday's Child*.

"Isn't that the painting?" Mark asked. He frowned, sounding perplexed.

Billy Jo was so shocked she couldn't speak. Walking closer, she looked at the painting carefully—shifting her gaze from the water, to the children, to the beach. It was identical to the painting she had just seen at the home of Mrs. Walcott. She reached forward and although she knew she shouldn't, with the tip of one finger she gently touched the tiny multi-shaded blue, green, aqua and azure paint strokes with which the artist had created the water. Each brush stroke was separate and she could feel individual daubs of paint. This was no copy. This was an original. Jeremy Iverson-Jones had painted the same scene twice. Now she knew why there were two titles.

"Compare it to the one on your phone," Mark said and Billy Jo pulled out her phone and used her fingers to stretch the image of *Wednesday's Child*. She matched each corner of the painting on the easel to the same corner of the painting on her cell phone. She enlarged the artist's signature and compared it. "The signatures are identical," she murmured.

"Did you see that faint shadowy image on the left side?" Mark asked. "That's the only difference I see."

"Where?" Billy Jo asked and Mark pointed to a barely visible penumbra on the left side of the painting. It was an indistinct contour of a woman in a broad-brimmed summer hat. They looked at it from several angles. Sometimes it appeared and sometimes—depending on the light—they couldn't see it at all.

"The profile is that of Mrs. Wendy Brookover," a woman said as she entered the room. An elegant older lady, she had silver hair and was dressed in a dark skirt, a pink silk blouse and flat heeled shoes. "I'm Betty Poitou, the Curator of paintings here. Jeremy Iverson-Jones is our famous local impressionist and portraitist. This painting is called

*Children by the Lakeshore* and was done for Dr. Cedric Brookover a century ago. It's a painting with a sad history as both the artist and Mrs. Brookover, the mother of the children, died shortly after the completion of the work."

"We are pleased to meet you, Ms. Poitou. I'm Billy Jo Bradley and this is my friend, Mark Schneider. We're here to learn more about the artist and his work."

They shook hands and Billy Jo continued saying, "Did you know there are two originals of this scene? The one I'm familiar with is in Tennessee. It's entitled *Wednesday's Child*," she said and showed the woman the photos on her cell phone.

Betty Poitou didn't answer right away. She seemed thrown by the news and took a breath before saying, "I had heard rumors of a duplicate painting but was unable to confirm them. It's called *Wednesday's Child*, you said? What's the date on it?"

"1920."

"*Children by the Lakeshore* was painted first then, it's dated 1919."

"When did Mrs. Brookover die?" Billy Jo asked.

"Late in 1919, just before Christmas," Ms. Poitou said and a troubled expression crossed her face.

"I wonder if there is somewhere we could talk privately?" Billy Jo asked. Some visitors had entered the Society and were chatting loudly.

"It seems you and I have a quite lot to talk about," Mrs. Poitou said and turned toward her office. After a quick whispered exchange with Mark, Billy Jo followed.

CURATOR POITOU OFFERED BILLY JO COFFEE AND A SEAT. "What have you learned so far about the artist?" she asked.

"I know that Wendy Brookover and Jeremy Iverson-Jones fell in love while he was painting the portrait of her children," Billy Jo said.

"That seems to be true," the Curator said cautiously. "However, we don't discuss that with visitors because we don't want to embarrass the family. The descendants of Dr. Cedric Brookover are still living in the area."

"Not because you think Wendy Brookover was murdered?" Billy Jo asked, raising falsely-innocent eyebrows.

Ms. Poitou looked horrified. "Certainly not! That's absolutely not the case. Mrs. Brookover fell down a flight of stairs and broke her neck. It was an accident and no investigation was done."

"I'm sorry, I didn't mean to upset you but I wonder if you think her death could have been caused by the curse?" Billy Jo said.

Betty Poitou's facial expression didn't change, but her eyes looked hooded and her body went completely still. She was clearly more troubled about this topic than about the presumed love affair. "I have heard tales about it," she conceded quietly. "I don't believe it, of course. Curses are the stuff of Hollywood thrillers."

"They are indeed, but I wonder if you think the Brookover family could believe the painting is cursed?"

"Of course not. It's nonsense," Ms. Poitou said firmly.

"I'm not so sure," Billy Jo paused. "As you probably know, shortly after Mrs. Brookover died, the artist killed himself and then a few years later, Wendy's youngest daughter died. Those deaths could have made the Brookover family believe in the curse."

"I guess it's possible," Ms. Poitou said, but her tone was guarded.

"On another note, I wonder if you have an address for Dr. Cedric Brookover's grandson, Richard. I believe he's still living locally and I'd like to meet him," Billy Jo said.

Ms. Poitou said she did. She looked up the address on her computer and read it to her.

Billy Jo jotted it down. "Please don't mention this curse when you meet with him, or the presumed affair between his grandmother and the artist," she said firmly.

"I'm sorry Ms. Poitou, but I've been hired to document the provenance of *Wednesday's Child* and the only way to do that is to ask questions, and follow the clues where they lead," Billy Jo said.

The Curator kept her facial expression neutral as she said good-bye, but Billy Jo could tell it took effort.

BACK IN ROSEDALE, PD WAS SITTING RESTLESSLY AT HIS DESK. He had hesitated a dozen times, but finally took a deep breath and dialed the phone number of Mrs. Gladys Bonner, his son's ex-wife.

"Hello," a woman's throaty voice answered. She sounded like a smoker, a woman who spent a lot of time listening to music in bars—one of the few public places where smoking was still permitted.

"Good Morning. My name is Patrick Devlin Pascoe. I'm your ex-husband's father and I have some questions for you. The funeral home in Rosedale tracked me down. Do you have time to talk?"

She didn't respond right away but then said, "For a little while. This is a closed chapter for me. Ryan's dead, we've been divorced almost twenty years, and I've remarried. Besides, you ran out on his mother who died in an auto accident when he was only a few weeks old. You don't have the right to know a single damn thing." Her husky voice had turned harsh.

"I can see how you would feel that way, Gladys, but I never knew Amy was pregnant. I was in the Army and was shipped out to Viet Nam only a few weeks after we met. I wrote dozens of letters to her. All of them were returned. Until the Rosedale Funeral Home called last week, I didn't know of my son's existence. So, I do think I have the right to some information, don't you?"

"Hmmm. Well, that does change things a bit. What do you want to know?"

"Who ended up raising the baby? And why didn't they contact me, at least after I got out of the service?"

"I met Ryan in college and for a long time he was very tight-lipped about his family. He eventually told me he had been raised by his grandparents and treated as a burden—an illegitimate bastard. When we got engaged, I insisted on meeting them. His grandmother was a nice woman, but his grandfather was a piece of work. When I asked what happened to Ryan's mother, I was told she died in an auto accident. Asking about Ryan's father, I got blasted by a string of objectionable language from the grandfather."

*It must have been Amy's father who returned my letters*, PD thought. "If you don't mind, I was wondering something else. Did you and my son have children?"

"That was one of the issues between us. I wanted a family, but Ryan didn't feel he could be a good father and kept saying no."

"So you didn't have any children?" PD asked. He watched the door to any further involvement on his part begin to close.

"Actually I do. I have a son named Liam," she said.

"But you said Ryan didn't want a child. Was the pregnancy the reason you divorced?" PD asked.

"No, to my surprise, the opposite happened. Despite his fears about fatherhood, once the baby was on his way, Ryan wanted us to reconcile. We had been separated."

"Go on," PD said.

"During the time of our separation, I'd been seeing a man named

Carl Bonner, who became my second husband. We had fallen in love and he wanted us to be together, but was in the midst of a divorce himself and their litigation had been going on forever. I was living with my parents, but decided to give the marriage another try and returned to Ryan."

"The child was his, I take it?" PD asked

"Yes, it was Ryan's child."

"What was the reason you eventually divorced?" PD said.

"Over time, Ryan's moods became darker and more unstable. He was eventually diagnosed as endogenously depressed. But, he distrusted anti-depressants and refused all treatment, even psychotherapy. He had bouts of rage that were uncontrollable. It became harder and harder to live with him. By the time Liam was in Kindergarten, Carl was free. I got a divorce and we married. Ryan legally relinquished his parental rights and Carl adopted my son."

"Well, thank you for the information, Gladys. I appreciate your time," he said and was about to hang up. He assumed since Carl had adopted the Liam at such a young age, and Ryan had relinquished his rights to the boy, that Liam hadn't kept a relationship with his biological father. The young man wouldn't want to know him.

He could return to his current life having closed this door, except for disposing of his son's ashes. The sleek brown surface of the Little Harpeth River wash soon away any vestige of his son's short life. He thought back again to the brief glorious time he shared with Amy and felt a stab of remorse that he had never known his son.

"Don't go yet, Mr. Pascoe. There's something else I should tell you. Liam was in Hawaii when Ryan died. He's very interested in nature photography and saves up until he has enough money for a trip. He just got back. Now that he knows about his father's death, I'm certain my son will to want to meet you. His relationship with Ryan was challenging, but he loved him and despite his father's mental health problems, they were close."

"How old is Liam by now?" PD asked.

"He's twenty-two," Gladys said. "What should I tell him if he wants to contact you?"

"Please give him my phone number," PD said. He read it to her and bid the woman good-bye.

*It seems I have a grandson after all*, he thought and found himself smiling. Liam could provide a window through which he could learn about the son he'd never known.

# FIFTEEN

THE MORNING AFTER BILLY JO RETURNED FROM HER TRIP, all four members of the Rosedale Investigations team were seated at the conference room table.

PD opened the meeting saying, "We need to do a case review, but first I understand Wayne has something personal he'd like to share, and I do as well. Go ahead," he said nodding at his partner.

"All of you know that I wanted to locate Lucy's sister as my gift to her for marrying a broken-down old cop," he gave his crooked rueful grin.

"All that time in the gym is paying off, partner. You look anything but broken-down to me," Dory said and smiled jauntily at him.

"Thanks, Partner. Anyway, I got extremely lucky and found Lucy's sister last night."

"Wow, that's amazing," Billy Jo said, knowing how mobile street druggies were and how hard they were to track down.

"She's been admitted to the Rosedale Drug Detox unit. I don't want Lucy to see Anne before the wedding. I met with the staff and they know the date. They looked a bit daunted but said they would try their best to have her clean and presentable by then. I wonder if I got her dress size whether you might buy her a dress for the wedding. Would you, Dory?"

"My pleasure, although I presume you have absolutely no idea what colors Lucy has selected for the wedding. Or the wedding dress shop she is using?" When Wayne shook his head, she rolled her eyes and said, "I'm not surprised. You'll have to find that out, but then I'll take on the assignment."

"Thanks," Wayne said, quickly writing a note to himself.

"I have a personal item as well," PD said. "I called my son's ex-wife yesterday and found out I have a grandson. I am awaiting his call." He glanced at Billy Jo, who quickly turned her face away. It occurred to him the previous night that she might not like the idea of him having another grandchild, but assumed she would understand. That might have been hoping for a bit too much. "Changing the subject, let's move on to discussing Abigail Forester's case. I understand you had a productive meeting with Fr. Dominic, Dory. What did you learn?"

"Abigail Forester met with her priest for counseling before her death and told him she was hammered by guilt. She'd discovered she was terminally ill and felt ashamed that she had lost contact with her brother's only son. Abigail's brother, Oscar, was an alcoholic. When his son was a senior in high school, he came to visit and asked for money to send Steve to college. His request was denied. Abigail disagreed with her husband's decision. She thought they ought to help the young man. Her husband felt pretty sure the money wouldn't go to Steve at all and would only be used to fuel Oscar's addiction."

"Pretty likely," Wayne said.

"Anyway, when Abigail met with Fr. Dominic, she told him she was determined to leave some of her estate to Steve. It's going to take some of Billy Jo's brilliant computer skills to track him down, but I think it would be worth it. I believe he's key to solving this case."

"Why?" Wayne asked. "Not following your thinking."

"If Steve felt his future was blighted by Abigail's husband's refusal to help with his higher education, he might have been resentful enough to run her off the road," Dory said. "His last name is Pennington, by the way. That was Abigail's maiden name."

"I take it you didn't discover this relative, did you, Billy Jo," PD said frowning.

"I tried, PD, but had no luck," she said.

"Try again, harder this time," PD told her frowning. "It's been over twenty years since the Foresters refused to help Steve financially. I think it's pretty unlikely as the motive in this case but there could be other relatives out there. By the way, Billy Jo, we are almost at the end of the two weeks I gave you to work on the paintings case," PD scowled at her. "On another note, the sheriff has initiated a formal murder investigation into the Forester case. He's given the lead to Detective Rob Fuller, but has asked for our collaboration."

"What did the lab report tell us about the car that ran into Abigail?" Dory asked.

"It was an older car, a Ford painted what's called Apollo Green. We've determined that Jonathon Forester is no longer in the frame for the crime. He was seen cleaning Abigail's garage by a neighbor who stopped to talk with him at virtually the exact time of Abigail's accident. And his only car is a 2013 Dodge Viper," Wayne said.

"I checked the whereabouts of Jonathon's wife, Christine. She was having her hair cut and colored that morning. It's a time-consuming process called balayage that takes several hours. She was in the salon at the time Abigail was driving to Nashville. She drove their little red Vue to the appointment. It's visible on CCTV. She's out as well," Dory said.

"Sounds like Abigail's missing nephew, Steve, is worth hunting down. Since you didn't find the man—which was the job I gave you, Billy Jo," PD said with an irritable note in his voice, "I need you to locate him now but, be careful not to identify yourself. Remember this could be our killer."

"I really did try while I was in Erie, PD. He seems to be totally off grid," Billy Jo said. "Can I tell you what I learned on my road trip about the painting?"

"Go ahead," PD said.

"Mark and I visited the History Society in Erie and when we walked in, we were stunned by what we saw. There was only one painting on display on the easel in the main salon. To my surprise, the painting was *Wednesday's Child*."

She had their attention now, all of them turned their faces to her, silent and riveted.

"It turns out the artist did two paintings on the same subject. The painting in Erie, done in 1919, is identical to the one belonging to Mrs. Walcott, except for one interesting difference. That painting, called *Children at the Lakeshore*, contains an image in shadow cast by the figure of Mrs. Wendy Brookover. I discovered Wendy was born on a Wednesday and it was after her death that the artist did the second painting. During the time Iverson was painting *Children at the Lakeshore*, he and Wendy fell in love. I believe the artist titled the second painting, *Wednesday's Child*, as his farewell gift to her."

"Interesting. Did you find anything else out about the chain of ownership for Mrs. Walcott's painting?" Dory asked.

"Not so far, but while we were there, Mark and I visited with Grampa Richard Brookover, the grandson of Cedric who commissioned the artwork. He's in his 70's now, but very knowledgeable about the painting. For example, he knew about the curse." As soon as the word left her mouth, Billy Jo slapped her hand across her mouth.

"What did you just say? A curse? What curse?" PD asked. His dark eyes snapped furiously. Looking around the room he said, "Did all of you know about this curse business?"

Wayne and Dory nodded, looking sheepish.

"Sorry, PD. I thought knowing the painting was cursed might make you pull me off the case. May I continue?" Billy Jo asked. PD shook his head and took a deep breath. Finally, he nodded. "When Dr. Cedric Brookover came to the end of his life, he offered the painting to each of his two surviving children. They both declined. They blamed the curse for the death of their mother and the later death of their sister."

"Did Richard Brookover know about the affair between his grandmother and the artist?" Wayne asked.

"It took some careful probing, but yes, he did. In going through the attic after his grandparents died, he found a letter the artist had written to Wendy Brookover saying he could hardly wait for them to be together. He was thrilled she had decided to sue for divorce. It seems the divorce never took place because Wendy died only days after *Children by the Lakeshore* was delivered. She broke her neck falling down a flight of stairs."

"That sounds suspicious. Today such a death would have been looked into carefully, but in 1919, I'm sure they took the husband's word that she fell—without investigating whether or not she was shoved," PD said and his face darkened.

"How did *Children at the Lakeshore* end up at the History Society?" Dory asked.

"After Dr. Cedric Brookover passed away, his son donated it to the History Society. He didn't want to own it personally, but given the rising fame of the artist, thought it deserved exhibition."

"None of this tells you the provenance of our painting, *Wednesday's Child*, does it," Dory said. "Or how it ended up in a garage sale."

"No, it doesn't. I still have work to do."

"Not on this you don't," PD said firmly. "You need to find Mrs. Forester's nephew, Steve Pennington. Had you discovered him before you left on your little romantic junket, *which was the assignment I gave you,* you wouldn't have this hanging over your head," PD glowered. "I'm not approving any more time on the painting fiasco now until you track him down."

Billy Jo looked down at her lap, tears suddenly springing into her eyes. Then she stood up, pushed her chair back from the table abruptly and left the room. They could hear her crying as she ran down the hall.

"Well, I certainly hope you two are proud of yourselves," Dory said. Her mouth flattened in a line.

"Me? What have I done?" Wayne asked, looking defensive. "I always support Billy Jo."

"I will get back to you in a moment," she said. Then turning to PD, she continued saying, "You have been a total ass to Billy Jo lately. You blame her for not finding Steve Pennington today, of all days, when you just told her you have a grandson. She's bound to be hurt by that."

"Probably was pretty bad timing," Wayne said and PD nodded.

"I don't suppose it's occurred to either of you numbskulls that Billy Jo could quit her job and leave."

"Quit? That's ridiculous. She lives here. Where would she live or get a job?" PD asked.

"The Mount Blanc police post is looking for a person to head their IT unit. She would be highly competitive for that position. Plus, she and Mark are close and he just got a new apartment north of town. She could move in with him."

Wayne made a noise and Dory turned her head to see a thunderous expression on his face.

"See, this is what you do, Wayne," Dory said. "Billy Jo is twenty-two and every time Mark is mentioned storm clouds cross your face. The girl's allowed to have a boyfriend! You need to knock it off. They could even end up getting married. Not everyone waits until they are a *senior citizen* before they get hitched. And need I remind you that it was Mark who gave you the tip several years ago that enabled you to get your foster mother out of prison to die in the care of her family. Until he started dating Billy Jo, you sang Mark's praises."

Wayne, flushed in embarrassment said, "You're right, Dory."

"Okay, this meeting's over. Let's go get lunch and a couple of brews. What do you say, Wayne?" PD asked.

"Oh no you don't, Patrick Devlin Pascoe," Dory said. "You are not getting off that easily. You are going to march upstairs right now and apologize to Billy Jo. And further, you are going to stop blocking her from doing more advanced work for the business."

"What are you talking about? I let her do what she wants."

"No, you don't. Henceforth, you are going to give Billy Jo the responsibility for initial client interviews. She's going to be the person to recommend whether we take on new cases, or reject them. You are also going to give her a portion of the field work that Wayne and I usually do and let her go on stake-outs."

"You know I'm only trying to protect her," PD said

"She's a big girl and if she's partnered with one of us, she'll be safe and you know it," Dory said.

"Have you quite finished?" PD asked, his mouth quirked in irritation.

"Not quite. After you finish apologizing to Billy Jo and asking her forgiveness for your moronic behavior, you are going to tell her about these increased responsibilities and say you are considering her for a *partnership* in the firm. Upstairs right now, Detective, and don't come down until you have reassured Billy Jo that she is your adored *only* granddaughter and that you are deeply, profoundly, sorry for being such a jerk."

# SIXTEEN

After the senior team left that morning, Billy Jo sat at her desk sipping a cappuccino and searching the net. Since PD's apology the previous day, she'd been in excellent spirits. She assumed, given his assurances that she was being considered for a partnership, she had a bit of leeway about her wardrobe. No clients were expected, and she was dressed in old comfy pajamas and bunny slippers.

She started by searching for Steve Pennington on Facebook, Twitter and Instagram with no luck. Then she searched WhatsApp, Messenger, and WeChat, again finding nothing. The man simply did not have an obvious presence on the net. She was about to access a cell phone directory for all Steve Penningtons in the entire country when the office phone rang. She answered it absently saying, "Rosedale Investigations."

"Good morning, Billy Jo, it's Sylvia. Could we meet to go over what you learned on your trip to Pennsylvania?"

"Great idea. I have computer work to do this morning but how about getting together for lunch at the Bistro? I can be there by noon," she said.

"Sounds good," Sylvia said and clicked off the call.

After printing out a list of all the phone numbers for Steve Penningtons (with all the various spellings), she started the phone calls—it was a tedious process. Two hours later, still not having had any luck, she tripped upstairs, put on her newest acid-washed jeans, an apple green crop top, flip-flops and ran a brush through her dark curly hair. She usually made her bed and picked up her apartment before leaving the house but decided to let it go. She didn't want to be late to meet Sylvia.

THE ROSEDALE SENIOR TEAM, CONSISTING OF Dory, Wayne and PD, were waiting in the lobby of the sheriff's office to speak to Detective Rob Fuller.

"Do you think we should tell Detective Rob that we've already eliminated Jonathon and Christine Forester as suspects?" Dory asked, raising her eyebrows questioningly at Wayne.

"We should listen to his case presentation first," Wayne said. "Try to be patient, Dory. He's young, but very smart. He'll get there."

"If he seems to be floundering, I recommend we point him in the direction of Steve Pennington," PD said.

"In case you two have forgotten," Wayne said, frowning, "murder investigations start with first securing the perimeter—which the sheriff already did. Second, rapidly deploying the forensic team to the site. In this case, the crime scene is outdoors, and evidence can be destroyed quickly by weather."

"I stopped back there after leaving you and Camille at the office. The scene-of-crime people were there and so was the photographer, so that's underway," PD said.

"Since it looks like her car was hit from behind, I'm sure Abigail's vehicle has been impounded and is in the process of being gone over. Plus, Rob will be setting up an Incident Room with phone lines for tips, and he'll likely start George talking to anyone who reported seeing the accident," Dory added.

"When we meet with Rob, he should have the coroner's report, the data from forensics, the preliminary report on the car, and possibly the skid mark analysis. As you know, all this needs doing before *any* discussion of suspects," Wayne said firmly, hoping he effectively quelled Dory and PD.

At that point Detective Rob Fuller entered the waiting room, greeted the team warmly and escorted the trio downstairs to a large room next to the lab tech offices. He spoke briefly to Deputy George who nodded and left.

Multiple tables had been dragged into the room from storage closets and were set up with folding chairs. Extra phone lines and computers were being connected. Mrs. Coffin, the dispatcher and manager for the sheriff's office, was in the room organizing coffee and snacks. She said hello and passed out coffees.

Rob came over saying, "We very much appreciate the help and expertise of our local Murder Dream Team. You two," he said, nodding to

Wayne and PD, "are experienced detectives and we have all missed you here in the office, Miss Dory. Please take a seat at the table in the corner and we'll start reviewing the material that has already come in about the suspicious death of Abigail Forester."

"Will the sheriff be joining us?" Wayne asked.

"He's meeting with Abigail Forester's nephew. He'll join us later."

"Which nephew, Jonathon Forester or Steven Pennington?" Dory asked innocently.

Having failed to effectively instill any patience in Dory, Wayne rolled his eyes. He had tried.

"Is there another nephew we didn't know about?" Rob asked. He pushed his silver rimmed glasses up on his nose and ran his hands through his short hair angrily.

"There is. Steve Pennington is Abigail's brother's son," Dory said, grinning smugly.

"Just when did you discover this person? I thought this was supposed to be a collaboration. Damn it! What else haven't you told me?" Rob asked. Two red spots appeared on his cheeks.

"Apologies, Rob. Dory just met with Abigail's priest and found out about Steve Pennington. We are prepared to share everything we already know as soon as you have *finished* your presentation," Wayne said, giving Dory a fish-eyed look. "Go ahead."

Rob, still looking flushed and irritated, took a deep breath and began saying, "Mrs. Abigail Pennington Forester, a childless widow aged 62, died following a car crash. The accident was caused by another vehicle running into her back bumper at high speed. She lost control of her car, veered across the highway and into an open field stopping just short of a ravine . . ."

As Rob continued his case summary, Wayne found his mind wandering. Unless Sheriff Bradley had unearthed some new evidence, Jonathon and Christine Forester were already eliminated as suspects. Despite lacking a credible motive for the actions that led to Mrs. Forester's death, Steven Pennington would have to be found and interviewed. He hoped Billy Jo was having some luck finding the man.

AT THE BISTRO, SYLVIA WALCOTT JOINED Billy Jo at the ordering counter. "I'm excited to learn everything you found out," she said, as they got their lunches and took a seat at a table at the back of the busy lunch emporium.

"I can't wait to tell you about it. While in Erie, I discovered that there are *two* virtually identical paintings by the same artist—both feature the Brookover children on the shore of Lake Erie," Billy Jo grinned at Sylvia's look of astonishment. "My cell phone pictures don't do either painting justice, but take a look." She quickly pulled out her phone and showed Sylvia the images.

"They look exactly alike to me," Sylvia said.

"In the painting at the History Society, there is a faint shadow of Mrs. Brookover on the left side of the artwork. It's hard to see in these cell phone photos."

"Do you know which painting was done first?" Sylvia asked

"Yes, the one in Erie was the first. It is dated 1919. Your grandmother's painting was done a year later. I think I know why the artist painted the second one. The mother of the children, Mrs. Wendy Brookover, fell in love with the artist while he was doing the work. Only a few days after the artist delivered the painting to her husband, Wendy fell down a staircase, broke her neck and died."

"Wow, this is quite some story," Sylvia said, raising her eyebrows.

"I believe Jeremy Iverson-Jones put Wendy Brookover's shadow in the first painting during the time they were falling in love. After she died, he painted the children again, but her shadowy image doesn't appear in the second painting. Excluding her shadow was, I believe, his way of saying farewell to her. He committed suicide after completing the second painting."

"Those poor people. She died and then the artist killed himself. It's almost like Shakespeare's Romeo and Juliet," Sylvia said.

"Finding out there were two paintings also explains the two titles. The title of the 1919 painting is *Children by the Lakeshore*. Your grandmother's painting, as you know, is called *Wednesday's Child*."

"What does that phrase mean?" Sylvia asked.

"It's an old rhyme which tells a child's future from the day of the week they were born. It says that '*Wednesday's Child is full of woe*.' Wendy Brookover was born on a Wednesday and I think by falling in love with her, the artist believed he had caused her death," Billy Jo said, taking a shaky breath and feeling a profound remorse for the doomed lovers.

"This is all fascinating stuff, but how did *Wednesday's Child* end up in a garage sale? Did the artist give that painting to Mrs. Chase Wilson?" Sylvia asked.

"I haven't found out the answer yet," Billy Jo said.

"Did you meet with anyone from the Chase Wilson family?"

"I didn't have time. I was only there two days, and it took all the time we had to meet with the Curator of the Historical Society and Mr. Richard Brookover, the grandson of Cedric, who commissioned the original painting."

"I need to tell this to my grandmother. Perhaps she and I should go to Erie ourselves, meet with the descendants of the Chase Wilson family and see what we can find out," Sylvia said.

"That's a great idea. Your grandmother is the best person to make contact with that family, but I'm concerned about the security of the painting. What would you say to me keeping it at Rosedale Investigations during your trip?"

"That would definitely reassure my grandmother. Would you mind picking it up this evening?"

"I'll come by your grandmother's place when I'm finished working, probably around eight this evening. We have a large, locked closet in the office that has been fitted with a thick metal door and a secure lock. The painting will be safe there. I promise you."

Billy Jo gave Sylvia her promise blithely, but it was a pledge that would return to torment her in the days ahead.

AT THE SHERIFF'S OFFICE, THE CASE DISCUSSION with Detective Rob Fuller dragged on until almost six pm. Deputy George completed the interviews with people who had called in to report seeing the accident. Rob drew the attention of the group to the forensic report on the vehicle that had struck Mrs. Forester's car. Its tires left wide skid marks on the pavement. It was a significant finding—indicating whoever drove into the woman tried very hard to stop. Dory gave Detective Rob all the information she'd gleaned from her meeting with Fr. Dominic. Wayne gave Rob the information which effectively alibied Jonathon and Christine. At the end of the day, Steve Pennington officially moved into the frame as their prime suspect, although his motive remained obscure. He would be picked up for questioning—as soon as he could be located.

As Dory, Wayne and PD walked out to the parking lot, they discussed returning to the office, but decided to call it a day.

"This whole thing was a complete waste of time," Dory said.

"Hang on there, Dory. Rob is doing this right. He needs to build the case brick by brick in order to take it to the ADA. So far, all we have is a possible decades-old motive based on supposition and circumstantial evidence. Even the Foresters' refusing to pay for Steve's education is hearsay. There's nobody alive now to confirm that conversation."

"If the motive for the crime was Abigail Forester's husband refusing to pay for his higher education, I don't understand why Steve would run her car off the road now. It's been more than twenty years," PD said frowning.

Nobody had a good response to that point and they headed out in different directions. Wayne and Lucy were going to the jewelry store to pick out wedding rings. Dory was having dinner with her boyfriend Al. PD texted Billy Jo, saying he expected her report on Steven Pennington to be complete when they got there the next morning. He thought briefly of returning to the office, but decided not to. He was tired and headed out to his cabin for the night.

In the days to come, PD would be haunted by that spur-of-the moment decision.

# SEVENTEEN

D ORY WAS THE FIRST TO ARRIVE AT ROSEDALE INVESTIGATIONS the next morning. It was July third and she had picked up donuts. Each donut was topped with a little red, white and blue American flag. She was wearing a full-length cotton knit dress patterned in small red flowers on a navy background and a white silk plumerria flower adorned her hair. She didn't see Billy Jo at her desk but thought nothing of it. The girl would be downstairs soon.

PD arrived and asked where Billy Jo was. "I don't see her report on Steven Pennington," he said, flipping through the papers on her desk.

"She's probably still upstairs," Dory told him.

Wayne arrived and read the note Billy Jo had left the previous evening saying she was going out to the Walcott's to pick up the painting. Glancing at the clock, he said, "Why don't you go upstairs and check on her, Dory."

She did, but the girl wasn't there. The bed was unmade, a tumble of blue sheets and a white down comforter. It was a surprise. Billy Jo usually made her bed and picked up her apartment before leaving the building.

"She's got to be around here somewhere," Wayne said when Dory came downstairs saying Billy Jo wasn't in her apartment.

"Her car is in the driveway. She can't be far," PD said.

"I'll call Sylvia Walcott," Dory said. When she finished her conversation, she told the men that Billy Jo had left the Walcott residence with the painting at eight forty-five the previous evening. "Sylvia helped Billy Jo put *Wednesday's Child* in the back of her car. She was planning to bring it here and put it in our safe. Sylvia and Grandma Walcott were going to Pennsylvania, and they wanted the painting secure."

"I'll open the safe," PD said, but when he did so, the closet-sized safe was virtually empty, containing nothing except CDs of client interviews and a stack of legal-sized contracts.

"I'm getting worried now," Dory said—making eye contact with Wayne.

"Let's check her car."

They walked outside. The car was unlocked and Billy Jo's car keys were under the driver's seat, as was her cell phone. Her purse and shoes were on the passenger seat. They flipped open the back lift gate of the vehicle, but no painting was in evidence.

"Let's think this through. She got back here and must have started unloading the painting, preparing to put it in the office safe. Hang on while I check my phone. Damn it. She sent me a text last night asking for the combination for the safe. My speaker was off and I didn't get the message," PD clenched his teeth.

Wayne knelt down by the back of the car, peering at the bottom edge of the lift gate. Then he raised a worried face to his partners, saying, "There's a dark stain on the edge here. I think Billy Jo was lifting the painting out when somebody came up from behind and slammed the lift gate down on her. I'm going to look for blood spatter," he said as Dory and PD looked at each other in dismay.

Wayne followed the blood trail out to the street where the drops of blood stopped. "If this is Billy Jo's blood, it stops here."

"This all is my fault. I should have come back here last night," PD said. His face had gone gray.

"Don't blame yourself. I could have run by here as well. I believe the painting was the target. Billy Jo must have tried to prevent the thief from taking it and got injured in the process."

"Not injured, attacked," PD said grimly and held up a rock. It was streaked with blood.

"I'm calling Sheriff Bradley," Dory said.

"Hang on a minute. They have their hands full with the Abigail Forester murder. The three of us have more experience than Detective Rob or even the sheriff. Let's do what we can before we call in the law. It's unlikely anyone saw the abduction, but we should find out."

"I'll ring the doorbells for the houses across the street and next to us on both sides," PD said.

"I'll check the road for any more blood spots," Wayne added.

"How about I take the rock to the lab techs at the sheriff's office and make sure it's Billy Jo's blood?" Dory said. "Given my history of working with the office, I can probably prevail on them to fast-track the analysis without having the sheriff any the wiser."

"Do we have a record of her blood type?" Wayne asked. "I doubt the sheriff's office would have her DNA on file."

"There's no way the sheriff's office has a record of her DNA," Dory said. "She's never committed a crime." Worry etched the lines deeper on her anxious face.

"You're right. See what the lab techs can do with the rock. It's possible there are fingerprints on it. And if there's DNA from the creep who tried to steal the painting, he might be in the system."

"What are you and PD going to do?" Dory asked.

"We need to check the urgent care clinics and the hospitals in case Billy Jo showed up. After that, we should call on the art galleries in town to see if anyone tried to fence the painting."

Dory nodded, picked up her car keys and departed.

PD returned from having spoken to the people in the neighboring houses and said, "Nobody home next door, and none of the other people I talked to saw or heard anything. They were all watching TV or out for the evening."

"Let's divide up. I would usually check the medical facilities, but Lucy isn't on duty today. She and her Maid of Honor were getting final fittings on their dresses. How about we both go talk to art galleries?" Wayne asked, before noticing the extreme pallor on partner's face. He looked suddenly very old and frail. PD sat down heavily at Billy Jo's workstation, grabbing for the arms of the chair to balance himself. "Are you okay, man?" Wayne asked softly.

"Don't think I should be driving," PD said in a strangled voice.

"We're going to find her, PD. Try not to worry. We don't even know that the blood is Billy Jo's. It could belong to the thief. Maybe she was the one who chunked the guy in the head. In case she's at the hospital, I've left a text for Lucy."

"Could she have walked five miles to the hospital in the dark with no shoes or purse?" PD asked and Wayne felt his confidence fall precipitously, like a rock bounding down a canyon, leaving echoes on the air. He knew very well that most homicide victims were young and female.

"I'm worried," Wayne admitted, putting his arm around PD's shoulders. The man's whole torso felt cold. He was going into shock. He needed to get him warm and hydrated as soon as possible.

Dory returned an hour later, having given the bloody rock to the lab techs for analysis. "I was afraid they might ask a lot of questions, since I don't work there anymore, but apparently my *street cred* is still pretty high. Both of them seemed reluctant to cross me. Smart people. They said the studies would be done by tomorrow. Fingerprints too. Where's PD?"

"I took him upstairs and put him into Billy Jo's bed. He was going into shock, and I got instructions from Lucy. Luckily, Billy Jo has an electric blanket in her closet. I got him to drink some orange juice and made him lie down. He fell asleep after about five minutes. I was going to check art galleries, but decided to wait until you got here in case PD needed help," Wayne said.

"I'll start calling the urgent care facilities here and in Nashville. Luckily, I kept our phone and email lists from when we were working on the Blind Split case."

"Did you remember that Billy Jo's shoes and purse were in her car? If she visited a health facility, she would have arrived barefoot and without identification," Wayne reminded Dory.

"God, Wayne. Where is our girl?" Dory asked, and her voice was resonant with alarm and fear.

Billy Jo became slowly aware of a bright light and then the pain hit—so sharp she winced. She smelled bleach and felt a starched pillowcase under her cheek. Her head ached. Her feet were excruciatingly sore. Opening her eyes, she saw a white walled room. A green fabric drape surrounded her bed. There was an intravenous drip in her arm. She was in some kind of clinic or hospital. Moving her hands around on the blanket, she found the button for the nurse and pushed it.

"Need something, dear?" The nurse asked as she bustled in, looking competent and busy.

"What happened to me?" Billy Jo asked.

"Let me look at your chart." Having checked her tablet, the nurse said, "You arrived at the ER around eleven last night without any ID or shoes. Apparently, you walked some distance before getting here. Are you in pain?"

"My feet are sore and my head is killing me. I can hardly open my eyes," Billy Jo said blinking at the bright fluorescent lights overhead.

"Your feet were cut and bleeding last night. They bandaged you in the ER, but you were pretty out of it so they didn't give you anything for pain except Tylenol. You weren't making a lot of sense, saying something about a get-away car and a painting. Do you remember what happened?" The nurse looked concerned.

It came flooding back then—the pain as the lift gate banged down against the back of her head, falling to the driveway, skinning her knees, seeing a man lift the painting out of the trunk, struggling to get to her feet and then being hit her in the head. Falling to the ground . . . running feet . . . a car door opening . . . a vehicle speeding away. She had tried to stand up, desperate to see the license plate, but then everything went dark. "Yes. I remember. Can I have something stronger for the pain?" she asked.

"I'll check with the hospitalist. Try to lie still and rest if you can," the nurse said and left the room.

The hospitalist returned with the nurse a bit later, introduced himself and said they were adding some morphine to her IV. He said it was pretty fast-acting stuff and asked her for her name.

"Billy Jo Bradley," she said, but the pain-killer was already working, and her words were slurred.

"Do you have any identification?" the doctor asked. Billy Jo shook her head which made her headache worse.

*I have to call Dory,* she thought and tried to ask for her phone, but she was already falling asleep.

# EIGHTEEN

WAYNE NICHOLS WAS LEAVING THE LAST OF THE ART GALLERIES in Rosedale. The little town had become a mecca for artists and each place he visited told him the name of several other establishments he should check. After leaving several highly agitated owners, he modified his spiel by saying while he knew *their* gallery wouldn't accept a valuable painting without provenance, could they tell him any galleries that would? None of the owners would identify any gallery in town that would take an original oil painting without full documentation of ownership. At the last place, however, the young man he spoke to suggested he check antique stores.

"You said the painting was 100 years old, right? Being that old, it would be a natural for antique dealers to handle and some of them aren't too particular about documentation. Please don't tell them I said that," he added.

"How many antique dealers are there in town?" Wayne asked, feeling discouraged. It seemed a doomed hunt. Since the painting had been stolen, the person who took it could be halfway to New York by now. Unless he was a local, he would naturally want to put some serious distance between him and the great state of Tennessee.

"There are four antique dealers in Rosedale and an antique mall out by the freeway. They handle almost anything anyone brings in—dishes, vintage clothes, furniture and even dodgy artwork," the young man said with a rueful grin.

Wayne thanked him and left the gallery. On his way to the parking lot, he called Dory. "Have you heard anything back from the sheriff's lab techs yet about the rock?" he asked.

"Just got a call. Luckily Billy Jo's blood type is unusual. It's O negative. That's only about 7% of the U.S. population. So, unless the perp is also in that 7%, which is pretty unlikely, it's our girl's blood," her voice quavered, and Wayne could hear her swallow as she said the last words.

"Any DNA match?" he asked.

"Nobody in the system," Dory said.

"What about fingerprints?"

"No, the perp wore gloves. Stupid TV police dramas are making them way too smart these days. I've been checking on PD every fifteen minutes. He's still sleeping. And I've called all the Urgent Care clinics in town with no luck. What have you found?"

"Nothing. I went to the art galleries and one person suggested the antique shops, as well as the Antique Mall out by the freeway. It's been a total waste of time. The violent psycho who assaulted Billy Jo is probably long gone by now anyway. It's been over twelve hours and the longer a person is missing . . ."

"The more likely it is that they are dead," Dory said, finishing Wayne's sentence with a shaky inhale.

"Don't even think that. Hang on, I'm getting a call from Lucy." He quickly pressed the accept call button. "Hi, thanks for calling. Sorry for interrupting your day off, but as I said earlier, Billy Jo is missing."

"I'm not positive, Wayne, but there's a pretty good chance she's been admitted to Rosedale General. A young woman about five feet three inches tall with dark eyes and wild curly hair came into the ER late last night. She wasn't making much sense, had no ID and wasn't wearing shoes. She had a concussion but is listed as in fair condition."

There was a long and significant pause before Wayne and said, "If I hadn't already proposed to you, I'd be down on my knees right now."

Lucy chuckled and her voice was warm and lazy when she said, "As I recall, the kneeling component of your proposal was conspicuously absent. I might just insist on it before the ceremony."

"You will have it and while on my knees, I will repeatedly and fervently kiss your toes," Wayne said. "Sorry, Honey. Dory's on hold. Have to go. In case I haven't mentioned it lately, I absolutely adore you." He clicked back to Dory and said, "Lucy thinks she's at Rosedale General. I'll call to see if the hospital allows visitors. All of us should go. We are her family after all. Check on PD and see if you can wake him," Wayne said.

"There is one more family member who should be notified, Wayne," Dory said in a chiding tone.

There was a brief hesitation before Wayne said, "Right. Calling Mark now." He heard Dory's amused chuckle before ringing off. Wayne dialed Mark's cell and when he answered told him that Billy Jo was in the hospital, they were going to visit her. Mark could meet them there.

Almost running as he headed to the parking lot, Wayne found himself singing, "Walking on Sunshine." He was tone-deaf and the song was drastically off key. A passerby gave him a raised eyebrow, but he didn't give a fig what anyone else thought just then. Their girl was alive. He practically skipped.

HALF AN HOUR LATER, THE ROSEDALE INVESTIGATIONS TEAM was at the Patient Information Desk at Rosedale General. A large sign outside the Hospital read, *"Masked visitors may enter the lobby to obtain patient information. Only 1 visitor per day permitted in patient rooms."* At the Patient Information desk was a sign saying, *"Visitors to patient rooms must provide proof of vaccination or recent test and be symptom free."*

"We should have thought of this," PD said. "Only one of us is going to be allowed in. Who gets to go?"

"Mark," Dory said, smiling at the unshaven, unkempt desperate-looking kid. He was pacing the lobby and looking dreadful with messy hair and a T-shirt with an open neck that showed the fiery mouth of his dragon tattoo. The body of the dragon had been inked on his back, but the fire-breathing head snaked around to the front.

"How is that you get to make this decision?" PD asked irritably.

"Because I am so wise by now that I know the right answer for everything," Dory said calmly. PD rolled his eyes.

Once informed of Dory's decision, Mark showed the attendant his vaccination card, rapidly completed the required health questionnaire and has his temperature checked before being allowed to go upstairs.

"Come back soon and give us a report," Wayne said as Mark got on the elevator.

"We'll wait here," Dory added.

REACHING THE NURSE'S STATION ON THE 4$^{TH}$ FLOOR, Mark stopped to get final approval to see Billy Jo.

"Did patient information tell you that I need to see your vaccination card and recent test results? I assume you completed the health question-naire?" the nurse asked.

Mark nodded, setting his vaccination card on the counter. He was tapping his fingers on the surface in impatience.

"She's in room 410, but isn't completely with us yet. Still a bit con-cussed," the nurse said looking at his documentation.

Not waiting for further permission, Mark dashed down the hall to room 410 and pushed open the door. He stopped short seeing Billy Jo lying there, little and silent in the hospital bed. Some of her hair had been shaved off and a white dressing covered her head wound. One small bare foot, bandaged and swollen, stuck out from under the covers.

Hearing the noise, Billy Jo opened her eyes and dodging IV's and bandages, Mark managed to kiss her repeatedly.

"Stop, stop. I'm okay, Mark," she said and gave him a crooked grin. "I'm at Rosedale General, right?"

"You are," Mark told her. His voice was tremulous. "Can you tell me what happened?"

Billy Jo took an uneven breath and said, "I was bringing the painting, *Wednesday's Child*, to the office to keep it safe," she shook her head and blinked away tears. "Some security guard I am. A bad ass hit me on my head with the lift gate of my car and I just laid there on the driveway for a minute. When I tried to stand up, he hit me again. Then he stuffed the painting into his trunk and drove away. I tried to see his license plate, but it was dark and," her voice trailed off.

"I'm sure that Wayne and PD will want to know anything that might identify him. Did you see or hear anything? Race, accent, clothing?" Mark asked.

"When he turned his cell phone light on to see the painting, I noticed he was dressed in a hoodie and wearing one of those Covid 19 masks, a black one."

"The team is on it. They will get the creep," Mark said.

"But the painting is gone," Billy Jo wailed. "I promised Sylvia and Mrs. Walcott that it would be safe. He could have already destroyed it! And today is the first of July. The two weeks PD gave me to look into the case are already over."

"Since you were attacked, PD will probably extend the time he gave you. I'll ask him. As far as the fate of the paintings, I think the guy who attacked you will probably try to sell it. It is worth $50,000. Wayne already went to the art galleries and he's checking the antique dealers. It will turn up. Stolen art almost invariably does." He forced himself to sound optimistic but knew it was going to be a long slog to get the thief and recover the painting—if it was even possible. "Did you walk all the way to Rosedale General from the office last night?"

"All I remember, after being knocked down in our driveway, was walking into a brightly lighted room with sore feet and holding my head. Are Wayne, Dory and PD here?" she asked hopefully. She was clearly looking brighter by then. Seeing him had lifted her spirits.

"They sure are, and dying to see you, but the hospital only allows one person per day in to see the patient," Mark said.

"That's disappointing," Billy Jo said.

"Honey, I'm so sorry you were hurt. I feel just dreadful that I wasn't there for you," Mark said. "I wish I had known you were in trouble."

"There was no way you could have known, Mark, but right now I have to tell you something. I simply can't wait any longer." To his surprise, given her condition, he saw that her eyes below the head dressing were dancing.

"Go ahead," he said, with a confused frown.

"You are in love with me," she said.

Mark looked stunned for a moment but then a slow smile spread across his face.

"Don't tell me you are doing to deny it. You are a hopeless case," Billy Jo said.

"I wouldn't even try," Mark said and kissed his girl again. After a bit more awkward cuddling while trying not to dislodge her IV, he asked her if they were now an exclusive couple.

"Of course we are, Dragon boy. So if you have any other girlfriends you've been hiding, you better tell them good-bye. Now kiss me again."

Mark rode the elevator back down to the lobby. Despite Billy Jo's being in the hospital, he couldn't help smiling thinking about her saying he was in love with her. It was true and he assumed she felt the same.

The team were all seated near the elevator with expectant faces.

"She's fine, guys. A mild concussion is all. She'll probably be released tomorrow. Sends her love," Mark said and turned to PD. "She asked if you would give her a bit more time on the paintings case."

"That original deadline is irrelevant now. You can tell her I said that."

# NINETEEN

Billy Jo called Mark the next morning to say her discharge papers would be signed by noon. He arrived at the hospital, pulled out his vaccine card, once again completed the health symptom questionnaire, had his temperature checked and went up to her room. A bevy of medical staff in a swirl of white coats speaking in medical code were just leaving. One young resident, who said her name was Emily Feathers, stayed to talk with them.

"I'm sorry, but the attending didn't sign her discharge papers after all. She needs to stay another day at least. She's nauseous and can't get out of bed without falling. We'll get an otolaryngologist in to check her balance. Sorry, guys," she said and gave them both a weary smile before heading out to catch up with the others.

Mark looked at Billy Jo who was trying not to cry. "Hey, it's only one more day. No biggie," he said, striving for a cheerful tone.

"I just want to get out of here, back to my little apartment and my job. I never found Steve Pennington and he's the prime suspect in the Abigail Forester murder." Her voice was choked.

"How about I go back to Rosedale Investigations and try to find him? I bet I can locate the guy. What have you already tried?" Mark asked.

"He has no presence on the net, and no local phone number. I have a cell phone index which I checked without success. I assembled a bunch of phone numbers nationwide for all Steven Penningtons, using multiple spellings. The list is in my top desk drawer. I crossed off the people I already talked to. Thanks, Mark. You are such a whiz I'm sure you can find him faster than I could anyway," she smiled, looking humble.

"Glad to help. Have you had any breakfast?" Mark asked.

"The food people came around 7:00 this morning, but I couldn't eat anything. This whole thing sucks! I feel like such a failure. I promised Sylvia the painting would be safe and look what happened. I haven't even had the guts to call and tell her it was stolen." Her last words came out in a wail.

"No hurry about that. When do they get back in town?" Mark asked.

"They were going to be gone this whole week," Billy Jo said.

"By then the team could already have retrieved the painting," Mark said and forced himself to sound confident. He was trying hard to sound upbeat but had been an IT consultant to Nashville's finest long enough to know that some cases never got solved. "By the way, PD said the deadline he gave you to finish the paintings case is irrelevant now. He just doesn't want you to do anything that would put you at risk." Billy Jo nodded. "Do you want me to go get you something for lunch?" he asked.

"Good idea. The nausea is gone for the moment. Could you go to Noodles & Co and pick me up some Mac 'n cheese, a chocolate chunk cookie and some sweet green tea? And please swing by the office and see if they found my phone," she said.

"On it," Mark said, smiling and saluted his commanding officer.

AT ROSEDALE INVESTIGATIONS THE THREE PARTNERS had been waiting for their girl's arrival. Dory was working desultorily on billing clients. She wasn't making much progress and kept one ear cocked for the sound of Mark's car. Wayne and PD were in the kitchen. PD called out asking if there was anything to eat. Dory had made sun tea earlier and told him they could get it from the picnic table in the back yard.

"Is it that sweet crap?" Wayne asked. Having come originally from the north, he despised the saccharine taste of southern ice tea.

"It sure is," she chuckled. "The rest of us like it, you know. And it wouldn't kill you to make some without sweetener—even an old male chauvinist pig like you could put tea and water into a jug."

"I'll grab what you made," PD said

He was chatting with Wayne when Dory heard the welcome sound of a car pulling into the driveway. She got up and went to the front door, intending to be the first to greet Billy Jo. To her surprise it was Deputy George Phelps from the sheriff's office. He was dressed in his brown sheriff's uniform. It was too tight which served to accentuate his pudgy face and chubby silhouette. When he got out of the car, however, he was moving noticeably faster than usual.

"I've got something," he said in a near-excited voice.

"Come into the kitchen," she said. "Wayne and PD, George is here, and he has something for us."

"Got anything to eat?" George asked hopefully as he came inside.

"Sweet tea is about it," Wayne said. "What do you have?"

"Sheriff Bradley made me stay really late last night looking at the CCTV footage from both roads out of Rosedale for the guy who assaulted Billy Jo. I tried to get out of it, told him we didn't know what kind of car the creep drove, but he said it was an order."

"What did you find?" Dory asked, pouring him a glass of tea.

"Our new equipment allows us to do a close-up on the license plates and I have a list," he said, sounding extremely proud of himself.

"You figured out how to use the software?" Wayne asked in a doubtful voice.

"Well, Detective Rob and Deputy Cameron had to show me, but I printed out the list all by myself," he said.

"That's good, George. Did you include what direction they were going?" Wayne asked.

"I have the roads and the directions," he said smugly.

"What about the times?" PD asked.

"There is only one north/south road and one east/west road out of town and just a dozen cars were on those roads between 9:30 and midnight. One of the SUV's was speeding and travelling north," George said, looking self-satisfied.

"That's great, really great," Dory told him and patted him on the shoulder. "By chance, did you check the owner of that particular car?"

George's pudgy face crumpled, looking like bread-dough. "Can't you do that?" he asked plaintively.

"We certainly can," Dory said. "No problem. I did find a somewhat stale donut for you," she said and handed it to him. He thanked her gratefully.

As the front door shut behind their former colleague, Wayne said, "Well, that was a bit of a surprise."

PD snorted. "That dumbbell is a complete Muppet. Can't believe he didn't check the vehicle registrations for the owners." He sounded disgusted.

"Yes, PD, that was an oversight and George may be a Muppet, but he is *our* Muppet, and don't you dare criticize him," Dory said, narrowing her eyes.

"Sorry, Dory," PD said.

"Mark just drove in," Wayne added and all three of them walked out to the porch to greet Billy Jo. Seeing the car, their faces fell. Mark was alone in the vehicle.

WHEN MARK DEPARTED, HAVING INFORMED THEM ABOUT THE VERTIGO and the delay in Billy Jo's release, he had her laptop, purse and cell phone. Dory had assembled a set of clothes and handed him a tote bag.

Afterwards, PD said they should divvy up the tasks for the two crimes they were now investigating. "Since we've got Abigail Forester's murder, as well as the assault on Billy Jo, we need to agree on who is doing what. Dory, why don't you follow-up on the drivers George identified from CCTV? That's likely to be the most relevant to solving Billy Jo's case."

"Agreed. Think I'll start with that SUV speeding north George was so proud of finding. Probably will need to check all the cars on his list, though. Maybe there will be a driver's name I recognize," Dory said. "I have a question, PD. What happened to Rosedale Investigations having CCTV? I thought you were going to get that."

"I ordered it but it hasn't arrived yet. I wanted a system that had better resolution of the video. Still waiting for it. Supply chain issues," PD said.

"I'll follow up. What are you going to do now?" Dory asked.

"I'm going to the sheriff's office to talk to Detective Rob again. I'll give him a hand with the tip lines. Someone might call in having seen Mrs. Forester's accident," PD said.

"I just realized both of these cases involve cars—the green Ford that ran into Abigail Forester's car and the unknown vehicle of the thug who took *Wednesday's Child*," Dory said.

"Right. We're going to have to keep the cases—and the cars—separate in our minds," PD said. "What are you doing, Wayne?"

"I'm going to visit Camille Raines," he said. "She'll have Abigail Forester's attorney's phone number and I want to talk to him. Given how guilty Abigail felt about not giving Steve money for his education, it's possible she sent her lawyer an e-mail or a text with the changes she wanted to make to her will."

"Good. Let's all meet back here at five o'clock for a close-of-day review on both cases, Billy Jo's assault and the Forester murder," PD said.

"Hold on just a minute there, guys. As I recall, you two were totally opposed to Billy Jo investigating the paintings in the beginning. I assume now that she has been mugged, you have realized the error of your ways," Dory said.

"Indeed," Wayne said

"Totally on board now," PD said. "I already told Mark to tell her as long as she didn't put herself at risk, she could have all the time she wanted to work on the paintings."

"It's about time," Dory said, giving them a narrow stink eye.

WAYNE CALLED CAMILLE FROM HIS PHONE IN THE TRUCK. She was at her trailer home conducting a garage sale and sounded tickled to hear from him. He told her he was coming by. When he pulled in to the trailer park, he saw two long trestle tables set up in front of her mobile home displaying items for sale. Several neighbors were handing her money and taking their finds away. The big black dog was sleeping beneath one of the tables.

"Hi there, Mr. Fine-Looking," Camille greeted him coquettishly. Her strawberry blonde curls bounced as she walked up to meet him. She was wearing a shapeless blue shirt and loose trousers. The outfit did nothing for her physique, but the delight on her face at his appearance was unmistakable. "Come on in. These folks are just leaving. There's nothing much left inside, or even on the tables for that matter. It's so hot, I've been having a cold beer. Want one?"

He did. The trailer's dinette was built-in and although the rest of the furniture had been sold, the table and benches were still in place. Wayne took a seat and Camille pulled two Miller Lites from her refrigerator.

"Thanks for the beer. I thought we should review your situation. Plus, I've a couple of questions," Wayne said.

"I can hardly wait to be interrogated by the law," she said giggling. Her blue eyes twinkled.

"Do you mind telling me what you received from Mrs. Forester? I gather that you did get the house."

"More than that. I now own the house, which incidentally is paid off, and a lifetime annuity. It's a monthly disbursement which will be deposited directly into my bank account and is large enough to pay for the taxes and insurance. It was incredibly generous of Abigail and I'm so grateful. Me and Sally, who is now officially my dog, are going to have a fine old time of it with me being Lady of the Manor," she dimpled.

"I'm delighted for you. What about Jonathon and Christine? Did she leave them anything?"

"As it turns out, she did. Abigail's husband had a large life insurance policy on himself and a separate policy on her. The policies listed each other as primary beneficiaries. Abigail hadn't collected her husband's insurance and since Jonathon was listed as the secondary beneficiary on both policies, the company is going to pay the total amount to him. It was half a million dollars and they get it all."

"That should definitely make it easier to get him out of the house," Wayne said.

"They are already looking for real estate in Ohio. He said the money would allow them to start over and even congratulated me on having received Abigail's home. They are leaving right after her funeral. I understand both of them have been eliminated from consideration as suspects. Have you made any progress on finding the driver who ran my dear friend off the road?" Her face, usually wreathed in smiles, had quickly turned sad.

"We are trying to locate Mrs. Forester's other nephew, a man named Steven Pennington. He is in the frame as a suspect. Haven't found him yet, but Billy Jo is looking and the sheriff has an APB out on him. Since Jonathon and Christine are now cleared, I doubt you are in danger any longer. What do you think?"

"I'm totally fine. I've seen the police cars drive by every evening but please tell the sheriff he can call off his deputies now," she said. "I thought all along that Jonathon was all talk. Once he got his money, he's been all smiles to me."

"That's good to know, but if anything changes or you feel you are in danger, please call me. Changing the subject, do you have Mrs. Forester's attorney's contact information by chance?"

"I have it right here. I'll text it to your phone. Do you mind telling me why you are contacting him? Want another beer?" Camille asked.

Wayne nodded and she rose to grab another beverage from the fridge. The sun came in through the kitchen windows, lighting the flowered curtains. It was warm and cozy in the small trailer and Wayne was reminded of his distant family member, Waseta, who lived in Michigan's

Upper Peninsula. She had generously cared for his foster mother after her release from prison until her death. The scent of the foods Waseta cooked, and the warmth from her little black pot-bellied stove, had evoked his earliest memories of life on the Native American reservation. He needed to go back and visit her again. It was always a powerful trip, filled with nostalgia.

"Thanks," he said, accepting the beverage. "I thought I'd see if Mrs. Forester texted or e-mailed her attorney any instructions about what changes she planned to make to her will when she was driving to their appointment," Wayne stopped talking then, noticing a look of abject desperation flooding Camille's peaches-and-cream complexion.

"If she did, could I lose the house, do you think?" she asked anxiously. "I already accepted an offer to sell my trailer and I've sold almost everything I had."

"I'm pretty sure it wouldn't impact your inheritance. She told you about her intentions right from the start, provided you cared for the Bernese."

"I would have done that in any case. Will you call me right away with what you find out?" she asked, and he assured her he would. Camille hugged him when he left, but her face was decidedly apprehensive.

Wayne's phone rang as he walked out to the truck. Opening the door, he pushed the button to accept the call. Dory's face showed up on the screen.

"Did you find something?"

"On George's list there was one name I recognized immediately. The SUV he caught speeding north is owned by none other than Mr. Henry Brookover." She sounded jubilant.

"Fantastic. I can't wait to put the screws to the bastard," Wayne said and grinned evilly.

"And I can't wait to assist you," Dory said.

"I'll be coming by the office shortly," Wayne said. Then knowing how anxious Camille would be to know whether Abigail Forester had texted any instructions to her lawyer about her will, he dialed her attorney. After providing him with the number of his private detective's license and explaining the connection he had with the Forester investigation, he asked, "Did Mrs. Forester email or text you any instructions about the changes she wanted to make to her will?"

"I can only say this. If a person finds themselves in a life-or-death situation and types a text message to their attorney that begins, *This is my last will and testament,* followed by who they want to receive their most-prized possessions and ends the message with their full name, it turns out the will is valid. It's been upheld by courts after suicides."

"But Mrs. Forester didn't commit suicide," Wayne said.

"I'm aware of that," the attorney said, sounding irked. "However, if she texted her wishes to me before the accident, I believe it would be legal. Most of the precedents are in other countries, but I assume it holds here as well."

"Very interesting. Can you tell me if she did text you any last wishes?" Wayne asked.

"I cannot, sir. I need to consult some experts about this matter." Sounding prissy and uptight, he said, "As you know, it is my right to decline. It's lawyer/client privilege."

Wayne knew it was ridiculous to deny him the information. He had only asked *whether* Abigail had texted the attorney her wishes, not the content. "Here's my problem. As you informed her, Camille Raines inherited Mrs. Forester's house and a lifetime income. If Mrs. Forester changed her will via text, Camille's concerned that her inheritance could be threatened."

"Then she needs to call me but," the attorney hesitated and his voice warmed, "you can tell her she's a very lucky girl."

Wayne immediately left a message for Camille telling her to call Mrs. Forester's lawyer. He also told her the attorney said she was a very lucky girl. He knew it would raise a smile.

# TWENTY

THE ROSEDALE INVESTIGATIONS TEAM ARRIVED EARLY at St. Martha's on the afternoon of Mrs. Abigail Forester's funeral. It was the first week of July and the village of Rosedale seemed trapped in a bowl of unremitting heat. The service was to begin at 4:00 p.m. but the team wanted to be in position early in order to i.d. everyone who appeared. Although mostly discredited by law enforcement today, sometimes unsophisticated criminals returned to the places their victims had frequented.

Organ music drifted out into the parking lot as they walked toward the entrance. First to drive into the parking lot were Abigail's nephew Jonathon and his wife Christine. With them was Camille Raines. Jonathon opened the car door for Camille, giving her a hand out of the back seat.

Wayne waved and she walked over to join them. "Good afternoon," he said and introduced her to PD and Dory. Camille was dressed in a simple black sheath but the dress was too tight and emphasized her chubby curves. Wayne glanced at Dory who was no doubt dying to give the woman fashion advice, probably about underwear. "We were wondering if you could help us identify the people who are arriving."

"Nice to meet you all. I'll do my best," she said smiling and Wayne could tell her normally buoyant personality had returned.

At that moment, a group of middle-aged women walked up to the sanctuary. Fr. Dominic, in his full-length black cassock, was standing at the door of the church welcoming everyone. He seemed especially glad to see that particular group.

"Those are the ladies who play Bingo at the church on Saturday nights," Camille said. The next to arrive was Nancy Webb. She was with two men, one her age, and one much younger. "You probably recognize Mr. and Mrs. Webb and that's their son, Troy," Camille said.

More people started arriving. Camille knew one group who belonged to Abigail's book club and others who were the members of the Rosedale garden club. Almost all those who came to pay their respects to Abigail Forester were women and Wayne knew women were less likely than males to run cars off the road.

"We're probably looking for a man who caused Abigail's accident," he told Camille.

"Yes, and it's likely to be someone younger than Abigail, probably in his thirties or forties," PD said.

"So, I'm helping identify the culprit?" Camille asked with wide eyes. "Cool."

"We need to make our way inside," PD said as Sheriff Bradley, in his dress uniform, and Detective Rob Fuller, in a suit and tie, walked up to join them. Deputy George trudged behind them. He looked hot and kept running his fingers around his tight uniform collar.

Once the congregation was seated, the casket was brought down the aisle. It wasn't carried by pall bearers but proceeded down on a wheeled cart. A young priest walking beside the cart was sprinkling the casket with holy water and holding an ornate crucifix in front of him. When the casket arrived at its position in front of the altar, Fr. Dominic blessed the occupant.

"May the grace and peace of God our Father, who raised Jesus from the dead, be always with you," he intoned.

"And also with you," the congregation responded.

"Welcome my brothers and sisters. Let us pray." When Fr. Dominic closed his prayer saying Amen, he did a reading from Ecclesiastes saying, "There is an appointed time for everything, and a time for all things under the heavens. A time to be born, and a time to die; a time to plant, and a time to uproot the plant. A time to kill, and a time to heal; a time to tear down, and a time to build . . .

As the priest continued his reading, the back door of the cathedral opened and a bright whoosh of air entered the sanctuary before the door slammed shut. Dory's attention remained focused on the reading, but Wayne and PD both looked back to see a young white male with a scruffy beard who had entered the church.

"We need to check out the cars in the parking lot when we leave," PD whispered. Wayne nodded.

When Fr. Dominic asked if anyone from the audience would like to share some memories of Abigail, Jonathon Forester rose from his front row pew and ascended to the pulpit. After a few personal remarks about his aunt, he read from the Bible saying, "The souls of the just are in the hand of God and no torment shall touch them. They seem, in the view of the foolish, to be dead; and their passing away was thought to be an affliction and their going forth from us, utter destruction. But in God, they are in peace. As is my beloved Aunt Abigail." He looked moved as he returned to his seat in the congregation.

"Anyone else?" Fr. Dominic asked.

Camille rose from her seat. Reaching the pulpit, she looked down at the Congregation and said, "For those of you who don't know me, I'm Camille Raines. Abigail Forester was my employer and best friend. She's gone from my sight but will never be gone from my heart. I'd like to read a poem by Elizabeth Fry for her.

"*Do not stand at my grave and weep. I am not there. I do not sleep. I am a thousand winds that blow. I am the diamond glints on snow. I am the sunlight on ripened grain. I am the gentle autumn rain. When you awaken in the morning's hush, I am the swift uplifting rush of quiet birds in circled flight. I am the soft stars that shine at night. Do not stand at my grave and cry; I am not there. I did not die.*"

Camille was in tears by the end of the poem. As she rejoined the congregation, Nancy Webb came up to the pulpit and said that Abigail had been a religious woman. "Her strong beliefs are a comfort to me and I imagine she is already welcoming our departed pets into heaven."

The service continued with the priest offering a well-crafted homily to Abigail. He then asked those who would like to take communion to come forward and most of the congregation rose.

Wayne slipped quietly from his seat at the end of the pew. "Checking the parking lot," he whispered to PD who nodded. Walking toward the back of the church, he looked for the bearded man who had come late to the service. To his consternation, the pew was empty. Heading quickly outside, he was just in time to see an old Ford exiting the parking lot. The paint on the car was the color Dory had showed him on a paint swatch. It was called Apollo Green. Standing in the hot sun, looking after their quarry and almost quivering with frustration, Wayne dialed the sheriff's office.

"Sheriff's office," Mrs. Coffin answered. "How may I help you?"

"Mrs. Coffin, it's Wayne Nichols. The person who forced Abigail Forester off the road and caused her death is just leaving the parking lot of St. Martha's Catholic Church. It's an old green Ford. He turned right onto Broad Street, heading into Rosedale. It's imperative, absolutely *imperative*, that he doesn't escape. Get one of your deputies to pull him over ASAP, will you?"

"I will indeed, Detective," she said, and Wayne felt the pain of losing his rank with the sheriff's office fade into oblivion. He re-entered the church with a sense of relief. The congregants who took communion had nearly all returned to their seats. He sat down in the pew next to PD.

"I noticed that Scruffy Beard left. Did you see his car?" PD whispered.

"Yes. He was driving the old green Ford we were looking for. I called the sheriff's office. They are going to pick him up," Wayne said quietly.

"Good work," PD said.

Fr. Dominic intoned a blessing over the casket with incense and said, "Let us pray." The Lord's Prayer resonated in the large sanctuary. He then nodded to the organist to begin the recessional and the music flowed over the departing congregation.

As THE TEAM LEFT THE CHURCH AND WALKED OUT into the hot sunlight of a summer afternoon, Wayne's phone rang. "Sorry, Detective, we missed him," Mrs. Coffin said.

"Goddamn it," Wayne said, feeling a wave of fury rise in his body.

"Hold on. It was not a total loss. Deputy Gomez got his license plate number. So, we know who owns the car. As soon as the sheriff gets back here, he will put out an APB on the vehicle and ask Nashville to do the same."

"Who was the owner of the car?" Wayne asked, trying not to let his irritation show in his voice.

"It's a guy named Topper Gaines," she said.

"What?" Wayne asked, feeling stunned. *Who the hell was Topper Gaines?* They hadn't considered anyone other than Steve Pennington. The appearance of Scruffy Beard arriving at Mrs. Forester's funeral driving the car that had shoved her off the road had completely changed the trajectory of the investigation.

"I checked and Topper Gaines has a record," Mrs. Coffin continued.

"What was he in for?"

"Drunk and disorderly, driving while under the influence, and you will love this one, Detective. He was a suspect in a road rage incident. Looks like he ran a car off the road last year."

"Excellent news. When he's picked up, please let me know."

"You bet," she said and rang off.

When Wayne told Dory and PD that the driver of the Apollo green Ford was named Topper Gaines, the team were all equally baffled. It was going to be necessary to start the investigation completely over.

# TWENTY-ONE

**B**ILLY JO CAME HOME THE FOLLOWING AFTERNOON RIDING IN STATE. She was in the passenger seat of Mark's car, virtually hidden in a nest of blankets. Parking the car in the Rosedale Investigations driveway, Mark came around to her side and lifted her out. Carrying her inside, he put her down very gently on the small couch in the entryway.

"Hi everybody," she said, and the partners came over to welcome her home.

The irrepressible Dory couldn't help telling Mark that normally the bride wasn't carried over the threshold until *after* the wedding before adding, "We have big news for you, Billy Jo. A car registered to a Mr. Henry Brookover left Rosedale at 9:37 pm the night you were attacked. He was caught on CCTV," Dory said. She was grinning like a Cheshire cat.

"Following up on that sighting, Sheriff Bradley called the Erie, Pennsylvania police and they have agreed to pick him up. We are aware that the evidence against him is only circumstantial, but it's pretty strong. And if they can get a judge to give them a search warrant for his house, it's likely they'll find the painting," Wayne said.

"Thank God," Billy Jo said with relief. "I couldn't summon up the courage to call Sylvia and tell her *Wednesday's Child* was missing. I still feel just terrible that I promised her the painting would be safe. She texted me saying they've extended their trip and won't get back until the middle of next week, so maybe I won't even have to tell her."

"Once we have the painting, which I'm convinced we will get, the creep is going to be locked up for quite some time," PD said.

"You guys are just the best," Billy Jo said.

"What did the doctors say about your vertigo?" PD asked.

"The otolaryngologist found nothing structural that explained it. He said my ear canals were fine. There's no doubt I have it, though. Every time I tried to get out of bed the whole room spins. I think they took me seriously, but whenever a doctor has no clue what's wrong with you, they always say it's in our heads," she rolled her eyes.

"Especially if it's a woman," Dory said sympathetically. "The funny thing is that the condition of vertigo *is* actually in your head. Go on, honey."

"I asked the neurologist why I was so dizzy. He said the vertigo was probably related to the trauma from the head injury and it would likely go away in time. He took the time to walk me up and down the corridors in the hospital. Once I'm on my feet, I can do fine. Unfortunately, going downstairs is impossible, the whole staircase spins, and as you know I live upstairs," she said, in a discouraged tone.

"Guess Mark will have to come over every morning and carry you downstairs, or he could just sleep with you every night," Dory said chuckling.

"Dory, stop," Mark said. "You're embarrassing both of us. If Billy Jo closes her eyes, and has someone walking beside her, she can do the stairs."

"We're so glad she's back home, alive and well," Wayne said. He was virtually beaming.

"Almost well anyway," Billy Jo said. "And exceptionally hungry. Anything to eat around here?"

"There sure is. Dory went home last night and cooked up a storm. It's all set up as a picnic in the back yard," PD said.

"Well, what are we waiting for?" she asked.

They emerged into the backyard to see a picnic table virtually groaning with food. There were pulled pork sandwiches, bratwurst sausages and hot dogs. There was a funky salad Dory called "Cowboy Caviar." There were two types of potato salad, one with red potatoes and one with white. Hot baked beans were simmering in an electric pot. A banquet of fruit graced the table with strawberries, raspberries, blueberries and green grapes. There were pies, cookies and a cake with frosting that read, "Welcome Home, Billy Jo." Dory had even added a little table-sized easel with a paper replica of *Wednesday's Child* she had printed off. Billy Jo got teary-eyed—feeling all the love from her family.

CAPTAIN PAULA CRAWLEY, CHIEF OF NASHVILLE PD, called Sheriff Ben Bradley the following morning. They had picked up Topper Gaines and he was being held at their station. She wanted more information before making a formal arrest.

"We are pretty sure Topper is the person who ran Abigail Forester off the road causing her death. The state lab report said that she was hit by an old Ford painted Apollo green which matches the color of Topper's car. And according to the state lab report, there were some chips of paint that color on Mrs. Forester's back bumper," Sheriff Bradley said.

"Okay. We'll pick up his car and have our forensic people check his front end for any indication of damage from contact with other vehicles. What was Mrs. Forester driving?"

"A blue Subaru Forester. It was a 2019, I believe."

"I'll get back to you with what we find, and I'll personally interrogate the prisoner as to his whereabouts the day and time of Mrs. Forester's accident," Chief Paula said in a grim tone.

"One last thing, his record at our office shows that he was questioned and later released after an episode of road rage. That was a couple of years ago. He wasn't arrested, but we were definitely suspicious. Thanks for your help," the sheriff said.

"It's my pleasure," Captain Paula said.

# TWENTY-TWO

Based on the evidence Deputy George found on CCTV the night of Billy Jo's assault, Sheriff Bradley contacted the Erie, PA police and after discussions with their Captain, Henry Brookover was brought in for questioning. Captain Schlachter agreed to call the sheriff back after Brookover's interrogation. The sheriff then called Wayne to see if he wanted to listen-in on that conversation. Unsurprisingly, all three partners at Rosedale Investigations wanted to hear what Henry Brookover had to say for himself and were present to eavesdrop on Sheriff Bradley's conversation with the Captain Schlachter of the Erie PD.

"Hello, Captain," Sheriff Bradley said as the call was connected. "I understand you had a conversation with Henry Brookover today."

"I did. And I'll tell you what I learned, but first I'd like to go over what you have on your end," Captain Schlachter said.

"We faxed our crime report to you, but I'll summarize," the sheriff said. "A young woman named Billy Jo Bradley was assaulted in Rosedale by an individual who stole a valuable painting from her. She was transporting the painting from its owner to be placed in a safe at Rosedale Investigations where she is employed. We believe the motive for the assault was to obtain possession of the painting."

"Here's my problem, Sheriff. Henry Brookover is one of Erie's long time valued and well-to-do citizens, and he is loudly proclaiming his innocence. I'm wondering why you think he would want this painting badly enough to attack a young woman to get it?" he asked and even over the phone lines he sounded dubious.

"My understanding is that the reason goes back a long ways. Henry Brookover's great grandfather, Dr. Cedric Brookover, commissioned a painting called *Children by the Lakeside* a century ago. The subject was his three children. Shortly after the painting was completed, Brookover's wife, Wendy, died. A year later, the artist painted the scene again and called it *Wednesday's Child*. That's the painting which was stolen from Miss Bradley."

"Hold on. How did Mrs. Brookover die?" Captain Schlachter asked.

"Falling down a staircase and breaking her neck. There is evidence that Wendy Brookover was planning to leave her husband for the artist who did the painting, which made us suspicious, but no investigation was done. Apparently, the artwork has always been considered unlucky, and bad things happened to the family because of it."

"Hmm," he paused. "I'd say someone has a very vivid imagination. If the painting is that unlucky, why go to such lengths to get ahold of it? And, if Henry Brookover took it, which I seriously doubt, it seems more likely he wanted to sell it. I understand from the staff at the History Society that it's valuable."

"I don't quite have a complete handle on it, but Brookover's vehicle was caught on CCTV leaving Rosedale within a few minutes of Billy Jo's assault and given his family's hundred-year history with the painting, we want to know whether he took the painting and what he was doing here so far from home," the sheriff said.

"The problem is that it's all circumstantial, Sheriff. You don't have enough evidence either for an arrest or for me to go to the trouble of transporting him to you."

"Would you be willing to have one of my officers come to your city and interview him?" the sheriff asked.

"In order to do that, given how far Rosedale is from Erie, I'd have to arrest him. You know I can only hold him for twenty-four hours before I have to let him go or make an arrest."

Ben rolled his eyes at the Rosedale Investigations team. "Sir, may I remind you that Miss Bradley was hit on the head with a rock. The rock had her blood on it, and might have his DNA on it. The thief also pulled the lift gate of her SUV down on her head, so there might be evidence on her car as well. Would you be willing to ask Brookover to agree to a DNA swab and send the results here?"

"I'll ask him, but I doubt he'll acquiesce. I can't order it, you know."

"If he won't allow you to take a DNA swab, you can tell him if he returns the painting, I'll ask the judge to go easy on him. If the painting hasn't been damaged, I doubt he would have to serve any time. Probably just pay a fine."

"What about the assault?"

"That would be up to Billy Jo. She might possibly drop the charges."

"With your encouragement?" Captain Schlachter asked.

Sheriff Bradley snorted. "Hell no. He hit her on the head twice and could have killed her. She's been left with a serious case of vertigo and besides that, we're related. She's a distant cousin. I'd appreciate you trying to talk him into giving you a swab."

"I'll ask, but as I said, I'm doubtful. If I get a sample and his DNA is on the young woman's vehicle, we can pick him up again. He's not going anywhere. His family has lived here forever. And, I just don't see the man as dangerous to himself or others."

"Thanks, Captain. To the extent I understand it, this is all about getting ahold of the painting for some reason known only to Henry Brookover. And, though I firmly believe he's guilty of assaulting Miss Bradley, I don't think he's dangerous to anyone else either," Sheriff Bradley said and rang off.

However, as the investigation progressed, the sheriff's belief that Henry Brookover wasn't dangerous would be badly shaken.

DORY, PD AND WAYNE THANKED THE sheriff for letting them listen to his conversation and left the station. Walking out to Wayne's truck, Dory said, "Guess we'll have to wait and see what happens next with Mr. Brookover. Hope he agrees to a DNA test. Or confesses to have taken the painting."

"Meanwhile, Mark is still at our office trying to find Steve Pennington for the Abigail Forester case, but we are now operating under the assumption that it was Topper Gaines, *not* Steve Pennington, who was driving the car that ran into Mrs. Forester. There just aren't that many old Ford vehicles on the road that color," Wayne said.

"This doesn't sound to me like the usual road rage incident," Dory said thoughtfully. "Several eye witnesses reported that Abigail was travelling just below the speed limit and she wasn't talking on her phone—the behaviors that often lead to road rage. What we have here is a crime without a triggering event. A crime seemingly without a motive."

PD suddenly snapped his fingers. Wayne and Dory looked at him curiously.

"I just remembered something. A long time ago, I knew a man I think was Topper Gaines' grandfather. I'm going to contact him. Perhaps he can shed some light on the motive or might know where he lives."

It was late that afternoon when PD set off for Topper Gaines' grandfather's farm. The place was south of Rosedale in a rural area. It had rained the night before and the gravel roads were potted with puddles. He swore repeatedly as he dodged around potholes as big as cows. When he arrived at the Gaines farm and drove up the driveway, he saw no sign of occupancy. There were no cars parked outside and despite dark clouds threatening rain, no lights were on in the place.

PD sat listening to the clicking of his engine as it cooled. His mind circled back to his conversation with his son's ex-wife. He frowned, realizing that he hadn't gotten a call from his grandson, Liam. He wondered if the boy would eventually call. Perhaps he should contact the mother again. No, he didn't want to push the situation. If the boy wanted to contact him, he would. He just needed to be patient.

Setting aside his thoughts about Liam, he took a look at the old Gaines place, remembering the first time he came out here as a young cop. At the time, he was there to talk to Peter Gaines about an ongoing dispute between him and his belligerent neighbor. It was something about the neighbors stock grazing on his land. He and Gaines had struck up an unlikely friendship that persisted on and off for decades, although he hadn't seen him now in fifteen years.

"Probably a wasted trip," he groused irritably, but got out of his car and walked up to the front door. The air was heavy and felt like a wet blanket covering the property in cool gray mist. The house badly needed painting, and a broken gutter hung down over the front porch. Swatting the hanging gutter out of the way, he rang the doorbell. Hearing no sound, he pounded on the door. It had a tiny window about the size of a piece of typing paper. He peered inside, seeing nothing but furniture and an old television from the 1980's. He was about to give up when he saw a shape in the kitchen area. A man was sitting at the kitchen table, hunched over and not moving.

"Are you deaf, man? Open the door," he shouted and saw the old guy turn his head.

Moments later the door opened and a suspicious face looked out through the opening.

Seeing no sign of recognition, PD said, "Gaines, it's Pascoe. I'm not a cop any more. Are you going to let me in?"

The door opened and Peter Gaines, looking decades older than PD remembered, gestured for him to come in.

"Want some whiskey?" Gaines asked in a husky voice. When PD shook his head Gaines said, "I'm drinking, so you're drinking with me."

Gaines turned around and led the way back into the kitchen which was cluttered with dirty dishes and trash sacks filled to the brim. PD could smell garbage. Flies were buzzing around. Peter Gaines sat down at the table and sloshed whiskey into his own glass. Then he looked around and seeing a glass that was cleaner than most, poured a generous tumbler-full for PD. The bottle had the label of Buffalo Trace straight Bourbon whiskey. It was PD's least favorite beverage.

"This will put some hair on your chest," Gaines said and gesturing to the chair across from him said, "Have a seat."

PD sat down, feeling a wave of sadness about the old drunk across the table from him. If his recollection was correct, Gaines had ended up with most of the responsibility for raising his grandson, Topper. The kid's parents had experienced a variety of calamities and Topper kept getting dropped off with Grampa.

Gaines lifted his glass in a salute and their glasses clinked together. "Didn't expect company this morning," he said, gesturing to the kitchen. "Place's a pit. Good to hear a human voice. Are you still working?"

"Yup, but I'm not a cop now. Started a PI business in Rosedale. In fact, I came out here this morning to talk to you about your grandson, Topper."

"What's the kid done now?" Gaines asked. His voice was low and tinged with apprehension.

"Ran a woman off the road."

"Big deal. The way people drive these days, it's enough to drive a man crazy," Gaines said. "Topper's done it before. His temper gets the best of him. Usually it's not enough to bring an old detective out to see me, though," he said and his eyes narrowed in suspicion.

"The woman died, Peter," PD said, looking directly at his host.

Gaines coughed and cleared his phlegmy throat. "Should have drowned the damn kid as a pup," he said. Then, his face turned morose as he added, "He was a sweet little boy once upon a time. A happy laughing little tyke."

"Well, it's possible Topper was coerced or paid to do it, in which case he might be able to take a plea and get a shorter sentence—if he fingers the guy who ordered it. The woman he ran off the road was named Abigail Forester. Her maiden name was Pennington," PD looking intently at Gaines.

"Pennington, Pennington, now that's a name I recognize," Gaines said tapping his fingers on the sticky table. "Let me think. Yes, I remember now. There was a kid named Pennington that Topper was friends with in elementary school." He topped up his glass again and held the bottle out to PD who waved it away.

"Do you think Pennington is still around here?" PD asked.

"I'd say so. His father drank himself into the grave years ago. Steve never made anything of himself and it's likely he still lives with his mother. The mother remarried and took the husband's name. It's Blake. But, Mr. Blake died shortly after the marriage. She's widowed again now."

PD drank with the old wreck for a while before shaking hands and promising to inform Gaines of the date for his grandson's trial. Despite the poverty and alcoholism of his old acquaintance, PD walked out to his car feeling a rise of satisfaction. His old brain had remembered Peter Gaines and that he was Topper's grandfather.

Thinking it through as he drove back toward Rosedale, PD came up with a theory of the crime. He assumed Steve Pennington had hired Topper, his pal from elementary school days, to run his aunt off the road for some unknown reason. Something had gone wrong though, because when they met with Detective Rob Fuller, he said there were broad skid marks left on the highway. Whoever was driving had tried to stop but was going just too fast. That fact would help Topper once the case came before a judge.

Somedays PD felt he was getting too old to be a detective, but not today. A grin tweaked the corner of his mouth. He'd found what they needed to solve the case—a strong connection between Topper Gaines and Steve Pennington. Once Billy Jo found the address for Pennington's mother, he'd go out there and bring the kid in personally.

# TWENTY-THREE

The middle of July saw Rosedale hit by a line of thunderstorms and heat lightening. With the thunder and pounding rain, Billy Jo had hardly slept. The ringing phone woke her from uneasy dreams. She was still in bed and her voice was tinged with sleep when she answered saying, "Rosedale Investigations."

"Is this Billy Jo Bradley? This is Betty Poitou."

"Yes, it's me," she said. She was surprised to hear the elegant Curator of Paintings from the Erie History Center sounding distinctly angry.

"There's been a theft here at the History Society. The easel in our grand salon is empty."

"What?" Billy Jo asked. She could hardly believe what she had just heard.

"*Children on the Lakeshore* was stolen before we opened this morning. I've already spoken to the police and they are on their way here. I've given them your name as being responsible for this theft." Her voice was crisp and unwavering.

"I'm sorry, I don't understand," Billy Jo said. She was having a hard time processing the information.

"I'm sure you remember the painting, the one we talked about when you visited, *Children by the Lakeshore*? As I said, it was stolen. It's gone and whether you took it personally or not, the theft is your fault," Ms. Poitou's said accusingly.

Billy Jo didn't respond right away—she had been through quite an ordeal since she last talked with the stylish older woman. Still struggling with fatigue as well as vertigo, the accusation hit her like an arrow in her heart. She felt anger rising like a summer storm in her body.

"Just hold on a minute there, Ms. Poitou. When I got back from visiting you, I was assaulted. *Wednesday's Child*, the Iverson-Jones painting we had here in Tennessee, was stolen from the back of my car. The thief hit me with a rock, I got a concussion and had to spend a couple of days in the hospital. I could have been killed trying to prevent the loss of *Wednesday's Child*. I'm in no frame of mind to be accused of art theft."

Ms. Poitou hesitated a moment but then said, "I'm sorry that happened to you, Billy Jo, but now that you tell me *Wednesday's Child* is also missing, I'm even more convinced that you are at the heart of this. Hang on a minute, I can hear sirens—the police are pulling up in front."

She set the phone down and Billy Jo, still fuming from the unjust attack, could hear the front door of the building open, footsteps on the stairs and voices. Then Ms. Poitou came back on the line.

"There's a police officer here, a Sargent Sanders who wants to talk to you."

Billy Jo waited, controlling her temper with difficulty. It wouldn't do any good to lose her cool on the phone with the police. She needed to sound calm and collected, even if inside she was feeling outraged at the totally baseless accusation. She bit her bottom lip.

"Is this Miss Billy Jo Bradley?" the officer asked.

"This is she," she said and took a deep breath.

"Ms. Poitou said you came here recently and met with her about the painting, *Children at the Lakeshore*. Is that correct?"

"It is, Officer," she said remembering to breathe and pitch her voice in a low register.

"I want to make sure I have this right. The painting was stolen and the theft occurred shortly after you and your companion, a Mr. Mark Schneider, were here. Now Ms. Poitou tells me that a second painting by the same artist has been stolen from where you live in Tennessee. Is that correct?"

"Yes, sir, but I am innocent of both thefts. In fact, we are confident we know who took our painting. Are you aware that Captain Schlachter, who is your *boss* I believe, recently interviewed Mr. Henry Brookover about this matter? He did so at our sheriff's request because Brookover's license plate was caught on CCTV leaving Rosedale, Tennessee the night I was assaulted and the painting stolen."

She was dying to put him on the spot by asking if the right hand knew what the left hand was doing at his police post, but stopped herself in time.

"Hold on a moment. I need to confer with Detective Carol Wright. She's just arrived."

She could hear male and female voices, but the words were indistinct. Then he came back on the line. "Detective Wright would like to speak with you," he said.

"Miss Bradley, this is Detective Wright. I understand from speaking with Curator Poitou that you are researching the provenance of a Jeremy Iverson-Jones painting called *Wednesday's Child* and toward that end you visited our fair city recently. A painting on the same subject and by the same artist called *Children at the Lakeshore*, was stolen from the History Society this morning, and Ms. Poitou has told us you are responsible. Art theft from a museum is a serious crime and will be prosecuted to the fullest extent of the law. Do I have this correct?"

"Yes, ma'am. I am a private investigator with Rosedale Investigations in Tennessee." She actually wasn't, but wanted to seem on an equal level with the uppity cow. "I'm always happy to collaborate with the police, but in this case will refer you to our local Sheriff, Ben Bradley. He's been working with your superior, Captain Schlachter, on this matter. Mr. Brookover is responsible for both these thefts. And I'm wholly innocent of these terrible crimes."

There was a pause before the detective said, "I'll check with my Captain. Thank you, Miss Bradley. Ms. Poitou just informed me that you were injured trying to prevent the theft of the second painting. I'm sorry you were hurt and hope you are feeling better now."

Slightly appeased, Billy Jo said, "I'm getting there. Please tell Curator Poitou that I am shocked and dismayed that *Children by the Lakeshore* is missing and I hope you can retrieve it soon. I am confident that both paintings will be found in the possession of Mr. Brookover."

The detective thanked her, said they might have to talk to her again, and bid her good-bye.

Billy Jo clicked off the call. To think both paintings were missing made her feel sick to her stomach. She envisioned the knowledgeable grandfatherly Mr. Brookover, the man she had interviewed in Erie, sitting in his living room and reminiscing. It seemed ridiculously unlikely that the old guy would have driven nine hours to Rosedale, hit her over the head and stolen *Wednesday's Child*. And even less likely that he would have broken into the History Society in his home town and stolen *Children by the Lakeshore*.

Somehow the little project that she had fought so hard for—researching the provenance of a painting for pity's sakes—had turned violent and near-deadly. The worst of it was she had a sinking sensation that Ms. Poitou was right. If she hadn't dug up all the old family pain around the artist, his love affair with Wendy Brookover and the *curse,* this might never have happened. She sat up, intending to get out of bed, but vertigo made the room spin and she fell to the floor.

Lying with her face mashed into the carpet, and the room spinning around her, Billy Jo felt so miserable she wished she could die.

PD drove to the Nashville police post that morning, hoping to participate in the interview with Topper Gaines. Once flecks of paint from Abigail Forester's car had been identified on the front bumper of his vehicle, Topper was arrested by the Nashville police and charged with the murder of Abigail Forester. Although PD had worked at the post for many years before his retirement, Captain Paula denied his request to assist with the interview.

"Sorry, PD, but this is a capital crime. Can't violate procedure by the slightest micrometer. I'm sure you understand." She did agree to him providing background on the case to Detectives D'Angelo and Stoneman prior to their interrogation of Gaines.

When PD reached the interview room after briefing the detectives, Sheriff Bradley was already present to observe. The room had a one-way window from which they could see and hear the interview with Topper Gaines. The prisoner, with dirty hair, a straggling blonde beard and wearing an orange prison jumpsuit, was escorted into the room by a uniformed officer. Upon entering the room, he was shown to a seat at the table.

As soon as Topper was seated, Detectives D'Angelo and Stoneman entered the room. Stoneman was a hard-looking man in his early fifties. He had a narrow face and graying hair. He sat down across the table from Topper. Detective D'Angelo took his position standing in the back corner of the room. The uniformed cop who brought Topper in was dismissed.

"Good Morning, Mr. Gaines. My name is Detective Stoneman. My partner, Detective D'Angelo," he gestured to the far corner, "is present in the room. In the adjacent viewing room are Sheriff Bradley from the Rosedale Sheriff's office and Detective PD Pascoe from Rosedale Investigations." He gave the time and date of the interview for the tape and then said, "You are Mr. Topper Coolidge Gaines and you have been arrested and read your rights in conjunction with the wrongful death of Mrs. Abigail Forester. Do you understand?"

"Yes," Topper said in a sullen tone.

PD felt his phone vibrate, looked down and saw a text from Billy Jo. The message was simple, just three letters—SOS. He turned ice cold and his breathing caught. Then he noticed it was a group text, sent to both Wayne and Dory, and exhaled in relief. Whatever was going on with Billy Jo, they would both be leaving immediately to help.

"I got an SOS text just now from Billy Jo," he whispered quietly to the sheriff. "It also went to Wayne and Dory. I'm sure they will respond."

"Let me know what happens," Sheriff Bradley said, just as the door to the interview room opened for the third time.

"I'm Mr. Gaines' attorney," a young man said. "My name is Robby Willoughby and I'd like some time alone with my client."

RECEIVING BILLY JO'S SOS, BOTH WAYNE AND DORY'S VEHICLES entered the driveway of Rosedale Investigations at virtually the same moment. Wayne jumped out of his truck, leaving it still running with the driver's door open. Dory rolled her eyes, walked over to his truck, shut it off and closed his door. The front door to the agency was ajar and she could hear both Wayne's and Billy Jo's voices. The girl was sobbing and talking at the same time.

Dory walked inside. Seeing Wayne at the top of the stairs walking Billy Jo down the steps with an arm around her waist, she could tell the girl was okay. If this was a prank she was going to smack the kid.

Billy Jo raised her eyes to Dory's.

"What is going on, Billy Jo?" Dory asked.

To her surprise, Billy Jo's tears stopped instantly and she started to laugh. She pointed at Dory chuckling, "Have you seen yourself?" she said.

"Yes, do take a look," Wayne said with a wry grin of his own.

"What are you two talking about," Dory said. "This had better not be some practical joke, Billy Jo."

"You are dressed in your bathrobe," Wayne said.

Dory looked down at herself. To her shock, they were right. She was still wearing her robe and slippers. "Oh my God. After all my nagging here I am in my night attire at work! I can't believe I ran out of the house like this. I'm so embarrassed, I could die. It's all because you sent us the SOS," she said. "This emergency had better be worth it."

"Setting aside your glee at seeing Miss Dory embarrassed, I think you better tell us what triggered the SOS," Wayne said. "I'll get us all some coffee. And, since you sent the text to PD as well, I'll let him know you're fine."

"But I'm not fine. I'm not fine at all," Billy Jo wailed and her tears threatened again.

"What's the problem, little person?" Wayne asked patting her shoulder.

"The original Jeremy Iverson-Jones painting, *Children by the Lakeshore*, was stolen from the History Society in Pennsylvania. Both the paintings are now missing, and it's all my fault," she wailed. Wayne and Dory looked at each other in mystification.

"We're not getting this," Dory said frowning.

"I've been accused of stealing *Children by the Lakeshore* and the Erie PD have already questioned me," Billy Jo told her in a choked voice.

"How the hell did they come up with that?" Wayne asked sounding exasperated. "We didn't leave the office until after six last night and you were still here then. It's a nine hour drive to Erie, PA. I guess it's theoretically possible, if you drove all night, but you haven't been driving since your doctor told you not to, while you were on anti-seizure meds."

"And I don't see why a phone call from the cops to you warranted an SOS to us," Dory said.

"Because they are right. I am guilty. I'm guilty as sin," Billy Jo said and sat down in her chair, crumpled in shame.

# TWENTY-FOUR

Detective Stoneman's interrogation of Topper Gaines was not going well. Stoneman was a senior detective well known in the Nashville PD for having a short fuse. At the moment, his jaw was clenched and he was turning red. Clearly his fuse had been lit and was just about to blow. The spark that had ignited his temper was Topper's young attorney.

Attorney Robby Willoughby, who had represented Poppy Delaney in her appeal to the Parole Board during the Blind Split case, had advised his client not to answer the majority of Detective Stoneman's questions.

Topper just kept saying, "Upon the advice of my attorney, I decline to answer." Stoneman was getting more furious by the moment. Steam was practically coming out his ears.

Unable to take it any longer, Detective Stoneman slammed his hands down on the table making a loud startling smack. "What the hell were you doing at Abigail Forester's funeral, Topper? You were seen at the service driving away from the parking lot. We have your license plate number. No use denying it."

For once, Topper ignored his gesticulating attorney and shrugged saying, "I just decided to go."

"So you admit you were there. How did you know the woman?"

"I didn't," Topper said.

"You just decided to go to the funeral of a woman you didn't know, is that it?" Stoneman said sarcastically, shaking his head.

"I sometimes go to funerals for the food," Topper said looking put-upon.

Stoneman raised his eyes heavenward. "Right. And you pealed out of the parking lot before the service ended without getting anything to eat.

I'm going to ask you again, and this time I want the truth. Why were you there? Did somebody ask you to go?"

Topper looked down at his lap, saying nothing.

"We have paint on the front bumper of your car and it matches paint found on the rear of Abigail Forester's vehicle. You ran her off the road which led to her death. We already know that. Why the hell you would do such a stupid thing?" Stoneman asked.

Again Topper shook his head mutely.

Stoneman shook his head. "Topper, you say you didn't know the Forester woman. You admit to attending her funeral, and we have both eyewitness reports and forensic evidence that you were the person who ran her off the road before she died. Someone else told you to do this. Are you really going to take the hit for a capital crime?"

Topper shifted uneasily in his chair and grimaced, but didn't respond.

"You didn't think this up all by yourself, Topper, you're just not that smart. Somebody hired you to run Mrs. Forester off the road. If you don't tell me who it was, you are going down for felony murder and I'll push for first degree and premeditation. It's won't just be a short stint in the big house this time. You will be there for the rest of your dumb useless life."

Topper darted a quick frightened glance at Robby Willoughby who said, "I'd like a private word with my client."

Stoneman grimaced, stood up and joined Det. D'Angelo in the corner of the room. From the observation room, PD could see that D'Angelo trying to calm his partner down. When the conversation between Robby Willoughby and Topper ended, the attorney gestured for Det. Stoneman to return. He did so and sat down at the table.

"So, who was it, Topper? If you tell me, I'll tell the judge you cooperated."

"It was a friend of mine, a person I've known since I was a kid. His name is Steve Pennington," Topper said.

"We're done here," Stoneman said and stood up abruptly. He and D'Angelo left the room together, meeting PD and Sheriff Bradley in the hall.

"Let's go down to the coffee room," Det. D'Angelo said. He was a good-looking single Italian guy who was the heart-throb of all the women working at the post. He'd been partnered with Stoneman both to learn from him and help keep a lid on his temper.

ONCE THEY WERE SEATED IN A SMALL CONFERENCE ROOM, and Stoneman had mostly regained his composure, he asked PD to explain his theory of the crime.

"I believe the motive for this crime goes back over twenty years. Apparently, Oscar Pennington, Mrs. Forester's alcoholic brother, came to Rosedale for a visit when Steve was a senior in high school. He asked Abigail's husband for money to send his son to college and her husband refused."

"Go on," Stoneman said.

"Two decades later, Abigail Forester learned she had cancer and had less than a year to live. She went to her priest and told him she wanted to make amends to Steve before she died. She set out for a meeting with her attorney. My guess is that she was going to change her will to benefit him, but as we know she never made it."

"How did you get all this?" Stoneman asked.

"Investigator Dory Clarkson got it directly from Abigail's priest, Father Dominic," PD said.

"Hard to argue with a priest, and Father Dominic's a good one, but I still don't get why Steve Pennington would hire Topper Gaines to run his Aunt Abigail off the road?"

"Clearly a lunatic idea, but I wonder if that's really what Steve really told Topper to do. Perhaps he was only supposed to drive alongside Mrs. Forester, wave her off the road and talk to her. The skid marks show that Topper was trying to stop," PD said.

"We know from the state lab that Topper was going way too fast for their idiotic plan to work. Once Abigail's car went off the road, Topper probably panicked and left the scene," Det. D'Angelo said.

"Knucklehead. If he'd stopped after the accident and tried to help her, he might not be facing jail time," Det. Stoneman said.

"It's so ironic. Pennington launches this ridiculous scheme at the very moment that Abigail is on her way to her attorney to change her will. Turns out all he had to do was talk to the woman," Sheriff Bradley said, shaking his head.

"Those two numbskulls were never known for their intelligence," PD said. "It was a long time ago, but I remember them both as kids. They were always playing pranks and practical jokes. Steve was the leader and Topper the follower."

"Even if this theory holds together, I don't understand why Steve

Pennington didn't run his aunt off the road himself, or at a minimum talk to her personally," D'Angelo said. "What was so pressing that he needed to launch this crazy plan now? What the heck did he need the money for?"

"That's the first question I'm going to put to the man," Stoneman said.

BACK AT ROSEDALE INVESTIGATIONS, WAYNE ASKED BILLY JO if she was up to doing an in-depth background on Henry Brookover. "There is some reason he stole both the paintings and I'm hoping you can figure out what it was," he said.

"I'll see what I can find," she said but she was white-faced and as she walked into the kitchen to make herself a cappuccino, Wayne noticed she was walking unsteadily.

"If you're not up to doing this, I'll call Mark. We can have him do it," Wayne said.

"I'll do it. I'm the reason the paintings were stolen," she said quietly as she came back to her workstation and took a seat.

"I doubt that, but tell me why you think so," Wayne said.

"If I hadn't met with Grampa Brookover and talked about his grand-mother's affair with the artist and the curse, I think both the paintings would be safe."

"So you think it was something you said to Grampa Brookover that triggered his assaulting you and stealing *Wednesday's Child*? And then you think he broke into the History Society and stole *Children by the Lakeshore*? What was it exactly that you said to the man?" Wayne asked looking perplexed.

"When I mentioned the curse for the first time, Grampa Brookover got a far-away look in his eyes. He'd been showing us his old photo album and when I said the word curse, he snapped the album shut. I believe he came some conclusion then, and that's what led to the thefts," Billy Jo said.

"I can think of only one reason he would steal the paintings. He needs the money. Together they would be worth at least a hundred thousand dollars," Wayne said.

"I think it's more likely he wants to destroy them," Dory said thought-fully. "He may think doing away with them would bring an end to a curse that has dogged that family for a century. I checked with Evangeline Bon Temps, our local authority on such matters, and she told me burning a cursed object can stop the curse."

I need the restroom," Billy Jo said and stood up abruptly. She swayed and then her arms and legs jerked wildly. Her body stiffened and she fell to the floor in a cataclysm of juddering movements.

"Call an ambulance," Wayne yelled.

THE AMBULANCE ARRIVED WITH LIGHTS AND SIRENS on ten minutes later. Dory and Wayne had picked Billy Jo up off the floor and carried her to the couch in the waiting room. The seizure had ended and they kept asking her if she could hear them. She didn't respond. The paramedics burst through the door and one of them asked, "Is she breathing?"

"She is," Dory said.

"Conscious?"

"No."

"Did she fall? Hit her head?"

"She stood up, said she needed the bathroom and then hit the floor," Wayne said.

"While she was lying on the floor, she had a seizure. Earlier today she told me she fell after getting a phone call from the police," Dory said.

The two paramedics exchanged significant glances. "Has she spoken since the seizure?"

"No," Wayne said. "But she opens her eyes partway from time to time."

"What's her name?"

"Billy Jo Bradley."

The paramedic leaned down close and said, "Billy Jo, can you hear me?"

There was no response. "Okay, I'm going to get her blood pressure, oxygen saturation and a heart rate before we transfer her," he said. He placed the blood pressure cuff on Billy Jo's arm before placing his stethoscope just below the cuff. Listening for her heartbeat, he pumped it up. He then clipped an oxygen sensor on her finger before turning to his partner saying, "BP 140 over 90, $O^2$ 92%, heart rate 120. I want to do a finger stick too."

"What's that for?" Dory asked.

"Checking her blood sugar in case she's diabetic and might be hypoglycemic." He pricked Billy Jo's finger and said, "It's 102. That's normal."

They had brought a stretcher into the room with them, a long yellow backer-board on a wheeled cart. They positioned it parallel to the couch. "We're going to transfer her now. On my count, one, two, three," the paramedic said and the two men lifted Billy Jo on to the stretcher. "We're taking her to Rosedale General if you want to follow us," he said. Then they wheeled Billy Jo out the door, down the rose-bordered sidewalk, and loaded her into the ambulance.

As the ambulance drove away with lights and sirens blaring, Dory turned to Wayne and said, "Is Lucy working today?"

"Yes, I'll call her."

"Funny how things happen, isn't it. Turns out, it was worth our girl sending that SOS after all," Dory said giving her partner a long somber look.

"Indeed," Wayne said. "Let's not tell PD about Billy Jo's seizure for a bit. I want to get some more information about her condition before I call him."

# TWENTY-FIVE

PD WALKED OUT OF HIS LITTLE CABIN INTO THE FOREST in the gray pre-dawn. The sun wouldn't be up for an hour, but the sky was already lightening. He could see his car, a looming dark presence in the driveway, and felt a cool breeze on his face. Climbing into the vehicle, he started it and turned on his headlights. A young buck standing in the weeds turned toward him, raised his white tail, and vanished into the woods.

Driving slowly down the mile-long dirt driveway, PD reviewed his plan. Billy Jo had finally found an address for Steve Pennington's mother, Edna Blake. Having no presence on the internet, no phone and no vehicles, she had to resort to property ownership records and at last learned Mrs. Blake lived in a decrepit mansion not far from his place. It had been a long slog and PD told Billy Jo he was impressed by her commitment. She had smiled broadly when he said, "Well done."

During the years he was a detective, PD often pounced on criminals by arriving early in the morning. Most of them were hung-over and sleep-fogged. Using the element of surprise, he was usually able to convince them to come into the station without using his gun. He'd brought it with him today, though. It was unloaded, but just the sight of a gun usually did the trick with dopey would-be criminals like Steve Pennington.

A golden chin of sun was just peeking over the horizon when he found the old place. It was a large two-story brick residence with a covered porch. Intricate white gingerbread trim had been used on the porch overhangs. The elaborate light fixtures on the porch were mostly broken now, but the place had obviously been the home of a wealthy person once. It spoke of old glamor—young girls in bright summer frocks and gentlemen in white jackets drinking mint juleps and smoking stogies.

PD parked his car in the driveway, pocketed his gun, took a small flashlight out of his glove compartment and walked onto the porch. He reached for the door handle and felt it give to his touch. He swung the door open and walked inside. He was unsurprised to find the house unlocked. This far out in the country, most people didn't bother locking their houses.

He walked into the living room, noticing cigarettes in ash trays and beer cans on the coffee table. Taking the corridor to the right, he passed several empty rooms, following the sounds of loud snoring. The door to the snorer's bedroom was open and PD looked in. It was Mrs. Blake. The woman must have weighed close to three hundred pounds. The blankets rose and fell with her breathing, her quivering belly looking larger than a giant bouncy ball. She was lying on her back and PD shined his flashlight on her face. A thin line of drool came from her open mouth.

He continued down the corridor, but the rest of the rooms were uninhabited, empty except for lovely old, faded wallpaper on the walls, threadbare rugs and dusty furniture. He returned to the main living room and took the left-hand corridor. The last room was occupied by his quarry. Steve Pennington was in bed and sound asleep. He was lying on top of the mattress, wearing nothing but a T-shirt and briefs. A crumpled dirty sheet lay across his legs. It was very hot in the room. A fan was running and the blankets had been thrown off the bed, landing in a tangled heap on the floor. PD pulled out his gun and in a loud voice said, "Wake up, Pennington."

Steve sat up, his eyes huge. Trembling in abject fear, he grabbed for the sheet and pulled it up to his bare chest. PD shook his head, amused by people who thought hiding a under a sheet would protect them against gunfire.

"Who the hell are you?" Steve asked.

"I'm Detective Pascoe and your worst nightmare. Let's not wake your mother. Put on your jeans." PD tossed them to him and Steve got out of bed awkwardly. He stumbled, hopping on one foot trying to put on his pants. "We're going down to the kitchen, I've got your shoes."

He made Steve walk ahead of him down the long hall, poking him in the back with his gun barrel several times. They reached the kitchen and PD sat down at the table. "Sit," he said, holding the gun steady as he put the man's shoes down on the dirty floor.

"What do you want, man?" Steve asked in a pleading voice.

"You bribed your old buddy Topper Gaines to run your Aunt Abigail off the road. Stupid plan. Don't know if he told you, but poor woman died afterwards. Topper's in custody and going down for murder."

Steven blanched and his mouth twisted. "Never meant for that . . ."

"Stop talking. You are going to do yourself a huge favor this morning, Pennington. You are turning yourself into the Nashville police. It will go a long ways toward getting you a shorter sentence. Topper already fingered you as the brains behind the operation. Let's go," PD said.

"Can't do that," Steve said crossly, shaking his head. "Can't leave Mama."

"She's sound asleep. Leave her a note."

To his surprise, Steve stood his ground. "She's old now, Detective. Has bad Alzheimer's, can't read anymore. You can shoot me where I stand, but I'm not leaving her." He drew himself up to his full height and at that moment looked truly valiant.

PD was a sucker for family loyalty, and to his surprise there seemed to be a strong vein of honor in Steve Pennington. "Can't you call somebody? Isn't there any other family?"

They waited several hours but eventually a disheveled woman in her mid-forties showed up. She cast a wary eye at PD and Steve, but said she'd stay with the old lady until something else could be worked out.

"You've got to get your Mama into a facility," she told Steve, shaking her finger at him.

"I know. Don't have the money," he called over his shoulder as they walked out to PD's car.

So that was it, Pascoe thought. That's what he needed the money for. The respect he felt for Steve's concern for his mother grew stronger. Having hardly any relatives himself, PD honored family commitment. It would be a terrible thing to love a person who needed care you couldn't afford. He would make sure the judge knew about Steve's dedication. It might strike a chord and get him less time in the big house.

LUCY WAS STANDING ON THE BACK DOCK OF THE HOSPITAL, waiting for the ambulance to arrive with Billy Jo. She was dressed in a pale-yellow blouse and navy skirt under her long white coat. It was a hot summer morning in August with a bright blue sky and puffy clouds. She took a deep breath, enjoying the breezy day and the short interlude of quiet from the hectic pace of the ER. It wasn't long before she heard the siren. *They're playing my song*, she thought with a wry smile.

When the ambulance pulled up, she recognized the driver. It was a paramedic named Will and his partner. Both were competent guys. "What's her status?" she asked, as they loaded Billy Jo onto a gurney and wheeled it up on the dock behind the ER.

"Our patient, Billy Jo Bradley, was partially conscious when we arrived, but she woke up in the ambulance. She had a seizure at her place of employment this morning."

"How long was she out?" Lucy asked.

"For about 20 minutes."

"What were her BP and heart rate?"

"Blood pressure's a little high, 140/90 and her heart rate was 120. The people she works with said she was left with a case of vertigo after being hit on the head," Will said. "According to the electronic medical record, she was seen here in at Rosedale General last week for a head wound that required stitches and subsequently experienced vertigo. Okay if we bring her inside now?" Lucy nodded.

"Billy Jo, it's Dr. Lucy, can you hear me?" she asked, walking along-side the gurney as the men pushed it through the swinging metal doors.

"Um hum," Billy Jo said quietly. Her eyes were closed and she seemed only minimally conscious.

Turning back to the emergency medics, Lucy said, "Billy Jo works with my fiancé, Detective Nichols and his partners. Thank you for pick-ing her up."

"No problem. I'm going down to grab something to eat at the cafete-ria," Will's partner said and took off.

"What do you think Billy Jo's problem is?" Lucy asked Will, who had stayed behind to talk with her.

"I was thinking it might be a post-traumatic seizure," he said.

"And I'm thinking it's about time *you* applied to medical school," Lucy said and grinned. "A post-traumatic seizure is just what I was thinking. Probably post-ictal. I'll get a second head CT done. One was done when she was here before, but I want a repeat scan or an MRI to rule out a bleed."

"Sorry, I'd like to talk some more with you, but I've got another call," Will said and pushed the button on his pager.

AFTER LUCY GOT AN ORDERLY TO lift Billy Jo from the gurney and on to a bed in the ER, her nurse appeared, moved the curtain aside and came up to the bedside. Nurse Channing Soldan was known for her unflappable cheer and for dying streaks of her hair to match the color of her outfits. Today she was wearing turquoise scrubs and her blonde bangs were perfectly color-coordinated.

"What do you think of the turquoise?" she asked Dr. Lucy.

"Just hoping that the day of the *wedding* you will at least dye your hair apricot, peach or salmon. Those are my wedding colors you know," Lucy said.

"Not to worry. Who is our patient today?" Channing asked.

"This is Billy Jo Bradley who works with Wayne and Dory. She's just coming around." Then addressing herself to the girl, Lucy said, "How are you feeling by now?"

"Okay," she said quietly.

"Glad to hear it," Lucy said. "I'd like to introduce you to your nurse, Channing. It seems you had a seizure this morning, do you remember that?"

Billy Jo shook her head. "No. The last thing I remember is standing up at my work station feeling like I needed to go the bathroom and then waking up in the ambulance."

"We need to figure out what caused this seizure, so we're going to do a repeat scan of your head and some routine blood work."

"Do I have to stay? I'm feeling better now," Billy Jo said.

"You need to stay. In fact, I'm going to admit you. You can probably go back home in a day or two, depending on the results of the scans and the blood work. The seizure could be a result of the assault you experienced. I'm aware that there's a police investigation into your initial attack and the results of the tests could be subpoenaed. Channing will take you to the CT suite now for the scan."

The nurse pulled a wheelchair up to the bedside and with Dr. Lucy's help they lifted their patient into the chair just as Wayne and Dory appeared. Both looked frantic.

Billy Jo waved good-bye weakly to her colleagues as she was wheeled away.

"How is she?" Wayne asked.

"She just got here, Wayne. I'm going to need a little time to review her case and look at her scans," Dr. Lucy said.

Wayne shook his head. "Unfortunately, Doctor, time seems to be our enemy in this case," he said. Dory nodded in silent agreement.

# TWENTY-SIX

"**W**HO DO WE HAVE HERE, DETECTIVE?" the duty sergeant asked from his raised tower as PD Pascoe and Steve Pennington entered the reception area of the main Nashville police post.

"This moron, Steve Pennington, is wanted for questioning about a murder. Your Captain is going to want to be informed," PD said. He had returned his gun to his chest holster but had Steve gripped firmly by the upper arm.

"I'm turning myself in," Steve said loudly.

"Yes, he wants everyone here to know that he's come in of his own volition," PD said giving the sergeant an oblique look.

"Looks to me like he had a little encouragement," the sergeant said and grinned. "Have a seat and I'll buzz Captain Paula."

PD and Steve took seats on the old wooden chairs that lined the exterior walls of the entry area. Officers and perps were arriving and leaving. One scantily dressed young lady with a male escort slapped him across his face. An officer grabbed her arms and held them behind her back, telling her to calm down. It was the usual activity at the post where PD had worked for twenty-plus years before founding Rosedale Investigations.

He had visited a drive-thru on their way to the post, and Steve was hungrily downing a double cheeseburger, when Captain Paula in her sharp blue uniform walked in. The two detectives who had interrogated Topper Gaines—Stoneman and D'Angelo—were right behind her.

"Good morning, Captain and Detectives," PD said. "This is Steve Pennington who is here of his own accord to talk to you about his pal Topper Gaines and their hair-brained scheme to run Mrs. Abigail Forester off the road."

Stoneman had a wintry smile on his face. He rubbed his hands together. D'Angelo, no doubt seeing the signs of his partner's rising temper, touched his arm. Stoneman frowned.

"Thank you for bringing him in, Detective," Captain Paula said. "You can turn him over to the detectives now. I can tell you've had a busy morning. Would you like a cup of coffee?"

"I would," PD said, and he and the Captain walked to the coffee room and helped themselves.

"Did Pennington say anything to you about the reason he talked Topper into driving poor Mrs. Forester off the road?" Captain Paula asked.

"He didn't say anything directly, and of course my report to you is hearsay anyway, but when I was trying to get him to come with me, an interesting thing happened. Even with my gun on him, Steve refused to leave his mother. I told him to leave a note about where he was going but he stood firm. His mother has Alzheimer's and can no longer read, so a note would have been useless. He actually said I could shoot him where he stood, but he wasn't leaving his mama. We had to wait until a neighbor came over before Steve would go with me. I must say at that moment, I respected him."

"Sounds like you not only found the connection between the two men, and convinced Steve to turn himself in, but also may have discovered the motive," Captain Paula said. "Nice work, Detective."

"Does Topper Gaines have an attorney?" PD asked.

"Yes, it's a young guy from Legal Aid named Robby Willoughby."

"I want to make sure Pennington is represented by counsel. Could you see if Willoughby will represent both of them?"

"No problem," Captain Paula said. "I think the judge would have the cases conjoined anyway."

They chatted a bit longer before PD departed.

On his way back to Rosedale, he called Wayne. "What's been going on?" he asked.

"Billy Jo is back in the hospital. She had a seizure. Scared the hell out of me. I'd never seen someone seize before. Lucy called it a post-traumatic seizure, probably left over from her assault."

"Can we see her?" PD asked, and his old voice cracked.

"Not for a bit. The doctors need some time to review the new scans."

AN HOUR LATER AN OFFICER CAME TO ESCORT STEVE PENNINGTON into interrogation. Detectives Stoneman and D'Angelo were standing in the hall. As the officer and Steve walked by, D'Angelo turned to his partner.

"How about me doing the interview with this guy?" he asked.

"Okay," Det. Stoneman said shortly. They walked to the interrogation room where Pennington was already seated.

D'Angelo walked to the table and introduced himself. "I appreciate you coming in of your own accord this morning, Steve," he said.

He nodded.

"Why don't you tell me the whole story? Just start at the beginning," he said, encouragingly.

"It goes back a ways," Steve said.

"We have plenty of time this morning," D'Angelo told him, glancing quickly at his supervisor standing in the back corner of the room. Detective Stoneman raised his eyes to the ceiling in exasperation.

"When I graduated from high school, I wanted to go to college. My folks didn't have the money, but my dad had a well-to-do sister. Dad thought she and her husband might help."

"And her name was Abigail Forester?" D'Angelo asked, writing a note on his notepad. Steve nodded. "Go on," he said.

"My dad went to see them and asked her husband for the money to pay for my tuition. I wanted to be a nurse," he said and a brief spasm of regret crossed his features.

"Did Mr. & Mrs. Forester give you any money?"

"No. Uncle Anthony turned my dad down. He assumed Dad would drink it all and wouldn't give the money to me."

"I take it your dad was an alcoholic?" D'Angelo asked.

"That's right. He died of complications from cirrhosis of the liver when I was twenty-two."

"So why didn't you go to see your Aunt and Uncle yourself after your father's death?" D'Angelo asked.

"Around that time, I got a ticket for driving under the influence and lost my license. There was an accident involved and my car was totaled. I couldn't visit her because I didn't have a car."

"I see. What about your mother? Couldn't she have asked them for help?"

"She always thought they were rich and stuck-up. Mama didn't want to lower herself by asking for help. Plus, by then I was already past the age when kids usually go to college and had a decent job. I was working as a mechanic at Joe's Garage."

"You said all this took place some time ago. How old are you now, Steve?"

"I'm coming up on forty," he said.

Det. Stoneman, unable to stand the deliberate pacing of his partner's questions, had joined them at the table and was drumming his fingers in frustration.

"So why did you need money from your Aunt Abigail now?" D'Angelo asked.

"It's for my mama. She's pretty sick."

What is your mother's medical problem?"

"Mama has Alzheimer's. I have this neighbor, Mrs. Clarke, who drives her to her doctor's appointments. She told me there's a new medication that helps with her condition. The doctor prescribed it and Mrs. Clarke went to pick it up, but we don't have health insurance and it was too expensive," Steve wiped a hand across his forehead.

"And that's when you thought of your old pal, Topper. I take it you've known each other quite a while."

"Since first grade. I asked Topper to follow my Aunt Abigail's car, get her to stop and talk about my mama needing to be placed in a memory care facility. He was just supposed to drive up alongside her and wave her over. Said I'd pay him $50. It was every penny I had."

"He was to ask her for money for your mother's care, I assume," D'Angelo said.

"That was the plan, but the dumbbell ran into her. He was going way too fast," Steve said sounding regretful.

"I am still confused about a couple of things," D'Angelo said. "If you needed money for your mother's care, why didn't you just visit your Aunt personally?"

"Can't leave Mama," Steve said stubbornly. "If she's left alone too long, even being so overweight, sometimes she manages to get out of the house. It happened last winter and I found her lying by the back stoop. She'd fallen and was damn near dead from exposure."

"Couldn't you have called your aunt on the phone?"

"Phone got turned off. Can't pay the bill," Steve said wearily.

"I'm sure you have your license again by now. Don't you have a car?

Couldn't you have driven over to see Aunt Abigail while Mrs. Clarke was with your mother?"

Steve shook his head. "Sold the car to pay her medical expenses," he said.

"And you have no current source of income?"

"Already told you, I can't work now because Mama can't be left alone."

Det. Stoneman said he had something to add and took over. "I'm sure Detective Pascoe told you after your numbskull friend Topper ran your Aunt off the road that she died," he said coldly.

Steve grimaced.

"And what I'm about to tell you now is going to make you feel even worse. Your Aunt Abigail told her priest that she felt terrible about not helping you with college. She recently learned that she had cancer and only about six months to live. She was on her way to meet with her attorney to change her will—intending to leave you a big chunk of money," Stoneman looked intently at Pennington.

"Oh God," Steve wailed and put his head down his folded arms.

Detective Stoneman stood up, looming over Steve said, "And in case you think you will get your hands on her money now, I'm here to tell you since you and Topper caused the woman's death, you won't get a single dime. Your poor old mother's going to die at home alone."

D'Angelo frowned at his supervisor and touched Steve's shoulder. He waited until Det. Stoneman left the room and leaned down to whisper to the young man whose body was wracked with sobs.

"You need to talk with your attorney, Steve. If Topper's charge gets changed to involuntary manslaughter, they wouldn't be able to make a case against you."

Steve raised his head to look at Det. D'Angelo. "I don't understand," he said.

"Just talk to your attorney," D'Angelo said and quickly left the room.

# TWENTY-SEVEN

B Y THE FIRST OF AUGUST, WITH Abigail Forester's case having been resolved and moved forward to the courts, Dory, Wayne and PD were turning their full attention to finding the perpetrator of Billy Jo's assault. Although PD was opposed to the provenance investigation initially, he and Wayne were now fully on board.

"Just a couple of things about the Forester case before we put that one to bed," PD said. "The young attorney, Robby Willoughby, who helped get Poppy Delaney out of jail during the Blind Split Case, is going to serve as the lawyer for both of those two boneheads—Topper Gaines and Steve Pennington. They are coming before the judge shortly and he will decide whether to place them on remand."

"That's normally a no-brainer. Anyone who kills a person is automatically kept in jail until trial," Wayne said.

"True, but in this case I think a little leniency is warranted and I've set up a time to talk to their attorney. If Willoughby is okay with it, I've agreed to appear before the Judge personally and request that Steve Pennington be placed under house arrest with an ankle bracelet until the trial."

"Do you think the judge will buy it?" Wayne asked. He raised his eyebrows, sounding doubtful.

"I think there's a chance. Here's why. When I went to drag Steve Pennington out of bed the morning he turned himself in, he impressed me with his dedication to his mother. He actually said I could shoot him, but he wasn't leaving her. We had to get a neighbor to stay with her before Steve would go with me. And, although he paid Topper $50 to try to get his aunt Abigail to give him money for his mother's care, Steve wasn't the one driving. Plus, he insists he only told Topper to drive alongside her and wave her over. Steve's mother's life is coming to an end now and there is no support for her other than her son. I think it's possible the judge might let him be remanded to house arrest."

"Good luck with that," Wayne said. "Let's move on to Billy Jo's situation now, okay?"

PD and Dory nodded.

"Are you going to pick her up later today?" Dory asked.

"Yes, she's supposed to be released at 3:00 p.m. A neurologist provided most of her care, but since Lucy was the on-duty physician who saw her in the ER and admitted her, she is going to summarize his findings and recommendations."

"If there are any concerns about her living alone, she's welcome to stay with me until she's okay on her own," Dory said.

"Thank you. I'll let her know and see what the doctors say," Wayne said.

"I'm very glad she's well enough to come home. In terms of her case, let's start by reviewing what we know about the missing paintings," PD said.

"The only thing we know for a fact, is that both paintings featuring the Brookover children have been stolen, and Henry Brookover's license plate was caught on CCTV leaving Rosedale the night Billy Jo was assaulted," Dory said.

"We also know that he has denied any involvement with the attack on Billy Jo. He says he is baffled as to how his car could be in Rosedale and claims he's innocent. Captain Schlachter of the Erie, PD post believes him," Wayne said.

"Has Erie PD searched his house for the paintings yet?" PD asked.

"They have. They couldn't get a warrant, so Captain Schlachter asked Brookover's permission to do a search of his home. He agreed and the search was comprehensive."

"Did the officers find anything?" PD asked.

"Absolutely no luck locating either painting. And it gets worse. Henry Brookover has an alibi that looks unshakable. Captain Schlachter told me he is a lay pastor with the youth ministry for the Methodist church and was giving a talk to over fifty students the night Billy Jo was attacked. His speech was videotaped and there are time and date stamps. He definitely wasn't in Rosedale that night," Wayne said with a frown.

"What about when *Children at the Lakeside* was taken?" PD asked.

"Unfortunately, he has an alibi for that morning, too. He was attending a Rotary Club meeting and didn't leave until around noon. There are a dozen men who can attest to him being there. The alarm on the door of the History Society went off at 10:00 a.m. That was two hours before Brookover left his meeting. He's in the clear," Wayne said with an irritated quirk to his mouth.

"But it was definitely his car that was in Rosedale the night of Billy Jo's assault, right?" PD asked.

"Well, it was his license plate, but probably not his car. He drove himself to the Methodist church the night of Billy Jo's attack and was seen getting into his car by several people," Wayne said.

"What about a license plate switch?" PD asked.

"That was my thought as well," Dory said. "Maybe someone in that family traded license plates with Mr. Brookover and is the guilty party."

"I am not giving up on that family being the perps," PD said.

"I agree. There are a lot of generations here. I'm going to write down the genealogy on the board. I can't take credit for all this. Mark and Billy Jo assembled this information." Wayne stood up and went to the front of the room. The task took some time, but when he was finished, the partners looked closely at his chart.

| Name | | | Children |
|---|---|---|---|
| Dr. Cedric Brookover | | | Married to Wendy Brookover. She died in 1919. Three children Sarah, John & Emily. Emily died in 1922. |
| John Brookover<br><br>Son of Cedric | | | Takes "Children at Lakeside" painting to History Society in 1967 after father's death. Married to Catherine. One child, Richard |
| Living | | | |
| Richard Brookover<br><br>Grandson of Cedric | | Age 72 | Met with Billy Jo and Mark when they visited. Married to Irene, she died two years ago. One son Henry |
| Henry Brookover<br><br>Great grandson of Cedric | | Age 50 | Married to Bethany. Son Kyle (age 16), daughter Erica. (age 6)<br><br>His car's license place caught on CCTV in Rosedale |
| Kyle Brookover<br><br>Great great grandson of Cedric | | Age 16 | Has driver's license. |

"We're focusing on the three men listed at the bottom of the chart. We know it wasn't a woman because Billy Jo saw a male who assaulted her. We initially thought it was Henry Brookover, because his license plate was caught on the CCTV in Rosedale the night of the attack. But, we now know his alibi is rock-solid. He isn't our guy," Wayne said.

"Which just leaves Grampa Richard. He's 71, but has a current driver's license," Dory said.

"We can't forget to check if 16-year-old grandson Kyle is involved in any way," PD said. "Let's have Mark do a background on him. I'd like to know if he's been in any trouble with the law."

"Good idea, but we are missing a motive. That was our situation with the Abigail Forester case too, until you came up with one, PD. So, if you think 16 year-old Kyle needs to be considered, I'm with you," Wayne said.

"As am I," Dory agreed. "I just texted Mark to see if he could help and he didn't respond. In fact, I don't know where he is today, so I'll see what I can find out about the kid. I'm not Mark or Billy Jo, but I'll give it a try."

WAYNE DROVE TO ROSEDALE GENERAL THAT AFTERNOON to pick up Billy Jo. Lucy had brought her to the front of the hospital in a wheelchair and they were chatting when he drove up. Leaving his car in the loading zone with the flashers on, Wayne walked over to where the women were waiting.

Ever since Billy Jo's seizure and second hospitalization, he had felt time bearing down on him. Dory's comment that the Brookovers might decide to burn the paintings to end the century-old curse, kept returning to his mind. Wayne could easily envision the back yard of Brookover's home, which he'd seen on Google Earth, and the family collecting wood for a bonfire.

"Hi, Lucy," Wayne said and gave her a hug before turning to the wheelchair occupant. "You're looking much better, Billy Jo. How's the vertigo?"

"As a matter of fact, it seems to be entirely gone," Billy Jo said grinning.

"That's great news. What's her status now, Lucy?" he asked.

"The neurologist has her on some anti-seizure meds which she needs to take for a week. So far she's tolerating them well," Lucy said. Then turning to Billy Jo she added, "Sleepiness and fatigue are normal side effects of this type of med, but if you experience double vision or major mental confusion you need to come back."

"Is she good to stay by herself?" Wayne asked.

"No. It's better if she stays with someone for a while," Lucy said. "It's important for her to take it easy while she's on seizure meds. We don't want a recurrence."

"Or for the vertigo to come back," Billy Jo said smiling. "It's such a relief to have it gone."

"Indeed," Wayne said and helped her out of the wheelchair and into his truck.

As THEY DROVE SLOWLY BACK TO THE OFFICE, Wayne counted the hours left in the day. If he left that afternoon, he could be in Erie at around 1:00 a.m. in the morning. An old man like Grampa Brookover would be sound asleep at that hour. He had no doubt he could rattle the curmudgeon into a confession, even if there were consequences later. He grimaced, envisioning the arrest sheet that would list the charges against him: 1) breaking and entering, 2) threatening an elderly man with a weapon, and 3) beating or injuring him.

His career would be over and he would have gone against the rule of law he'd honored his entire life. In the depths of his heart, he didn't give a damn, but knew it would be smarter to wait until Kyle Brookover's background was completed before setting out to become what he'd most despised—a vigilante.

# TWENTY-EIGHT

W AYNE AND PD WERE TALKING QUIETLY IN THE KITCHEN of Rosedale Investigations the following morning as the coffee brewed. The pleasing scent filled the air as they heard the sound of the front door opening.

"Good morning all," Dory's cheery voice rang out. She was dressed in an ivory suit and navy blouse with heels. A summer thundershower was predicted for later in the day, so she had brought her red raincoat and umbrella. She put the coat on the hook just inside the door, setting the umbrella in a tall Chinese vase that Billy Jo had purchased when she updated the office.

"Where's Billy Jo?" Wayne asked when Dory came into the kitchen.

"No hello or even a good morning?" she asked with her hands on her hips.

"We were just wondering if Billy Jo was coming in," PD said, meekly.

"Nope. She's working from my place."

"Does she seem to be doing okay?" Wayne asked. He was wearing black pants and a white striped shirt with a buttoned-down collar and a tweed sport jacket. It was a nice outfit, but Dory could see he looked tired. Billy Jo's attack, combined with their inability to discover the culprit, was getting to her partner.

"To tell you the truth, she's a little down. And Mark seems to be MIA," Dory said.

"Do you mean to tell me that he didn't even go to the hospital?" PD asked. He was bristling.

"Nope. He left her a message saying he was going to be gone for a few days. She's worried that he's been attacked or injured in connection with the painting case," Dory said.

"Should we start checking accident reports?" Wayne asked.

"I already did and Lucy checked hospital admissions for me. We found nothing. I also talked with Deputy George who looked at CCTV for the day Mark disappeared. He spotted his car at the stoplight in town at seven a.m. Because the camera looks directly down into the cars there, we could see it was him and he was alone. On the camera, he could see a sack lunch and a thermos, all of which indicated a planned departure."

"What does Billy Jo think now?" PD asked.

"She keeps calling him, but he's not answering. She's worried. "

ALTHOUGH MARK WAS UNAWARE OF HIS GIRLFRIEND'S newest medical issue, he'd sensed she wasn't herself since the theft of *Wednesday's Child*. The last time they had worked together she'd been tired and distant. That evening she'd confessed her fear that the vertigo could prevent her from completing the provenance for *Wednesday's Child*. She'd already asked her professor for an incomplete grade in the Art & the Law course she was taking. And she dreaded telling Sylvia and Mrs. Walcott that *Wednesday's Child* had been stolen. Her admission was what had spurred Mark to make the trip to Pennsylvania. His plan was to dig deeply into the provenance on *Wednesday's Child* and possibly complete it.

When he arrived in Erie that evening, Mark called Mrs. Walcott and Sylvia from his hotel, knowing they were still in the city. They agreed to meet him at the History Society at ten o'clock the following morning. He considered calling Billy Jo, but like Detective Wayne Nichols, he had a surprise planned and was determined that nothing would spoil the reveal.

MARK WOKE EARLY THE NEXT MORNING, never able to sleep well when he was out of town. The sun was rising and the sky was streaked with red and orange. He pulled on sweats and went for a run. Returning to the hotel, he took a quick invigorating dip in the hotel pool, remembering his previous trip with Billy Jo when they sipped strawberry daiquiris as the sun went down. He checked his watch seeing that it was 9:30 a.m. He just had time to shower, don his suit and chow down the free breakfast the hotel provided, before his meeting with Sylvia and Mrs. Walcott. He left a quick message for Ms. Poitou, the Curator, asking if she would join them. It was a short drive to the History Society. Parking behind the building, he went inside. He could hear a woman's voice talking knowledgeably about art as he paused in the entryway to listen.

"Jeremy Iverson-Jones is a master of what is called Vanitas, a technique in art that portrays the evanescence, brevity and essential unimportance of a single human life. He's known for his seascapes and we are proud to say that they were all inspired by Lake Erie. As you know, we are holding a major retrospective of his work in the fall and have asked everyone who owns one of his paintings to lease it to the show. We will have around twenty of his masterpieces on display. Before we start the tour of the facilities, does anyone have any questions?"

It was the voice of Ms. Betty Poitou, the connoisseur of the work done by Iverson-Jones. She was showing a group around the facility. Not wanting to interrupt, Mark decided to wait in the lobby until Mrs. Walcott and Sylvia arrived before entering the main salon. Glancing back at the parking lot, he saw them driving in.

Mrs. Walcott was walking slowly using a cane and Sylvia, nicely dressed in a red suit, with her blonde hair tied back, took her arm. Mark opened the door for them. They greeted each other and located a room off the main salon where they could talk.

"Thank you both for meeting with me. I'm here to fill in some of the holes in the provenance of *Wednesday's Child* on behalf of Billy Jo," Mark said. He deliberately did not tell them that the painting was stolen, or that his girlfriend had been injured.

At that moment, Ms. Poitou entered the room. When the introductions were complete, she said she was pleased to talk with them. When Mark met her previously she was well-groomed and looked elegant. Today, she seemed careworn and Mark knew it was the upcoming show and the loss of two major paintings that occupied her mind.

"Thanks for meeting with us," Sylvia said.

"No problem. I understand you are interested in what I might know about the provenance of *Wednesday's Child*. I'm sorry to say that I don't know a lot, and particularly now since it's been . . ."

Mark started waving his arms wildly, but Ms. Poitou went on relentlessly.

". . . stolen along with *Children at the Lakeside*."

"What?" Sylvia went wide-eyed and horrified. She seemed unable to take in the information. Mrs. Walcott blinked rapidly, looking stunned.

"Did you say that *Wednesday's Child* had been stolen?" she finally asked.

"Yes, I'm sorry. I thought you knew," Ms. Poitou said, with a frown. "The police are hopeful they will be able to retrieve your painting as well as *Children at the Lakeshore* which, I'm sad to say, is also missing. We've been in touch with Sheriff Bradley as well as Rosedale Investigations and officers from the Erie PD are patrolling the neighborhoods where both the Brookovers live. There's some thought that the Brookovers might plan to destroy the artwork . . ." Her voice trailed off before she added, "Oh dear. You really didn't know any of this, did you?"

"Are you telling us both paintings have been stolen?" Mrs. Walcott asked.

"Yes. With regard to *Children by the Lakeshore*, the police found motorcycle tracks on the driveway in front of the History Society they are trying to identify. We have a good alarm system here and it went off the morning the painting was stolen, alerting our facilities man, the Director, and me. The alarm company called the police. At first, we thought that Miss Bradley from Rosedale Investigations had stolen both paintings but . . ."

Mark raised his eyes heavenward, thinking, "*Give me strength.*"

"The police don't consider her a suspect now, since she was viciously attacked trying to prevent the loss of your painting, Mrs. Walcott," Ms. Poitou said.

At this piece of information Sylvia and her grandmother looked at each other in shock. Finally, Sylvia said, "Billy Jo was attacked? Is she okay?"

"She is," Mark said. "She had to spend a couple of days in the hospital, but other than a case of vertigo, she's all right." He turned to the Curator then and said, "Changing the subject, you started to say you didn't have much information about the chain of ownership for *Wednesday's Child*. Can you tell us what you do know?"

"We have some information to share as well," Sylvia said.

"Do you want to start with what you've learned, Mrs. Walcott?" Mrs. Poitou asked.

"Not yet. I'm still sort of reeling with the news about our painting." She rubbed her bloodshot eyes and folded her arthritic hands in her lap.

"This is what we know so far," Sylvia said. "My grandmother inherited *Wednesday's Child* from Mrs. Helen Chase Wilson. She's passed away now, but we located an elderly neighbor who told us an important fact.

She said the artist had a younger sister and thought *Wednesday's Child* might have been given to her upon his death."

"I've been checking with a lot of people since Mark and Billy Jo were here and can confirm that information. Jeremy Iverson-Jones did indeed have a younger sister, her name was Judith, and I have recently learned that all the paintings in the artist's possession when he died went to her," Mrs. Poitou said.

"That included *Wednesday's Child*, I assume?" Mark asked.

"Yes, apparently it was her favorite. My source told me Judith kept that painting until nearly the last day of her life. She had a hard time making ends meet financially and sold her brother's paintings reluctantly, one by one, until only *Wednesday's Child* remained in her possession."

"And what happened to it?" Sylvia asked.

"Her house and its contents were auctioned off when she passed away," Ms. Poitou said.

"Do you know how Mrs. Chase Wilson came into the picture?" Mark asked.

"According to family lore, Mrs. Wilson found *Wednesday's Child* in a garage sale," Sylvia said.

"I wonder if she could possibly have purchased the painting from the auction of Judith's possessions, instead of a garage sale," Mark said. He was thinking that there should be records of auctions going back that far. "Is there a firm in Erie that does estate auctions?"

"Yes, it's Mr. Peppermint's Auction House on Elm street," Ms. Poitou said. "I'm really sorry to have given you such bad news about *Wednesday's Child*, Mrs. Walcott. What do you plan to do now?"

"I think Sylvia and I should visit the police," Mrs. Walcott said. "I want to be sure they know I'm the owner."

"The person whose been handling the investigation is a Detective Carol Wright. She's the person to talk to."

"Thank you Ms. Poitou," Sylvia said and helped her grandmother to her feet. "One last question. You mentioned that the police are patrolling the neighborhoods where the Brookovers live. Why is that exactly?"

"The Brookovers are a prominent family in this city, active in charitable causes and solid citizens. It was Miss Bradley who set the police onto the family. I don't know what evidence she had for that terrible accusation," Ms. Poitou said frowning.

"She had completely solid evidence. CCTV in Rosedale captured the license plate of Mr. Brookover's car leaving town the night Billy Jo was attacked," Mark said.

Mrs. Poitou took a deep breath before saying, "Be that as it may, it doesn't seem very likely that our civic-minded Mr. Brookover would be involved in such a dreadful crime."

As Mark left the building intending to visit Mr. Peppermint's Auction house, he thought about Mrs. Poitou's skepticism. Although he had seen and personally trusted the CCTV evidence, it did seem unlikely that Grampa Brookover, an old man in his 70's, would drive nine hours to Rosedale, hit Billy Jo over the head, and steal *Wednesday's Child*.

*If it really was the old man, he would have needed a very powerful motive*, Mark thought and remembered the day he and Billy Jo met with the elderly man on their trip to the city. When Grampa Brookover heard the word *curse*, he had snapped the photo album shut, as if he had come to some critical decision.

# TWENTY-NINE

"**A**LL OF YOU ARE TO STOP LOOKING INTO THE ASSAULT on Billy Jo anywhere beyond Rose County as of now," Sheriff Bradley said frowning fiercely. The sheriff had stopped by Rosedale Investigations that morning to issue his formal command. "Pay attention, all of you. I'm ordering you to *cease and desist!* None of you have the slightest vestige of jurisdiction in Pennsylvania, which I suspect is where you have been thinking of going. The Erie PD is on this. I've had a number of conversations with Captain Schlachter, and he's agreed to have his officers patrol the neighborhoods where the Brookovers live."

"We already know about Henry Brookover's alibi," Wayne said, sounding dismal.

"Totally solid," Dory said.

"What about the old man, Grampa Richard Brookover?" PD asked.

"Captain Schlachter has talked to him twice. He said he was home alone watching TV the night of the attack. There is nobody to confirm his whereabouts as his wife died several years ago. Obviously, it's not much of an alibi, but the Captain believed him. He talked to the neighbors who saw the lights in the living room go off at ten o'clock, his usual bedtime, on the night of the assault. And nobody saw him drive his car out of the garage."

"That hardly rules him out," Wayne said. He was gritting his teeth, finding it difficult to control his frustration.

"No, Wayne, it doesn't. I'm well aware of that," Sheriff Bradley said in an irritated tone. "However, the man's in his seventies and has an old wreck of a car that hasn't left the garage in months. That's according to him and his neighbors confirmed. Can you really see a 70 year-old guy driving nine hours to Tennessee, hitting Billy Jo on the head and stealing the painting? It just doesn't add up. He's not your man and his son's alibi is solid as kryptonite. Now, I want your word—all of you—that you will not even *consider* investigating this crime in Pennsylvania." He looked at Dory, Wayne and PD in turn.

"Wayne, I want your agreement," Sheriff Bradley said and Wayne scowled but nodded.

"PD?" He also nodded.

"Since you two are both former cops, it's critical that you stay in town. Dory, you're an investigator, not a cop, but I won't have you helping either Wayne or PD leave town on some stupid art hunt either. Agreed?"

Dory gave a minimal nod, but behind her back she crossed her fingers.

THAT AFTERNOON DETECTIVE PD PASCOE, wearing an uncomfortable new suit Dory had insisted he had to buy (saying it had been so long since he spent any money that moths were starting to fly out of his wallet), was waiting in the courthouse for the city of Rosedale. The old courthouse was a two-story red brick building with a portico and four tall white columns that defined the entrance. The case of Topper Gaines and Steve Pennington was coming before the judge for the remand decision in two hours. Prior to that judgement, PD had scheduled a meeting with Robby Willoughby.

PD never had much patience with people being late for meetings and he was drumming his fingers on his knees waiting for Attorney Willoughby to appear. The young lawyer was fifteen minutes late. Then the front door to the courthouse opened and a tall skinny kid with brown curly hair, glasses, and a wide smile came inside. He was holding out his hand to shake. PD stood up.

"You must be Robby Willoughby, right?" he asked in an irascible tone of voice.

"I am and I'm pleased to meet you, Detective Pascoe. I know your colleague, Dory Clarkson, from when we worked together on Poppy Delaney's parole hearing. Sorry I'm late," he said.

Slightly mollified, PD shook hands with the young man. He decided not to grouse about the kid's lateness, since he was about to ask him for a big favor. He wanted Robby to petition the judge to release Steve on his own recognizance rather than being confined to jail until the trial. Lawyers usually had a strategy for remand hearings and he would be asking Willoughby to request something rarely granted in murder cases.

"There's a room for barristers in this building. If you want to follow me, I'll take you there and we can talk," Robby said.

PD followed him down a long tiled corridor and into a side room with an oval conference table and chairs. It was a high-ceilinged space with walnut paneling and large windows that looked out on a well-tended community garden. He glanced out the window seeing some multi-colored flowers called four o'clocks. A sudden memory came to him—an image of a sunlit day walking with Amy, the woman he should have married, through a garden filled with fragrant four o'clocks.

"You said on the phone you wanted to discuss the case of Steve Pennington," Robby said, gesturing for PD to be seated at the conference table.

"I don't know how much time you have had with Steve, or Topper for that matter. Are you aware that Steve's elderly mother is ill and that he's her only caretaker?"

"Yes, in fact Steve was so frantic that we get someone to look after Mrs. Blake that I called Hospice. Her doctor reviewed her chart and said she was eligible for in-home Hospice."

"How often can Hospice visit?" PD asked. He was aware that Hospice services were in high demand because of the pandemic and that they usually couldn't come more than once a week. Steve would be beside himself when he learned his mother would be alone except for a single weekly visit.

"They're really stretched to the max, but Steve told me about his neighbor, Mrs. Clark. I talked to her, and she agreed to stop in every day or call Mrs. Blake daily if she couldn't go over. She's got Meals on Wheels coming in with food."

"Sounds like you have things pretty well covered, but I'm sure Steve will still be desperately worried. When I went to bring him in to the police, he wouldn't leave his mother. He absolutely refused to go with me until Mrs. Clark was there to care for her. Despite his moronic idea of hiring Topper to shove his Aunt Abigail off the road, I respected him for his loyalty," PD said.

"I was also impressed with his sincerity. But, I must have missed something. I was told Steve turned himself in to the police," Robby said.

"He may have bent the truth just a bit. I went out there to convince him to turn himself in and I drove him to the post," PD said.

"Hmmm," Robby murmured and his lip twitched in a near-grin.

"What I want you to consider is a plea for Steve to be released on his own recognizance until the trial."

"That's an awfully long shot, Detective. The woman died and both those dimwits have confessed," Robby said.

"I'm aware. However, I am of the opinion that the condition of Steve's mother constitutes a mitigating circumstance and I'd appreciate you bringing it up. As you know, there are other options than jail, even for violent felons. Would you be willing to ask the judge if Steve could be confined to home with a house arrest anklets? As evidence of Steve's commitment to his mother, he quit a good job to nurse her through her final days. And the ridiculous plan he came up with was intended to get money from his Aunt Abigail to put his mother into a proper nursing home."

"I didn't realize that," Robby paused. "I'll give it a try, but if I plead for house arrest on behalf of Steve, isn't that throwing Topper under the bus? For all I know he may have elderly relatives too," the lawyer said.

For a moment, PD Pascoe could see Topper's grandfather the day the old drunk insisted that they imbibe whiskey together. He hesitated a moment before saying, "Topper's only family is his grandfather, but he's not ill. One other thing I wanted to mention. Detective Stoneman said he was going for premeditated murder, but Steve never told Topper to kill his aunt, just wave her over and talk to her. I think manslaughter, even involuntary manslaughter, would be the highest charge the prosecution could get," PD said.

"I'm going to talk to Steve again and depending on his exact instruction to Topper, I might be able to get the charge reduced. Sorry, but I need to let you go," Robby said. "I'm meeting with both of them before they are brought into the court. You've definitely given me some things to think about, Detective. Do you want to know the outcome?"

"Yes, and thank you for listening."

"Listening is my job apparently," Robby said, with a wry expression. "My grandfather told me when I was little that God gave mankind two ears and only one mouth because we are supposed to listen more than talk."

PD nodded, handed Robby his card and left the courthouse.

Driving back to Rosedale Investigations, PD got a call from a number he didn't recognize. No name was listed. He listened to it ring four times before he gave in and picked it up.

"Detective Pascoe," he said.

There was a silence on the other end of the call for a few seconds and PD was about to hang up, thinking it was one of those wretched telephone solicitors, when he heard a faint, "Hello."

"Who is this?" PD asked.

"It's Liam, your . . . well I guess I'm your grandson," the voice said.

"Hello, Liam," PD said, feeling a rush of pure elation. It has been some time since he'd spoken with young man's mother and he'd been afraid the boy wouldn't call.

"I was wondering if you'd like to meet me. Maybe have coffee or something?" Liam said. He sounded very young.

"I can be at the Donut Den in Rosedale an hour, if that works," PD said.

"It'll take me three hours to get there, but if we can meet later, I'll come. I'm wearing an orange T-shirt and jeans. Thanks and good-bye," Liam said.

PD clicked off the call with a bubble of pure delight rising in his heart

# THIRTY

D ORY WAS SITTING AT HER DESK trying to decide what was most
pressing. Client billing always needed doing, but it was her least
favorite job as CFO of Rosedale Investigations. Billy Jo hadn't come back
to work on-site since her seizure. Wayne had left a message saying he
was going to see what progress had been made with Anne Ingram, Lucy's
sister, who was recovering at drug rehab. PD called the office to say he
would come in after his meeting with Robby Willoughby.

She grabbed a blueberry donut from the kitchen and was standing in the conference room looking at the Brookover genealogy on
the white board when she remembered her dream from the previous
night. It was a warm star-studded evening, and she and her escort were
walking up a set of broad stairs into an elegant art museum. She wore
a full-length gold velvet gown and was on the arm of a good looking
African American gentleman. They entered the building and walked
into a large room where the two Jeremy Iverson-Jones paintings hung
side-by-side on pale taupe walls. *Wednesday's Child* and *Children at the
Lakeshore* had gathered quite a group of admirers. Her escort handed
her a bubbling champagne flute he'd secured from a passing waiter and
asked, "Are both of the paintings cursed?"

Recalling the dream, Dory realized it was the sentinel question—
one they had never asked themselves. She finished her donut and called
Evangeline Bon Temps, their expert on metaphysical matters, to see if
she had time for lunch.

"I've only got an hour and a quarter, but we could meet at the
Arboretum if you like."

"Lovely," Dory responded.

The Arboretum was a glass-sided cube that housed a new restaurant. It had been built in the center of a stand of old growth forest south of Rosedale. Dory had been wanting to check it out. She called Billy Jo and told her to get out of bed. They were going to meet Evangeline Bon Temps for lunch. She had a question to ask her.

"What question," Billy Jo asked, sounding tired and irritable.

"Whether both paintings were cursed, or only one."

"What difference does it make? We've lost both of them, Mark has left town for some unknown reason, won't return my calls, I've got a headache and don't want to get up," Billy Jo said.

"Listen up, crabby girl, this little question you don't think matters, might be the crux of the reason why the paintings were stolen and even the key to their recovery. I'll come by the house in twenty minutes to pick you up. I expect to see you nicely dressed and wearing real shoes."

Hanging up the phone, Dory grinned when she heard Billy Jo sigh.

WAYNE ARRIVED AT ROSEDALE DRUG REHAB AT NINE O'CLOCK. Only then did he read the sign in front of the building listing visitor hours. It didn't open for visitors until 9:30. The facility was some distance out in the country, having been built in a low dell surrounded by gentle hills. Behind the structure someone had created a garden with paths that meandered through a series of flower beds. It was nearly the end of summer though, and except for a few tired Black-Eyed Susans and a wave of beautiful blue Ageratum that edged a small pond, there was little in bloom. He took a seat on the bench in front of the fountain. A tired trickle of water dripped from its tulip-shaped spout.

A black squirrel dashed past with a green walnut in his mouth. They were storing up food for the winter. Wayne experienced a moment of nostalgia for summer's ending. When he raised his eyes to the grass-covered hills, he saw the figure of a young woman. She was striding quickly down the hill toward the garden. The sun touched her dark hair and it's red highlights shone. She walked right up to him.

"Are you waiting to see somebody here?" she asked.

"Yes, Anne Ingram. Have you worked with her, by chance?" he asked.

"I have spent a little time with her since she's been here. She's making decent progress. Mind if I sit with you? I'm one of the rehab nurses. Debbie's my name," she said. Not waiting for Wayne's assent, she plumped down beside him.

"I'm Wayne Nichols," he said. "Working all day with addicts who are throwing away their lives for a fix must be a discouraging job."

"There's always a reason they are here," she said, sounding philosophical.

"Why did you choose this line of work?" Wayne asked.

"The usual reason, I guess. My older brother got hooked during the opiate crisis and overdosed. I was an ER nurse at that time and on duty the night he was brought in. The doctors tried everything. They resuscitated him for a full half hour. When they gave up and called his time of death, I was awash with guilt because . . . well, I experienced a surge of relief," Debbie said with a little contrite smile.

"You said you had worked with Anne Ingham. I'm marrying Anne's sister, Lucy, in a couple of weeks. I hope to have her clean and sufficiently presentable to attend our wedding. It's on Labor Day week-end. What do you think the chances are?"

"Pretty good," Debbie said. "But there's a question I always ask family members who are involved with these patients. I ask them what will happen after the event. What plans have you made for Anne? Where will she be living?"

Wayne was silenced by her words. In fact, he hadn't thought that far ahead. He and Lucy were planning on a honeymoon in the Porcupine Mountains in Michigan's Upper Peninsula. He hated the thought that their special trip would be torpedoed by Lucy cancelling the arrangements or worse, having Anne accompany them.

Just then they heard the doors swing open to the facility. They stood up and walked inside together.

"Guess you don't have an answer for me, do you?" Debbie said, as she headed down a silent shining hall. "Better do some thinking," she called before disappearing around a corner.

DORY, AND A STILL-GRUMPY BILLY JO, met Evangeline Bon Temps in the parking lot outside the Arboretum. The restaurant was a cube made totally of huge sheets of glass. Its roof had been constructed from sliding glass doors that could be opened remotely to help with temperature control. It was the end of August and tiny golden leaves like near-translucent coins, rode the hot winds that signaled summer coming to an end. The clean scent of tall white pines washed the air. A cluster of bees darted in and out of a pot of golden poppies by the front door.

"Have you been here before, Evangeline?" Dory asked.

"Yes, this is my second visit."

"How's the food?" Bill Jo asked. She had been somewhat cheered by the innovative architecture and deep green forest. Plus, she was hungry.

"Excellent. It's an Italian restaurant, so they have artisanal pizzas, noodles with shrimp and sun-dried tomatoes, spaghetti with marinara sauce, lasagna and generous drinks," Evangeline said. She was an attractive family attorney who wore her hair cut short. It capped her face with its warm complexion and dark shining eyes. She was originally from New Orleans and had helped the sheriff's office with the Voodoo Village case several years earlier.

They walked in, asked for a table for three, and were seated. An hour later, all had enjoyed a delicious lunch and were having coffee and tiny frosted brownies, a specialty of the house.

"Was there a reason you asked me to lunch today, Dory? Or were you just missing my company?" Evangeline asked smiling.

"I do have a question for you, but we haven't gotten together in a while, and I'm not sure if you recall the case Billy Jo has recently taken on," Dory said nodding to her young compatriot to begin.

"I call this case *In the Frame*. It began when an older woman named Georgia Walcott inherited a painting. She subsequently approached Rosedale Investigations asking if we would construct a provenance for the artwork. It's a seascape in oil that was painted a hundred years ago and she was concerned that somewhere along the line the piece might have been stolen. I'd been making pretty good progress until the painting actually *was* stolen—from me! The thief hit me over the head and took it," Billy Jo said with a rueful look.

"This must be the painting you called me about the day we talked about curses," Evangeline said. Her expression had turned serious.

"Exactly. It turns out, the artist did two paintings on the same subject. The painting we had here in Rosedale is called *Wednesday's Child*. Two nights after *Wednesday's Child* was stolen, the near-identical painting called *Children at the Lakeshore* was taken from the History Society in Erie, Pennsylvania. It was Dr. Cedric Brookover who commissioned *Children on the Lakeshore* a century ago," Billy Jo said.

"We checked CCTV and saw the license plate of the car we presume was driven by the man who assaulted Billy Jo. However, it turns out the plates must have been switched because the owner of that car, Mr. Henry

Brookover, has a gold-plated alibi. We considered his elderly father who still drives, but his car is decrepit and hasn't left the garage for months," Dory added.

"Not sure I can help with this," Evangeline said, setting down her napkin and signaling for the check.

"I believe you can. There is little doubt that one or both of the paintings is cursed. It's been associated with three deaths. However, we don't know which of the artworks is implicated," Dory said.

"Who were these people who died? And how are they connected with the painting?" Evangeline asked as she totaled up the bill and added a generous tip.

"The first person to die was Wendy Brookover. She was married to Cedric, but fell in love with the artist during the completion of the work. The day the painting was delivered to her husband, Wendy fell down a flight of stairs, broke her neck and died."

"Go on," Evangeline said, frowning.

"The second death was that of the artist. He committed suicide after painting *Wednesday's Child*. Then, a few years later, one of Wendy Brookover's daughters died of a sudden cardiac arrest. She was only twelve," Dory said.

"Are both of the paintings cursed, do you think," Billy Jo asked.

"I would doubt it. Are the paintings identical?" Evangeline asked.

"Almost. *Children by the Lakeshore* has a faint impression of a woman's figure on the left side. We have learned it is Wendy Brookover's shadow. *Wednesday's Child* doesn't have that imprint," Billy Jo said.

"Now, as far as you know was *Wednesday's Child* ever in the possession of the Brookover family?" Evangeline asked.

"We don't think so," Billy Jo said.

"Then only *Children on the Lakeshore* is cursed," Evangeline said crisply.

"Are you certain, Evangeline?" Dory asked. "Thank you for lunch by the way."

"Definitely. Since *Wednesday's Child* was never in contact with Wendy Brookover or her daughter, and the artist took his own life—only *Children by the Lakeshore* is cursed. Furthermore, it seems the curse only affects members of the Brookover family."

They said good-bye to Evangeline outside the transparent eatery and walked to Dory's car, both of them deep in thought.

"It's good to know that *Wednesday's Child* was never cursed," Billy Jo said as they got into the car. "But I don't see how it helps us."

"I have a theory about the motive for the thefts," Dory said. "If the Brookovers are trying to eliminate the power of the curse before it can claim another victim, and since they don't know that only *Children by the Lakeside* is cursed, they had to acquire both paintings."

"Didn't Evangeline tell you that one of the ways to destroy a curse was to burn the object? Do you think they could be planning to set fire to both paintings?" Billy Jo asked in a trembling voice.

"I do," Dory said.

"We have to do something to prevent the destruction," Billy Jo said, inhaling shakily.

"The sheriff said we couldn't leave town," Dory said.

"But, we have to try . . ." Billy Jo's voice trailed off. Then she added, "Because if we don't find a way to retrieve the paintings and soon, the Brookovers are about to have a $100,000 bonfire." Her face crumpled, on the verge of tears.

"Hold on a minute. Let me think. You weren't in the office the day the sheriff told us we couldn't go to Pennsylvania, were you? He didn't make you promise to stop investigating the theft beyond Rose County, did he?" Dory asked.

"No, I was still in the hospital," Billy Jo said.

Dory's eyes narrowed as an idea dawned. "And the only promise I made was not to help *Wayne or PD* with an investigation out of our jurisdiction."

After a brief pause, the two conspirators met each other eyes and nodded.

# THIRTY-ONE

MARK WALKED DOWN THE STREET to Mr. Peppermint's Auction House feeling a breeze and appreciating that the long hot summer was coming to an end. A sign reading "We Value your Heritage" stuck out at right angles above the door to the auction house. Opening the door, he entered an enormous warehouse stacked to the ceiling with shelves filled with plastic-wrapped furniture, old books, cartons and artwork. The limited area at the front of the floor-to-ceiling shelving boasted a vintage car. Mark looked around for a receptionist. No one was at the front desk, but there was a bell on the counter. He rang it.

A young man dressed in a blue coverall walked out of the dim recesses and said, "Are you here about a property auction?"

"I am, but one that occurred many years ago, in the 1960's. It was for the estate of a woman named Judith Iverson-Jones."

"Do you have an exact year?" the young man asked.

"Sorry, no," Mark said, regretting not asking Ms. Poitou more questions.

"You are going to have to see the man himself about that. I'll take you back to his office."

The guide led him through the labyrinth of aisles, turning right and then left before reaching the very back of the building where an interior office had been created. It was well-lit by fluorescent tube fixtures and positively shone against the dusky warehouse. Inside the office, a large bald man was talking on the phone. An old-fashioned barber pole had been placed to the right of the office door. Its red-and-white striped cylinder rotated slowly within a glass casing. It resembled a candy-cane, a peppermint one. Mark caught the association to Peppermint's Auction and grinned.

"Ed, can you talk to this guy?" The young man asked as he opened the office door.

Still on the phone, Mr. Peppermint waved them in. He had China-blue eyes, no eyebrows to speak of and an almost circular cherubic face. When he concluded the call, he looked up at the two men expectantly. "What's up?" he asked smiling broadly. He seemed so delighted to see them, they could have been best friends who hadn't seen each other in decades.

"Good morning. I assume you're Mr. Peppermint, I'm Mark Schneider and I'm hoping your firm handled the sale of the estate of Judith Iverson-Jones in the 1960's. I'm looking for an inventory," he said.

"Mr. Peppermint's my nickname in the business, but I'm plain Ed Kolk. Call me Ed. It's nice to meet you," he said and they shook hands. He gestured to the chair in front of his desk for Mark to be seated. "Judith Iverson-Jones, now that's a name that takes me way back to the days when this business first started up. Her estate sale was one of the first our firm handled. She was the famous artist's sister, I believe. You can leave, Joe," he said to Mark's escort who departed.

"I'm hoping your auction records go back that far. She died in the 1960's."

"Our digital records only go back twenty years, but I know where the old paper lists are."

"Was there ever a Mr. Peppermint?" Mark asked, curious about the name.

"No. My grandfather was a barber and collected barber poles. After he died, my Grandmother started this business. I was just a kid then. She called it Mr. Peppermint's Auction House because of the red and white pole which stood outside Grampa's barber shop. It reminds people of red and white candy canes, old-fashioned Christmases and is memorable. Now you follow me, young man, it's a bit of a tortuous trail."

Ed got up from his chair, hitched his pants up to his ample waist and set out through the maze at a rapid pace. He stopped beside a tall stack of shelving and pointed to the top shelf. It looked dusty up there, as if nothing had been disturbed for decades. Multiple boxes, normally used to store reams of paper, had been shoved in higgledy-piggledy under the eaves.

Mark's heart fell when he saw some fluttering house sparrows who had established their claim to the rafters.

"You'll have to climb up, I'm afraid. I don't do tall ladders anymore," Ed told him.

"Where is the ladder?" Mark asked.

"On the floor around that end," Ed said.

Mark went in the direction indicated and spotted a two-story extension ladder lying on the floor. He managed to wrestle it around the corner and set it up below the shelf containing the boxes Mr. Kolk had pointed out. Climbing to the top rung of the ladder, he saw five boxes labeled for the decade of the 1960's.

"Are the files in alpha order?" he called down.

"Unlikely," Ed said. "Sorry, man."

Mark took a deep breath. It was going to be a very long day.

PD PASCOE WAS NERVOUSLY AWAITING THE ARRIVAL of his new family member, grandson Liam. He was sitting in a booth at the Donut Den sipping black coffee when he saw a kid drive up and get off his cherry-red motorcycle. He was tall and near pencil-thin. PD had an older brother who died in a traffic accident when he was sixteen. Liam looked uncannily like him. He got up and walked over to the door to greet the T-shirted youth who was entering the restaurant.

"I'm PD," he said and held out his hand to shake. He waited, but the boy didn't extend his hand. He pulled back, thinking it was probably too soon for physical contact when Liam opened his arms wide, stepped closer and with a huge smile gave his grandfather a bear hug. A stunned and very happy PD hugged him right back.

A few minutes later they were both seated in the booth PD had claimed earlier. Liam ordered a full breakfast; four fried eggs, a mountain of hash browns, bacon, biscuits and coffee. PD smiled, remembering the days he could eat like that and not gain an ounce.

"While you're eating, why don't I start," PD said. Liam nodded. His mouth was full and he was shoveling down more.

"I want you to know that I was deeply in love with your grandmother, Amy. We had only known each other a few weeks, but it was love at first sight for me. If she would have had me, I would have married her right then. When I was shipped off to Viet Nam, I wrote her dozens of letters. All of them were returned. When I returned stateside, I found out she died in an accident. I never knew she was pregnant. Had I known, I would have been there for her and my son," PD said and the terrible regret he felt was apparent in his gravelly voice and moistened eyes.

"That's good to know. My mom and dad raised me until I was in Kindergarten. As you know, she divorced and remarried then. Her second husband, Carl, adopted me. Mom told me my dad gave up his parental rights. I didn't understand at the time, and I really missed him. Five years later, he contacted me and we resumed our relationship," Liam said. He was mopping yellow egg yolk from his plate with a biscuit.

"Did you know that your biological father had issues with depression?" PD asked.

"Yes, he told me and whenever he was in a particularly troubled space, he refused to see me. He told me his depression came in waves, pulling him down into darkness like a strong undertow. He could feel it coming on like a steam train, but said there was nothing he could do to stop it. Learning about his mental health issues helped me understand why he gave me up, and my mother's choice to divorce and remarry."

"While you're eating, I thought I'd tell you a little about my life at present. Do you know I work as a private investigator? I head an agency called Rosedale Investigations."

"I already found out you're a detective. It's on your agency's website. Why did you decide to become a cop?"

"I became a cop because of my grandfather. He encouraged me to go to the police academy. He was a prosecutor and became disheartened by the number of criminals that got off—due to mistakes made by cops. So, I hung around cop bars and rode with Nashville's finest for a year before I turned eighteen. After my stint in the Army, I applied to the police academy. I was hired by Nashville PD when I graduated. But, I don't want to talk the whole time about me. Tell me about yourself. What are you interested in?" PD asked.

"I'm working at a camera shop right now, but I was captain of the football team in high school and my dream would be to coach kids in sports."

"Most high school coaches are teachers, I understand. Is there anything you could teach if you went in that direction?"

"I'd have to go back to college and finish my degree. I only had a year of college before I quit. But if I did, I could probably coach after school and in the summers I'd have time to focus on my photography," he said, sounding excited with the idea. "I've already entered my photos in several contests. Even won a few."

"That's great. I'd like to see those photos sometime. Can you stay in town a day or two?" PD asked and Liam nodded. "There's not much going on at Rosedale Investigations at the moment—Sheriff Bradley recently pulled us off a case involving the theft of two valuable works of art. But I'd like you to see the office and meet my colleagues. I work with a Detective named Wayne Nichols, an Investigator named Dory Clarkson, and we have a young associate. Her name is Billy Jo Bradley," PD said.

He wondered briefly if Billy Jo was still recovering at Dory's House. If she was in the office, this reunion that was going so swimmingly, might be derailed by what he assumed would be her unwelcoming reaction to his grandson.

They finished eating, PD paid the bill and set off for Rosedale Investigations.

# THIRTY-TWO

IT TOOK MARK THREE HOURS TO FIND MR. PEPPERMINT'S inventory of Judith Iverson-Jones' estate. It had been a dusty business, and he was coughing and sneezing when he finally pulled the list from the box. He carried the paper down the ladder to the front of the business in order to have enough light to read the contents. The list had been typed, but the ribbon on the old typewriter had faded and the key for the letter "e" was inoperable. Another hour passed before Mark tossed the list down on the desk in disgust. The painting wasn't included in Judith's belongings that went into auction. He walked to the office at back of the building, hoping against hope that something might have occurred to Ed Kolk.

"Hi, Mark," Ed said cheerfully. "How goes the search?"

"I found the inventory. Judith Iverson-Jones died in 1965 and your firm's stamp was on the list of her possessions," Mark said.

"That's right. I remember the family discussing it," Ed said. "What about the painting?"

"It wasn't on the list," Mark said and sagged disconsolately into the chair in front of the auctioneer's desk.

"Tell me a little bit more about the artwork. I've got a faint memory scratching around in my brain."

"It's called *Wednesday's Child* and was painted in 1920. The subject is three little kids playing in the water of Lake Erie. The artist gave it to his sister shortly before taking his own life. He'd fallen in love with the mother of the children in the painting and she died," Mark said.

"I remember the story now. It was Wendy Brookover that he fell for, right?" Ed asked.

"That's right. As I said, the painting wasn't on the list. Do you have any thoughts about what could have become of it? I'm plumb out of ideas," Mark said.

"My grandmother would probably know," Ed said.

Mark did a quick calculation in his head and assumed Ed Kolk's grandmother would be close to a hundred years old. *Grandma's got to be either dying or struggling with dementia,* he thought, feeling despondency wash over him. His plan to surprise Billy Jo was turning out to be a bust.

"I'll just give her a call," Ed said and dialed the number. He pushed the button to put the call on speaker. "Grandma, it's Little Eddie calling. How are you doing today? Feeling okay? Good. I've got a question for you. There's a young man here who is looking for a painting that belonged to Judith Iverson-Jones."

"Was it *Wednesday's Child*?" the old lady's squeaky voice asked. Mark could hardly believe his ears. He nearly laughed aloud in amazement.

"Yes, that's the one. It wasn't included in the estate sale list," Ed said.

"Of course not. Miss Judith wouldn't ever have let it go to a stranger. She had a dear friend who just loved that painting. She only gave it to her because she had no other family."

"Do you remember her name by chance, Grandma?" Ed asked.

Mark swallowed, breathing unevenly.

"Some days, Eddie, although I am an *octogenarian,* I believe my memory is better than yours. Of course, I remember her name. It was Julia Brookover-Sands. She was distantly related to the Brookovers, but sensibly didn't believe in that curse nonsense."

"I don't suppose she's still living, is she?"

"Probably not, I seem to be the last woman standing, but we were friends and she told me when she passed that she was going to give the painting to her granddaughter. The granddaughter's alive and well, I believe," Grandmother Kolk said.

"And her name?" Ed was poised with his pencil above a small note pad. Mark could barely breathe.

"Tanya Sands is her name. I met her recently. She moved into one of the condos just down the street from me. The complex is called Pine Tree Hills. Now, Eddie, you promised you would come over and help me with some gardening. Remember? My rose beds need mulching, and the leaves have to be blown off my grass."

"I remember, Grandma. I'll come over Saturday morning. Thanks," he said and handed Mark the note with the scribbled name of the woman.

Clutching the piece of paper as if it were the Golden Fleece, Mark stood up, hugged a completely surprised Ed Kolk and left the estate sale building a very happy man.

TWO HOURS LATER HE HAD LOCATED TANYA SANDS, a chubby blonde woman, and confirmed she'd inherited *Wednesday's Child* from her grandmother. She'd invited him into her attractively furnished apartment and offered him a cup of tea. Sitting on her couch, while his hostess went back to the kitchen for sugar, he noticed there wasn't a single painting hanging on her walls.

"I understand your grandmother didn't believe in the bad luck associated with the painting," Mark said when Tanya returned.

"It was a bit more than bad luck. Grandma told me about the curse, but she said it was like the placebo effect. If you believed in the curse, it increased the chance of it striking you. She didn't believe in it and neither do I."

She went on to say she had adored the painting, but a decade after inheriting it lost her job and was out of work for a year. With enormous regret, she decided to put *Wednesday's Child* in a garage sale taking place in her neighborhood.

"I never would have sold it if my grandmother were still living, but she was gone by then and the painting was practically the only thing I had of value," she told him in a voice filled with infinite regret. "It's worth a lot more now, but that was a long time ago. I put a price of $10,000 on it. I assumed I'd get no takers at the price and stood nearby, ready to pull it from the sale if the wrong sort of person wanted it."

"Who did you sell it to?" Mark asked, praying his quest was almost over.

"A woman named Helen Chase Wilson walked by and fell instantly in love with the painting. She didn't even try to bargain, just went to the bank. She came back with a cashier's check."

"Even so, it must have been hard to let it go," Mark said.

"It was awful," she said shaking her head. "I told her about the curse, hoping it might make her change her mind. She said she didn't care one whit, the painting had called to her. I cried when she put it into her car and when she saw how sad I was, gave me her address and told me to visit any time I wanted to see *Wednesday's Child*. I did so, and we became good friends over the years. I only wish I could see the painting now," Tanya said wistfully. She had tears in her eyes. "I still dream about it."

"You don't have any other paintings in your house, I see," Mark said.

"Nothing else even came close," Tanya said, taking a deep shaky breath.

"I can tell you that Mrs. Chase Wilson kept *Wednesday's Child* until the very end of her life," Mark said, and added that Mrs. Georgia Walcott, a distant relative from Rosedale, Tennessee had inherited the work. The painting was deeply appreciated he said, leaving it at that. He didn't want to increase the pain the woman still felt or reveal that the painting had been stolen. It was interesting how powerfully the painting invariably connected with its owners.

*To elicit such remorse, even decades after losing the artwork, was indeed a kind of curse,* Mark thought.

BACK IN HIS CAR, MARK WROTE DOWN THE NAMES AND DATES of the painting's owners. Now all he had to do was enter the entire provenance on the computer and he could return home. It was getting late and he decided to spend one more night in the hotel before heading back to Rosedale. He called Sylvia, who picked up immediately.

"Hi Sylvia, it's Mark calling. I'm going back to Tennessee in the morning. I got lucky and have all the information Billy Jo needs to finish the provenance on *Wednesday's Child*."

"It's not much use to us when the painting itself is missing," Sylvia said bitterly.

"I know and I'm sorry. Do you think the police can retrieve it?"

"My grandmother does. I know they are working hard. However, they searched Henry Brookover's house without finding a thing. They are still patrolling his neighborhood, I believe," Sylvia said.

"When are you going back?"

"We leave tomorrow as well. We'll probably see you on the road."

"Travel safe," Mark said and said good-bye.

After typing the list of owners in date order in a document on his laptop, Mark put it on a flash drive, went downstairs to the business center of the hotel and printed it off. Returning to his room, he decided to call Billy Jo. She had left multiple messages for him which he had ignored, afraid if he heard her voice, he'd crack and reveal the surprise. She didn't answer and he didn't leave a message. It wasn't important. He'd see her tomorrow and could hardly wait to show her what he'd done.

BILLY JO CHECKED HER VOICEMAIL AT DORY'S HOUSE that night and recognized Mark's number. He hadn't left a message.

"Look at this, Dory. Mark called, but didn't even leave me a message," she said.

"You two just need to talk," Dory said. "Mark might have a perfectly good explanation."

"He'd better have. Just wish he'd told me what he was really up to," Billy Jo said.

"Okay, honey, just calm down. Try not to think about it. If we're going to make any progress on recovering the paintings, we need to brainstorm. I've got an idea," Dory said.

"I'll get myself back under control in a minute," Billy Jo picked up her water glass and took a sip. "Okay, go ahead."

"You mentioned that the man who took *Wednesday's Child* had curly hair. Are you sure of that?"

"Yes, I am. When the creep opened the lift gate on my car, the overhead light came on and I could see his curls."

"And when you met with Grampa Brookover Sr. in Erie, did he have curly hair?" Dory asked.

"No. In fact, he was almost completely bald," Billy Jo said.

"Then I think for a variety of reasons—his age, his license plate not matching and his baldness, we can eliminate him. Moving on to Henry Brookover, we know he has a water-tight alibi and I asked Sheriff Bradley about his hair. He asked Captain Schlachter who told him Brookover tried to disguise his baldness with a bad comb-over."

"Dory, you are absolutely brilliant. It must have been the teen-ager, Kyle Brookover, who stole Wednesday's Child," Billy Jo said.

"There's another reason this works. We know that the license plate of the car caught on CCTV belongs to Henry Brookover, but since Kyle is only 16, the father's name would naturally be listed as the owner of the vehicle."

"Of course. Makes perfect sense. So, our next step is to figure out where the kid stashed the paintings."

"We know they aren't at his parents' house because it's been thoroughly searched. Where do teen-agers put things they don't want their parents to find?" Dory asked.

"He could have hidden it at his grandfather's house, I suppose. It's a big old place with lots of places it could be hidden. But if it's there, it would mean that Grampa Brookover was party to the plan to steal the paintings. I have a hard time thinking of him as a criminal, but I guess it's possible."

"If I were sixteen years old and had stolen two large paintings, where would I hide them?"

"Unless he cut the paintings out of their frames, they are too large to fit in his school locker," Billy Jo said.

"Since he put *Wednesday's Child* in the trunk of his car the night he stole it, it could still be there. That's the first place we should look," Dory said.

"I just wish we knew his motive," Billy Jo said wistfully.

"It would be helpful, but at this point all I'm focused on is getting the paintings back. We already know his license plate number and where the family lives. If we drove to Erie tomorrow, we could follow Kyle, wait until he parks his car, and jimmy the trunk," Dory said with a grim smile.

"I just hope they haven't already been destroyed," Billy Jo said with a deep apprehensive note in her voice.

"Don't think about that now. I believe we have a plan of action. I'd like to tell PD and Wayne, but it would only lead to them trying to stop us. Now, you try not to be too sad about Mark tonight. I trust him."

"I'm off to bed," Billy Jo said, but she blinked and Dory could see her eyes brimmed with unshed tears.

Entering Dory's guest room, Billy Jo walked into the bathroom. Her earlier frustration with Mark's lack of contact had disappeared. She just felt sad and confused.

"Mark, where are you? Why haven't you returned my calls?" she asked the mirror as tears ran tumbled down her cheeks.

# THIRTY-THREE

PD PULLED INTO THE DRIVEWAY AT ROSEDALE INVESTIGATIONS with Liam on his motorcycle right behind him. They walked up the porch steps and into the building. The bell hanging from the front door tinkled and he called out, "Is anybody here?"

"I'm in the kitchen," Wayne answered.

"Wayne, I'd like to introduce you to Liam, my recently acquired grandson. Liam, meet Detective Wayne Nichols," PD said.

"Welcome to the family," Wayne said and shook hands with the young man.

"Is Billy Jo around?" PD asked, looking a bit nervously at her empty workstation.

"No. She's still at Dory's place. It's a good thing I came in today because we got several calls."

"I was just telling Liam that we have been stymied on the art theft case. Let me show him around and then we'll talk," PD said. He showed Liam his office, the conference room, and Wayne and Dory's joint offices, while explaining the types of cases the agency investigated.

"What do these stairs lead to?" Liam asked when the tour was complete.

"Remember I mentioned Billy Jo Bradley? She's the IT guru for the firm, and several years ago I offered her a job here, as well as the apartment upstairs. She's my . . . granddaughter," PD said, deciding not to try to explain the complex series of events that led to that memorable adoption.

"So, you have two grandkids now," Liam said.

"Pretty good for never getting married," PD said grinning.

Wayne said, "Ready to hear about the calls?"

"Yup," PD said.

"The first call was from Robby Willoughby," Wayne said.

"Right," he turned to Liam and said, "Willoughby's the attorney for a couple of dopey perps named Gaines and Pennington who inadvertently caused a woman's death. They went before the judge this morning. The purpose of the hearing was to find out whether they would be kept in jail until the trial, or would be released on their own recognizance," PD said.

"Wow. I didn't think private investigators dealt with killings," Liam said. His eyes were wide. He seemed impressed.

"It wasn't a murder case originally. It was a missing person's case. What usually happens in those situations is the missing person is initially reported to the sheriff. The sheriff investigates to see if there is any evidence of a crime. If there isn't, and the person is an adult, the sheriff's office usually turfs the case to us. If it's a child, obviously the cops pull out all the stops, but adults can live where they want to live. Anyway, the woman's nephew contacted us after the sheriff checked Mrs. Forester's credit card statements, phone records, recent movements and found no evidence of a crime or a kidnapping," PD said.

"Sadly, Mrs. Forester showed up later as the victim of a traffic accident that resulted in her death," Wayne said.

"Did Willoughby tell you what the judge decided?" PD asked Wayne.

"He did. You will be pleased to learn that Steve Pennington has been placed on house arrest. Turns out Willoughby managed to have Steve appointed as his mother's legal guardian just before the hearing. And the judge, after learning the circumstances, agreed to an ankle bracelet that keeps him at home and automatically reports his movements to the Nashville PD."

"That's fantastic," PD said grinning. "What about Topper?"

"He stays in jail until trial," Wayne said.

"That was to be expected since he was the one driving the car that hit her. You said there was another call?" PD asked.

"Yes, Sheriff Bradley's office called to say that Erie PD matched the tire marks left on the driveway at the History Society in Pennsylvania to Kyle Brookover's motorbike tires. They are bringing the kid in for an interview."

"Let me bring Liam up to date. When we were having breakfast, I mentioned that there we were investigating two stolen paintings. It's great to know that the tire marks outside the History Society match the motorcycle belonging to the young son of the Brookover family. That family has been associated with the artwork for a hundred years."

PD turned to Wayne saying, "We came to the same conclusion—that it had to have been the kid who stole the paintings, but kudos to the Erie, police force," he said.

"We had the culprit identified, but they came up with the evidence. I hope the kid will confess, but apparently the family has hired the most successful defense attorney in the area," Wayne said gloomily.

PD grimaced. "We need to tell Billy Jo and Dory. I think I'll run over there, introduce Liam, and bring them up to date."

"I already tried to call them and didn't get an answer. It makes me nervous that neither of them is answering their phone. I'll hold the fort and ask the sheriff when he's going to get an update on Kyle's interrogation," Wayne said.

"Let's go, Liam," PD said and the two of them departed.

ENTERING THE FLOWER POT NEIGHBORHOOD with its brightly painted cottage-style houses, PD pulled into the driveway of a home painted lavender with dark gray trim. Dory's house was a neat one-story with a separate garage. Her window boxes were filled with purple petunias and trailing lime green foliage that cascaded down the siding. Her front porch was decorated with pots of orange zinnias, tomato plants supported by cages, a tray of herbs and a dog-watering dish.

PD knocked on the door. Nobody answered and he was surprised not to hear Dory's dog bark. He bent down and fished a house key from under her purple painted watering can. Using the key, he opened the door—to total silence.

"Dory, Billy Jo?" he called, but nobody answered. "Let's check the back yard," he said and they walked through the house and out through the back door. "True," he called and heard a sharp bark.

"Is it a little white dog?" Liam asked, looking at the back porch of the house next door.

"Yes," PD said.

"I think the dog is on the back porch next door."

Responding to the dog's barking, a woman came out on her porch to ask what they wanted.

"Just looking for Dory and Billy Jo," PD said. "I see you have her dog."

"Yes, they were going to be out of town for a few days. I'm watching True until they get back."

"Did they say where they were headed?" PD asked.

"Pennsylvania," the woman said and PD felt his stomach muscles clench.

"How long ago did they leave?" he asked. His voice was strained.

"An hour ago."

After thanking the woman and walking back inside Dory's place, locking up and replacing her key under the purple watering can, PD said, "I'm going to call the sheriff. It's possible one of his deputies can stop them before they leave the county."

"Why do they need to be stopped?" Liam asked looking confused.

"Because they are going to be in big trouble if they make it out of Rose County," PD said, and his expression was grim.

Driving back to Rosedale Investigations, PD asked Liam if he could stick around for another day or so. Liam said he could. PD wanted to show the boy his cabin in the woods, and on a sadder note, discuss where they should bury Ryan's ashes.

DORY WAS WITHIN A MILE OF THE BOUNDARY between Rose and Davidson Counties when she heard the sound of a siren.

"We better stop," Billy Jo said.

"Not on your life," Dory said, grinning and raising her speed to eighty mph.

"Dory, you need to pull over. It's the sheriff's office car."

"Drat," Dory said slowing down and edging toward the ditch. Her car came to a stop just off the pavement, but she left the car running. The police car pulled up behind them. Dory gulped when she saw it was Sheriff Bradley himself behind the wheel. He looked very official as he got out of the car and walked up to their vehicle. Dory put her window down.

"Investigator Clarkson, you've led me quite the chase," the sheriff said. He wasn't smiling. "I could give you a ticket for speeding, but I doubt it would keep you from heading to Pennsylvania, which is where I *know* you're going. I'm seriously disappointed in you, Dory. You gave me your word that you wouldn't leave Rose County," he said.

Dory, looking hangdog, gave him a guilty grin. "Sir, I actually only promised that I wouldn't help Wayne or PD go after the artwork . . ." Her voice trailed off as she looked at the granite-hard expression on the sheriff's face.

"Save it, Clarkson. Just zip it. You are in so deep here, I don't want to hear another word."

"Can I please ask one little question," she asked, sounding pathetic. The sheriff looked at her, taking a deep breath. Taking his silence for assent, she asked, "Are you going to give me a ticket, sir?"

"You know, I think I will," the sheriff said and turned back to his vehicle.

Just as he reached the police car, Dory yanked her steering wheel to the left and pulled back onto the road, spraying pebbles everywhere and pushing her accelerator to the floor. The lawman leapt into his vehicle and turned on his siren.

Despite a wild speeding chase, Dory's car crossed the county border a mere twenty feet ahead of the sheriff. He swirled his car around, stopped and got out. He yelled after her, but knew he couldn't stop her beyond Rose County—unless she had committed a crime. The sheriff's jurisdiction ended at the county line, and he hadn't had time to write the ticket. The damn woman had tricked him.

# THIRTY-FOUR

B ILLY JO'S PHONE RANG AS SHE AND DORY ENTERED the ramp on the freeway. It was Wayne. She put the phone on speaker.

"You two women are in serious trouble. The sheriff was red-faced and furious when he stopped by here. Dory, you gave him your word that you wouldn't go to Pennsylvania," Wayne said.

"Hand me the phone," Dory said and Billy Jo did. "If you will recall, all I promised the sheriff was that I wouldn't go with *you or PD* to Pennsylvania," she said, handing the phone back to Billy Jo.

"It's me again," Billy Jo said. She heard Wayne take a deep breath. He was obviously trying to control his temper.

"There is going to be hell to pay when you two get back, but you may as well tell me your half-assed plan. PD is here with me," he said.

"We figured out it was the teenaged Kyle Brookover who stole *Wednesday's Child*," Billy Jo said.

"We came to the same conclusion and so did Erie PD. It looks like he stole *Children at the Lakeside* too. They matched the tire treads on the kid's motorcycle with those left outside the Society. One of his tires had a recent puncture and left a distinctive tread mark. I think we can leave it to them now. They already picked Kyle up and will be interrogating him today," Wayne said.

"Has he got a lawyer?" Dory asked.

"Did you hear that, guys?" Billy Jo asked. "Dory wants to know if Kyle has a lawyer."

"Unfortunately, he does and it's one of the best defense attorneys in the state," PD said.

"We want you to turn around and come back to Rosedale," Wayne said firmly.

"Yes, you need to come back. It's not going to be very hard to break a teenager in an interrogation," PD said.

"Give me the phone," Dory said. "We are not coming back until we have retrieved both paintings. I'm sure the cops will do their best but think about it, all they have is circumstantial evidence at this point. They have the kid's tire tread marks, but there could be a dozen motorcycles in that city with those tires," Dory said.

They could hear Wayne and PD talking. They were discussing the CCTV image of the license plate from the night of Billy Jo's assault. Then they heard Wayne's voice say, "If they get enough evidence from the interview, they will arrest the kid and can legally take a DNA swab. Once they provide that information to Sheriff Bradley, he will have forensics go over Billy Jo's car, and he'll be nailed," he said.

"That's true, Wayne, but with a cagey attorney, they won't get a word out of him, much less a DNA swab. Remember, he's a minor and whoever he selects as his 'responsible adult' will say it's too hard for him emotionally. I'm laying twenty to one that Kyle Brookover will be released before noon," Dory said.

"You may as well tell us your plan," Wayne said in an irritated voice.

"Billy Jo will tell you," Dory said, handing her back the phone.

"We are planning to do a stake-out near the Brookover house tonight. We think that *Wednesday's Child* is probably still in the trunk of Kyle's car. It's possible he cut *Children at the Lakeshore* out of its frame and that it's rolled up in the motorbike's top box behind the driver's seat. If we get the paintings, we will come right back," Billy Jo said.

"For Pete's sakes, both of you know that if you even *touch* the paintings, the evidence will be compromised. I'm going to call the sheriff and tell him you think the paintings are in the kid's trunk and in the motorcycle box. Hopefully, he can talk Captain Schlachter into applying for a warrant to search the car and the bike," PD said.

"If they can get a warrant, will you turn around?" Wayne asked.

"Do you think we should?" Billy Jo asked Dory who took the phone again.

"There's a rest stop on the freeway ahead of us about an hour. There's a restaurant there where we can stop and get a bite to eat. That will give Erie PD a bit of time to get a warrant. If they get the paintings, I promise I'll return," Dory said.

"Not that your promises are worth a damn anyway," Wayne yelled. And with that parting shot, he cut off the call.

AN HOUR LATER, DORY PULLED INTO THE FREEWAY REST STOP where the restaurant was located and parked the car. As they were getting out, Billy Jo spotted what she thought was Sylvia's car.

"I think that's the car Sylvia Walcott drives. I'm going to peek in," she said. She looked into the car's windows and spotted Sylvia's black trench coat and red cloche hat lying on the back seat. It was definitely her car and that meant she was going to have to tell them about *Wednesday's Child* being stolen. She felt her spirits droop. "Dory, it's her car. God, I dread having to tell them about the theft," she said gritting her teeth.

"Might as well get it over with. At least we can tell them that Erie PD has Kyle Brookover in custody."

They had walked into the restaurant and Dory was surveying the booths, looking for Sylvia and Mrs. Walcott, when she felt Billy Jo stiffen beside her.

"Look, Mark's in a booth at the back and he's hugging Sylvia Walcott!" Billy Jo said furiously. She stomped off toward them with Dory frantically trying to catch up.

"Hi, Billy Jo," Mark said as he pulled away from Sylvia. His face was lit with a huge dopey grin.

"What the hell is going on, Mark? Why were you hugging Sylvia?" Billy Jo asked with furious note in her voice. Mark's mouth was open. He looked like a gulping goldfish, but no sound emerged.

"Sylvia?" Billy Jo asked pointedly.

"The *reason* I was hugging Mark, was to thank him for this piece of amazing research," Sylvia said. She gestured to the provenance document that lay on the table.

At that moment, Mrs. Walcott walked up. "Hello, Billy Jo," she said in a pleasant tone of voice. "How did you end up here this morning?"

After casting a long reproachful glance at Billy Jo, Mark stood up and helped Mrs. Walcott into her seat.

"Billy Jo, would you and Mark perhaps like a little time to yourselves?" Dory asked. "Maybe you two should go outside . . ."

"No, we are going to settle this right here and now," Mark said. "I went to Pennsylvania to finish the provenance for *Wednesday's Child* as a gift for you, Billy Jo, because you were struggling with vertigo. I haven't been in touch because I wanted to give you the completed provenance as a surprise."

"Oh no," Billy Jo said and covered her mouth with her hands. She looked at the floor, her cheeks flushed with shame.

"I was showing it to Sylvia and she hugged me to say thanks just as you and Dory walked in," he said. He picked up the provenance document from the table and held it out to Billy Jo with a flourish.

She took it from his fingers tentatively, as if it were a snowflake that could melt at her touch.

"I believe you owe Mark an apology, Billy Jo. He has been working very hard to prepare you a lovely surprise," Dory said meeting Billy Jo's eyes.

"Oh, Mark," Billy Jo said and burst into tears.

"Close enough," he said, smiling and taking her in his arms.

When Billy Jo had finished crying and wiped her tears away, she turned to Sylvia and Mrs. Walcott. "This is the most humiliating day of my life because I have to tell you something even worse. *Wednesday's Child* was stolen on my watch."

"We already know it was stolen. Plus, we are aware that you stood up to the thief in a dramatic way and ended up in the hospital. We're very sorry our painting endangered your life," Mrs. Walcott said and patted her hand.

Billy Jo then apologized to Sylvia about being upset about the hug. She just shook her head and smiled.

AFTER MUCH AMUSEMENT AT THE MISUNDERSTANDINGS, Dory said, "Let me bring you all up to date. We know it was the teenaged son of Mr. Brookover who stole *Wednesday's Child*. It seems likely he took *Children at the Lakeshore* from the History Society as well. He's being questioned today by Erie PD."

"What evidence do they have?" Sylvia asked.

"There are two pieces of evidence implicating him. First, CCTV in Rosedale caught the number of a car's license plate the night of Billy Jo's assault, and the car is registered to the boy's father. Second, Erie PD found tire tracks at the History Society left by a motorbike the day of the theft. The tires match a bike belonging to Kyle Brookover," Dory said.

"It sounds like it's all sewn up. Isn't it?" Sylvia asked.

"No, because all that evidence is circumstantial. We have no hard proof it was Kyle who assaulted Billy Jo. The CCTV doesn't show *who* was driving the car and it could be someone we haven't even considered who switched license plates with the Brookover vehicle. And there could be a dozen motorcycles in the city with that particular brand of tires. All of which leads to why we were driving north and found you three driving south," Dory said with a smile. "I'm really pleased we did. My travelling companion has been *impossible* to live with until this little issue about Mark got cleared up."

"Dory always trusted that you had a good reason to be gone, Mark," Billy Jo said shamefacedly, blushing a bit.

"It's a good thing *somebody* did," he said with the grin and kissed his girl again.

Billy Jo sat down next to Mark in the booth. She was glowing and Mark had the dazed look of a man hopelessly in love. He could hardly take his eyes off her and kept touching her arm and her face. He seemed to need reassurance that she was there, wasn't upset any longer and as deep in love as he was.

"Are you going on to Pennsylvania, Dory?" Sylvia asked.

"We are, because we think we know where Kyle Brookover has stashed the paintings, which is most likely his car and his motorcycle."

"What is your plan if the paintings aren't where you think they are?"

"Then, I shall *lure the young jackal from his lair* and force him to confess—at gunpoint if necessary," Dory said. She looked so severe that Billy Jo shivered.

"A goose just walked over my grave," Mrs. Walcott said.

# THIRTY-FIVE

W HEN PD AND LIAM RETURNED TO THE OFFICE after their visit
to Dory's home, Wayne asked whether they wanted to go to the
sheriff's office with him. If the Erie police were able to get a search warrant for Kyle's car and motorcycle, Captain Schlachter would call Sheriff
Bradley as soon as they found the paintings. If the paintings were recovered, the sheriff would call Dory and Billy Jo and order them to return to
Rosedale. Wayne wanted to be on hand for the news.

"I'd like to go with you but we should have someone to answer calls
here," PD said.

"Would you like me to stay here and get the phones?" Liam asked.

"Good idea, thank you. Just take messages. We'll be back soon," PD
said.

Driving to the sheriff's office, PD kept thinking about what to do
with his son's ashes that still rested in the pressed-board box at his cabin.
Although it had been many years, he suddenly recalled hearing that
his paternal grandmother, who died before he was born, had lived in
Rosedale. She was probably buried in the Rosedale cemetery. He could
contact the cemetery caretaker, possibly purchase a funeral plot and
Ryan's ashes could be buried nearby.

". . . so anyway, PD, how about it?" Wayne asked.

"What? Sorry, Wayne, I didn't hear your question," PD said.

"I just asked you if you'd be my best man at the wedding," Wayne said.

"Well, thank you. Yes, it would be an honor. Lucy's a grand lady and
I'm happy for you. I suppose I have to wear a tux."

"Yup. After we talk to the sheriff, I'll take you by the tux shop and
they'll get your measurements. I already had mine taken and know what

tuxes Lucy wants us to wear. I just had a thought. We could use another usher for the wedding. Mark already volunteered and I'm sure Lucy would be pleased if Liam would help out."

"I'll ask him," PD said just as his phone rang. "You go ahead inside. It's Robby Willoughby, Pennington and Gaines' attorney calling."

Wayne nodded, got out of the car, and walked toward the office where he'd worked for twenty years. PD saw him straighten his shoulders, knowing how difficult it had been for him to turn in his badge and gun—to become a private investigator instead of a detective. He had struggled with the same issues himself when he left the Nashville PD.

"Hi, Robby," PD said as he pushed the button to answer the call.

"To my total surprise, I was just notified of a trial date for the case of Pennington and Gaines," Robby said.

"That *is* a surprise. Trial dates rarely come up that quickly. Before I forget, you did excellent work getting the judge let Steve remain at home with an ankle bracelet until the trial."

"Thanks, I was pleased with the outcome. Anyway, I think the reason for the rapid court date is that the judge is trying to clear out a bunch of cases. I've heard he and his wife are going on vacation. I have more good news. Topper's charge has been reduced to involuntary manslaughter. He never meant to kill Abigail which means that there is no basis for a conspiracy charge. That gives me the ammo I need to ask that the case against Steve Pennington be dropped altogether. The trial will be a month from today at 10:00 a.m."

"Thanks for your good work, Robby." Clicking off the call, PD dialed the number for Peter Gaines and left a message with the date of Topper's trial. He then went on to say he'd been concerned when he visited about Gaines' drinking. "I kicked my own habit with the help of AA and a sponsor. I'd be willing to be your sponsor if you want to tackle this. Call me when you want to talk. We can have coffee and you can decide if you're ready." Then he called the office. When Liam answered the phone, he asked if he'd help usher at Wayne's wedding. He agreed and PD told him to turn the answering machine on and gave him the address for the tux shop.

DORY AND BILLY JO WERE WALKING OUT TO THE PARKING LOT from the restaurant when Mark suggested they take his car. It was black, so it would be hard to see at night—the perfect vehicle for a stake-out. Billy Jo and Dory agreed.

"I'll drive," he said.

"I'll ride shotgun," Billy Jo said and cheerily hopped in.

Dory got into the back seat. "No calls missed from Wayne or PD," she told the couple after checking her phone.

"That means Erie PD hasn't gotten a warrant to search the kid's car or motorbike for the paintings," Billy Jo said.

"How were you planning to tackle this, Dory?" Mark asked.

"After being questioned by the police, I imagine the parents will make sure Kyle is permanently grounded. That will mean his car and motorcycle will be parked outside the house or in the garage. There are often side doors into garages and if I can get in and his car is there, I have this special tool her that will pop his trunk," Dory said.

"Dory, that's against the law!" Billy Jo said.

"True, but what they did by stealing the art was also against the law. All I'm trying to do is return the artwork to the rightful owners," Dory said self-righteously.

"That sounds a lot like the playground taunt where the kid says, *he started it*," Mark said, grinning. "You said if the paintings weren't in the car or the motorcycle, you were going to lure the jackal from his lair. How are you planning to do that?"

"I thought I might use Billy Jo here as a honey trap," Dory said.

"You what!" Mark asked

"Just kidding, Mark. If burgling the garage doesn't work, I did consider having her knock at the front door of the house and say she was a reporter."

"I could pretend to be a reporter, I guess," Billy Jo said. "I could ask to speak to Kyle saying I want to know his side of the story."

"Hmmm, they would probably just close the door in your face," Mark said.

"Well, maybe I could pretend to be an insurance investigator and say I'm there to follow up on a claim made by the Erie History Society. The Society obviously has insurance to mitigate risks associated with thefts," Dory said.

"Mrs. Poitou told me all the holdings of the History Society are insured by the Erie Insurance Company. I'm sure the *real* insurance investigators are already on the case or will be shortly. Did you know the FBI has a dedicated unit that investigates art theft? What if the History Society or Erie Insurance has already called in the FBI?" Mark asked, which effectively squelched Dory.

After some time in silence, watching the late summer trees turning color as they drove by Dory said, "I'm going to pray that Kyle's car is in the garage, so I don't have to break into the house."

"Entering an unlocked garage is one thing, but breaking and entering a house is quite another," Mark said solemnly and the trip proceeded in silence.

WHEN THEY REACHED THE SUBURBS ON THE OUTSKIRTS OF ERIE, Billy Jo was impressed with the beauty of the many late-summer hydrangeas that has been planted around the houses. It seemed everyone had chosen the same variety.

"Look you guys, aren't all those blue hydrangeas lovely? I read somewhere that they are the symbol of grace and beauty."

"Apparently, the florists in Erie will deliver cut flowers or whole plants to any customers in the city," Dory said. She paused before adding, "On my cell phone it says the blue ones represent apology."

"Guess I should get one for you, Mark," Billy Jo said and smiled sweetly at him.

"I better buy some for Sheriff Bradley, Wayne and PD. I'm going to owe them all apologies for not returning to Rosedale when they asked me to," Dory said, just as her phone rang. "It's Wayne," she said, quickly flipping the call to speaker.

"Did Erie PD get the search warrant?" she asked him.

"They did and did the search, but had no luck. The paintings weren't in the car or the motorcycle box. Something else came up in the conversation that I wanted you to know, Dory. Henry Brookover has a permit for a Ruger pistol, 9mm caliber. The Captain said if you stupidly ventured onto the Brookover property, he couldn't guarantee your safety. You need to come back to town right now, Dory, before you and Billy Jo get into worse trouble," he said.

Dory hesitated a moment before saying, "Sorry, Partner," and clicking off the call.

"What's our plan now?" Billy Jo asked quietly, but for the first time since she met Investigator Dory Clarkson—the woman didn't have a single word to say.

# THIRTY-SIX

SINCE THEY WEREN'T TRAVELLING ON A BUSINESS ACCOUNT, Dory suggested they check into a local motel. Mark got a room for himself and Billy Jo. Dory was in the adjacent room which had a small living area where they could brainstorm.

"Give me twenty minutes. Then we can meet and decide what to do next," Dory said.

Sitting at the table later, the dispirited trio acknowledged it was too dangerous to venture on to the Brookover property. Silence reigned for some time before Billy Jo asked if anyone else was hungry. Mark ordered a pizza and they sat around eating mechanically. They were discussing whether they might as well return home, when Dory's phone rang.

"I don't recognize the number," she said, turning the phone on speaker. "Hello?"

"Is this Investigator Clarkson?" It was a powerful male voice, accusative in tone.

"It is," she said, meekly.

"This is Captain Schlachter of the Erie PD," he said. Dory darted a quick look at her compatriots with an alarmed face. "As you know, we have been cooperating with Sheriff Ben Bradley on the theft of two paintings. I understand you are a former investigator from his office. You are in my city, and we need to talk," His voice sounded very official and Dory winced.

"Shall I come to the police post in the morning, sir?" she asked, her voice sounding high and nervous.

"Be here by 8:00 a.m.," he said and hung up the phone.

The three of them looked guiltily at each other. Dory being summoned by the police made them feel like three kids standing in front of a schoolhouse with a broken window, holding slingshots behind their backs and steadfastly maintaining their innocence.

LATER, AS DORY WAS GETTING READY FOR BED, she turned on the TV and watched the local news that carried the continuing story about the lost masterpieces by Iverson-Jones. No new leads had surfaced, the spokesperson said. Her phone rang as she pulled back the covers on the bed and Wayne's face appeared on the phone screen.

"Dory?" he asked. "Did Captain Schlachter reach you?"

"He did. I take it you were the one that sic'd him onto us," she said. "It's not fair, Wayne. You and PD are ganging up on me."

"Calm down. PD and I have been worried about you. I called Captain Schlachter and asked if he and his officers would keep an eye out."

"Oh, okay. Thanks, I guess," she said.

"Also, PD and I had some ideas about what Mark and Billy Jo could do—*without setting foot onto the Brookover property*. I asked if Mark could meet with Grampa Brookover. Captain Schlachter said he had no lawful reason to prevent such a conversation. As far as Billy Jo goes, it seems that Kyle has been a busy young Casanova. He has a serious girlfriend named Brittaney Walsh and she attends Erie High school. We have her phone number. She calls or texts her boyfriend multiple times per day. So, I was thinking that . . ."

"Billy Jo would be the perfect person to question her," Dory said. She was starting to perk up.

"Another thing, when Kyle was being questioned, the responsible adult he asked for wasn't his father, but his grandfather."

"Hmmm. Very interesting. That tells me the old guy knows where the paintings are. I'll make sure both Billy Jo and Mark know this," Dory said.

MARK CALLED GRAMPA BROOKOVER FIRST THING the next morning and offered to buy him breakfast. He seemed hesitant at first but then agreed and suggested a local spot. Mark said he and Billy Jo would join him there.

The Sunshine Café was an eatery with a menu posted above the counter at the back. Decorated in the colors of the 70's—known as hamburger colors—the chairs around tables and the benches at the booths were all ground-beef brown, the seats were ketchup red and the dishes were the bright yellow color of mustard. The wait staff wore aprons in pickle green with the logo of a rising sun.

When Mark and Billy Jo entered the building, they didn't spot Grampa Brookover, and got seated in a booth. A waitress approached and handed out the menus.

"Coffee?" she asked.

"Yes, thank you. Black," Mark said.

"I'd like a cappuccino," Billy Jo said. The waitress looked uncertain, but wrote it down and went back to the ordering counter.

Ten minutes later the front door opened, and Grampa Richard Brookover entered the restaurant. Although they had seen him only a short time ago, he looked older and was walking with a cane. At their prior meeting, he had been smartly dressed. This morning he looked rumpled, like he'd thrown on last night's clothes. Both Mark and Billy Jo stood up to greet the elderly gentleman.

"Thank you so much for meeting with us," Mark said and they shook hands. They led him over to the booth and signaled the waitress.

"Coffee?" she asked, as if on auto-program.

"Yes, with cream and sugar," Grampa Brookover said. "I wasn't sure I should come this morning. The police questioned my grandson yesterday. I was there for the interview."

"We know," Billy Jo said. "You don't need to be concerned about this conversation. The police have approved us talking to you."

"I really have nothing to say."

"How about we tell you what we think happened and give you some information that might help your grandson," Mark said.

"Okay," the old man said, brightening a bit. "I'm willing to hear anything that will help."

"We know your grandson, Kyle, is responsible for stealing both Jeremy Iverson-Jones paintings, and that the motive for the theft was the century-old curse," Billy Jo said, looking closely at Grampa Brookover. His eyes shifted. Her assumption had hit home. "Furthermore, we are here to tell you only one of the paintings is cursed."

"Only one?" he said, raising his washed-out blue eyes and looking at her with dawning interest. "Are you certain?"

"Yes. We have a local expert in the occult, a lawyer in Rosedale, and she informed us that only *Children at the Lakeshore* is cursed, and further that the curse pertains solely to the Brookover family, no one else." Billy

Jo paused. When Grampa Brookover said nothing, she continued, "We are only interested in retrieving the painting called *Wednesday's Child*. In fact, if you will return it, provided it's in perfect condition, I will retract the accusations of assault against your grandson," Billy Jo said.

Mark frowned and gave her an irritated look. "You were put into the hospital because of him."

"You were?" Grampa Brookover asked looking startled and Billy Jo nodded. "I'm terribly sorry about that. Are you okay now?" he asked, and Billy Jo said she was.

"I'm willing to let the assault go because I believe your grandson stole the paintings in an effort to protect someone in the family from the curse. Am I right?" she asked, and Mr. Brookover hesitated but then nodded slowly.

Mark was still frowning. He started to say something, but she waved his comment aside, wanting to hear Mr. Brookover's response.

"Does your expert think that the curse pertains to the Brookover name or only to the Brookover bloodline?" he asked.

"Now that's an interesting question. Who is it your grandson thinks might be injured by the curse?" Billy Jo asked. She was feeling her way to the most important part of the theft. Recalling the genealogy of the family, she ran through the generations mentally.

"Your grandson is facing a long hard stretch in prison for this theft. I'm certain the DA here in Erie will try him as an adult which could mean incarceration with the general population of murderers and rapists," he said.

Grampa Brookover grimaced.

Billy Jo gave Mark a blistering look. Grampa Brookover partially rose from his seat. He was about to leave.

"Please stay a bit longer, sir. Believe me I would never want an adolescent to face hard time in prison. Would it help you to know if the curse pertains to the name or the bloodline? I can text our attorney right now," Billy Jo said.

Grampa Brookover sat back down, and she quickly texted Evangeline Bon Temps saying she had an urgent question. Mark signaled the waitress and asked her to take their orders.

The men both ordered scrambled eggs and bacon. Billy Jo couldn't think about food. Her attention was totally focused on her cell phone and what Evangeline might say. Then she heard the sound of the incoming text.

"She just texted back. The curse pertains only to Brookover bloodline. Does that help you?" Billy Jo looked sweetly at the old man.

"It does," he was silent for a long time before adding, "So *Wednesday's Child* was never cursed, and the cursed painting only affects Brookovers in the bloodline. Right?" Billy Jo nodded. "I'm afraid getting the paintings back to you will be like stopping a speeding train, but come to my son's neighborhood tonight at ten o'clock. His back yard adjoins a city park. You can hide behind the fence that separates the properties. I may be able to stop the . . . burning," he said. And despite all of their questions, he would say nothing further, finished his breakfast hurriedly and left the restaurant.

As Mark gestured for the waitress, Billy Jo pondered why Grampa Brookover wanted to know if curse applied solely to the family bloodline. Who was it they thought the curse would strike? Was it Mrs. Brookover? She had married into the family and thus wasn't related by blood.

THE BELLS AT ERIE HIGH SCHOOL RANG AT 3 O'CLOCK, signaling the end of the school day. Mark parked his car on a side street, and they walked to the paved court in front of the school. Billy Jo had called Wayne earlier to ask if Brittaney Walsh owned a car and found that the family owned three vehicles. She got the license plate numbers for each and gave them to Mark. He left to check the parking lot.

Billy Jo had sent a text message to Brittaney Walsh earlier in the day saying she had information that would help her boyfriend avoid a prison sentence. She hadn't gotten an answer, but saw the notations indicating that her message had been delivered and read. Waiting outside the school, Billy Jo sent the girl a second text saying she was waiting in front of the school wearing ripped blue jeans, a red T-shirt and a dark brown leather jacket.

Teen-agers were already pouring out, jostling, laughing, hitting each other on the back and running toward the buses. Billy Jo looked intently at each girl, mentally comparing her image with the photo Wayne had sent, but many of the girls were in small groups and it was hard to see their faces as they turned to talk with friends. Ten minutes passed, and the majority of students had left the school. Only a few stragglers were still exiting the building. Billy Jo was afraid she'd missed Brittaney, but then a slender girl with brown hair in a swinging ponytail walked up.

"Are you Brittaney?" Billy Jo asked.

"Yes. And you are Billy Jo?" The girl looked nervous and Billy Jo tried to think of something to reassure her.

"Thank you so much for meeting me. We are here to help your boyfriend, Kyle. Is there a place where we could talk quietly? I have a friend named Mark who will be joining us. Okay?" When Mark walked up, Billy Jo introduced him.

A still-edgy Brittaney walked them to a wooded area on a small rise above the tennis courts. There were some benches there, mostly used by parents watching their children practice. All three of them took a seat.

"Thank you for talking with us, Brittaney. We are here to get your boyfriend out of this jam about the stolen paintings," Mark said.

Brittaney just looked at them in silence. She looked like she could dart off at any moment.

"We know he's guilty of the theft," Mark said, and color rose in Brittaney's cheeks. "Unless we can stop the destruction of the paintings, which we think is planned for tonight, your boyfriend will be spending decades in prison," Mark said. When he said the word "decades" Brittaney's eyes widened and her breathing quickened.

"Who are you and how are you involved in this?" she asked with a sudden fierce note in her voice.

"Sorry, we will give you a bit of background," Billy Jo said and explained their connection to *Wednesday's Child* and reiterated their intention to recover it. "Who does the family think the curse will strike?" she asked.

"It's Kyle's little sister, Jamie," Brittaney said, looking miserable. She gazed across the tennis courts. Dark clouds were building up in the west. It was going to rain soon. "The transfusions aren't working anymore." Her voice was so quiet it was nearly inaudible. "She already lost all her hair to the treatment for childhood leukemia. She doesn't have much time left." She scrubbed tears from her eyes.

Mark and Billy Jo nodded at each other. They had the motive now. By planning to destroy the paintings, Kyle Brookover was trying to save his little sister's life.

"I am so sorry, Brittaney. I respect what your boyfriend is trying to do, but we have made an important discovery. *Children at the Lakeside* is the *only* painting that is cursed. Our painting, *Wednesday's Child*, is not. We just want it back. Won't you please help us?" Billy Jo asked and took

Brittaney's cold little hand in hers. There was a long wait and the rain fell steadily leaving drops on their jackets and tinseling their hair.

"We can't take the chance of entering the Brookover property, but since it adjoins a city park, we can wait there. Could you bring us the painting tonight?" Mark asked.

Brittaney took a deep breath and said, "I'll try to talk some sense into Kyle. He's dead set on destroying both paintings, but if I can convince him that your painting's not cursed, it might make a dent. Not making any promises, but I'll try."

Although Billy Jo felt a stab of guilt about making little headway on recovering *Children at the Lakeshore*, she said, "Thank you, Brittaney. That's all we are asking."

But as she and Mark walked back to the car, Billy Jo felt confused. *Why had Grampa Brookover wanted to know if the curse only pertained to the bloodline? Now that they knew it was Kyle's sister, Jamie, the family was worried about, his question made no sense. But, if it wasn't relevant, why had he asked the question?* She shook her head.

BACK AT ROSSDALE INVESTIGATIONS, PD TOLD Wayne that he and Liam were going to bury Ryan's ashes in the Rosedale Cemetery that afternoon. He had managed to purchase a plot for Ryan near his grandmother's grave. Knowing it would be an emotional experience for his partner, Wayne offered to drive him to the cemetery. Liam said he'd follow them on his motorcycle, as he couldn't stay long after the burial.

It was a blustery day, overcast and cloudy. *Suitable weather for the task,* Wayne thought grimly. They drove through the large wrought-iron gates, parked the vehicles and walked toward the section of the cemetery where a coverall-clad attendant was waiting. PD carried the box containing his son's ashes. Wayne caught the faint scent of leaves burning. Someone had started a bonfire and he could see a rising tendril of the bitter blue smoke.

PD handed the box containing Ryan's ashes to the graveyard attendant who lowered it into a dark hole dug in the trimmed grass. A small pile of dirt rested near the hole next to a shovel. The attendant asked if anyone had something they wished to say about the person who died.

Liam nodded, pushed a button on his phone and a lovely soprano voice began to sing. "I look over Jordan and what do I see?" The words were the first segment of a hymn composed by unknown slaves and passed down through the generations called, "Swing Low Sweet Chariot." The fine music was a moving plaint in the soft gray air.

Then Liam raised his voice to join the singer's. His fine tenor mingled with the soprano's lilting voice backed by the deeper notes from the chorus of a gospel choir. PD's eyes filled with tears as his grandson sang his lovely farewell tribute to his deeply troubled father.

Afterwards, PD hugged his grandson and said he'd see him again soon. The young man threw his long legs over his cherry-red motorcycle and drove off. PD remained at the gravesite for a while, praying silently.

Wayne walked unseeing among the gravestones, summoning what scraps of memory remained of his early years living with his foster mother, Jocelyn. Like Abigail Forester, he also had failed a family member. Jocelyn had been found guilty of murdering her abusive husband and spent decades in prison before Wayne discovered she'd been denied legal representation at her trial. He got her released, but had avoided dealing with the issue for so long it was almost too late. She was dying of cancer by then. He wrenched his mind away from his shame and turned his thoughts to Dory and Billy Jo. They could be walking into danger. He had failed Jocelyn; he couldn't fail them. His promise to the sheriff would have to be broken. When PD joined him, they got in the vehicle and drove out through the tall iron gates of the cemetery.

"It's over and I'm at peace now about my son, but I have a question for you," PD said.

"What's that?"

"Are we going to let the women handle this situation in Pennsylvania all by themselves? We know Henry Brookover has a 9mm Ruger. If they even venture on to his property . . ."

"We promised the sheriff we wouldn't investigate beyond Rose County, but I have a feeling they are walking into danger. I think the sheriff would understand if we felt we needed to protect them. If we left right now . . ." Wayne said, but even before he finished his sentence, PD nodded, and they headed for the freeway.

# THIRTY-SEVEN

IT WAS A FEW MINUTES BEFORE TEN P.M. AND THE TEMPERATURE had fallen dramatically. The afternoon rain had moved off, leaving near-frozen droplets shining on the leaves. The wind rose, moving tree branches that scraped against each other and the icy water droplets vanished. A heavy cloud cover blanketed the moon, for which Dory and Billy Jo were grateful. They had taken their positions at the back of the city park adjoining the Brookover property. Mark, dressed in black, said he had found a better position from which to watch. He departed, a slim dark shadow.

Dory kept shifting around uneasily, patting her side. It dawned on Billy Jo, with a sinking sensation, that she was armed.

"Damn it, Dory, are you carrying?" she whispered.

"Yes," Dory said quietly.

"Promise me you won't *shoot* anyone. Kyle's girlfriend, Brittaney, said she would try to bring us *Wednesday's Child* before the fire starts. And Grampa Brookover may help, too. What did Captain Schlachter say when you talked to him?"

"He reiterated that we are not allowed to enter the Brookover property, but I was able to convince him that the paintings were at risk of being burned tonight and he agreed to place two of his officers near the house."

"Is there any way you can contact his officers if this situation gets out of control?" Billy Jo asked. She was trembling all over and felt very cold. The dark night, the chance that both paintings would soon be burned to ash, and Dory's carrying a gun had reduced her to a state close to panic. Her eyes looked huge in the moonlight and her breath came in short bursts.

"The Captain gave me a miniature shoulder microphone. It's hidden under my jacket. If things get dicey, I just have to say the word "now" and his officers will come," Dory said.

"All I ever wanted to do was save *Wednesday's Child*," Billy Jo said sadly.

"We can't leave without at least trying to retrieve *Children by the Lakeshore*," Dory told her firmly.

"I'm sorry. You're right," Billy Jo managed.

In the middle of the Brookover's back yard was a fire pit surrounded by white Adirondack chairs. Solar lights had been placed in a circle around the chairs increasing the ceremonial—almost sacrificial—aura of the place. Dory and Billy Jo met each other's eyes, knowing exactly where the paintings would be set ablaze.

Just then the sliding glass door on the basement walk-out level of the Brookover house opened and three people came outside. The bright rectangle of light from the room outlined Grampa Brookover, curly-headed Kyle and his pretty girlfriend, Brittaney. Each of the two young people carried a painting; the boy had a dark red gasoline can in his other hand.

They could hear Grampa Brookover's voice say, "I'll stay here with the paintings while you get your parents and little sister." His voice carried well in the cold damp air.

The two teens who carried the paintings to the fire pit leaned them against the white chairs. Kyle set the gasoline can down in the dew drenched grass. They walked back toward the house as the old guy took a seat. He gave a little grunt as he settled himself and in that moment, Billy Jo knew he wasn't going to bring them *Wednesday's Child*. Without a second's hesitation, she hopped the fence between the park and the Brookover property—taking off toward the old man on a dead run.

"Stop," Dory called out in a harsh whisper, but it was too late. Billy Jo dashed up from behind his chair and when he heard her, Grampa Brookover jumped as if he had been shot. His terrified face was clearly visible in the solar lights. He must have recognized her though, because shortly thereafter Dory saw Billy Jo pick up *Wednesday's Child*. The old man wasn't trying to stop her. It looked like she was going to get away with it, when the back door to the house slid open again and a large middle-aged man strode outside. Billy Jo came to a sudden stop, seemingly unable to move. She stood frozen with the painting in her hands, her dark silhouette perfectly illuminated by the solar lights encircling the white Adirondack chairs. Grampa Brookover half rose from his seat.

"What the hell is happening out here?" Henry Brookover asked as he walked quickly toward the fire pit. Dory's breath caught in her throat as the moon came out from under the clouds and she saw a sharp glint of metal in the man's right hand. He was carrying the Ruger pistol Wayne had warned her about. That gun could fire eight rounds before reloading.

Dory, breathing hard, climbed over the fence awkwardly and started toward Billy Jo. She was bent forward, holding her gun ahead of her in two determined hands. Her footprints shone in the wet grass behind her. Henry Brookover and Dory arrived on opposite sides of the illuminated circle at the same moment. The man raised his pistol in the air.

"Put your gun down," Dory said, in an authoritative tone. She was panting hard from the exertion. "All we want to do is talk about this. The cops are in your neighborhood. They can be on-site in seconds. If you fire that gun at me, you will be arrested."

"They are more likely to arrest you for trespassing. Leave now or I will shoot you," Henry Brookover said. He raised his gun and braced his arm, pointing the pistol directly at Dory's face. She pulled her Glock from its holster. Then a noise distracted him and he saw Billy Jo.

"Don't let the girl take the painting, Dad," he yelled, and Grampa Brookover grabbed for the frame of *Wednesday's Child*.

Things were moving too fast. From other times she worked in hostage situations, Dory knew she had to slow the situation down. Sometimes that required a risk. "I'm going to put my gun down on the grass now," she said. Slowly, never taking her eyes off the nervous armed man, she placed her Glock on the wet grass. "As you can see, I'm unarmed. All I want to do is talk."

At that moment, the sliding door to the house opened for a third time and a woman came outside. The wind was blowing hard and her hair was a wild bright tousle. She was pushing a wheelchair. The little girl seated in the chair was completely bald. Her small head shone in the moonlight. The chemo to treat her childhood leukemia had taken each lovely tress.

Kyle walked over to stand beside his father. He bent down, removing the lid from the spout of the gasoline can.

"Pour the gasoline on the firewood, Kyle," Henry Brookover said in a not-to-be-trifled with voice. He was still pointing his pistol at Dory. The boy poured some gasoline on the kindling, set the can back down and pulled a cigarette lighter from his pocket.

Henry glanced approvingly at his son.

The second he took his eyes off her, Dory whispered the word, "*Now*." If the microphone worked like they said it would, the cops should be on the Brookover property in minutes. She started edging around the circle toward Mr. Brookover, taking just a single step at a time.

"Mr. Brookover, I want you to know that I applaud your commitment to your daughter. If I were in your shoes, I would do anything to save her. But there are things you don't know . . . things about the curse," Dory said.

"Light the fire now!" Mr. Brookover yelled, and Kyle struck the flint on his lighter and lowered it to the kindling. The gasoline-fueled fire caught. It made a horrible whooshing sound, sending high flames and bright sparks into the night. "The curse of the Brookovers ends tonight! Jamie's life will be saved."

"Stop for just a moment," Dory pleaded. "You can avoid jail time if you just listen to me."

"Stay back," he warned her. "Come one step closer and I will shoot you."

"I don't think you want to go to prison for shooting an unarmed black woman," Dory said. At that moment, Henry Brookover fired again and again. Six ferocious explosions echoed in the cold dark night. Dory grabbed at her chest and screamed. Her body twisted awkwardly and she tumbled heavily to the ground.

Billy Jo dropped *Wednesday's Child* and ran. Reaching Dory, she knelt beside her in the cold dew-drenched grass. Dory's eyes were partly open. She wasn't fully conscious, but she was breathing. "Can you hear me? Are you okay?" she asked.

Dory took a huge gulping breath of air, coughed and said in a strangled voice, "Just got the wind knocked out of me. I'm wearing a bullet-proof vest. You don't have a vest and he's got two more rounds in that gun. Get out of here right now."

Billy Jo stood up. Her fury at the man who had shot Dory flooded through her bloodstream. She didn't care that the man could shoot again, that he had two more bullets, that she was unarmed. The red mist rose and pure rage took over. "You put that gun down right now!" she shouted. Anger made her invincible.

Grampa Brookover approached his son from the opposite side say-ing, "The girl is right, son. You don't need to burn her painting. Only one of the paintings is cursed. Hers isn't." He was holding *Wednesday's Child* in his hand.

Henry Brookover didn't seem to be listening, but looking at Jaime in the wheelchair, he started to shake and seeing the man's anguish about his child, Billy Jo was moved. Her voice was filled with compas-sion as she said, "I'm telling you the truth, sir. You can still save your daughter's life. Look over there. My colleague is getting up. She's okay and you don't want to shoot an unarmed girl now do you? I'm only a little older than Jamie," she said and met his eyes. "I don't think this is the kind of man you are. You're not a man who shoots women and young girls."

Her kind words must have made an impression. Henry Brookover was beginning to waver. Dory scrambled awkwardly to her feet. Out of the corner of her eye, she saw two uniformed police officers creeping from shrub to shrub in the backyard.

"There's no need for anyone else to get hurt here or for either of the paintings to be burned. The curse only applies to the Brookover blood-line. Now give me the pistol," Grampa Brookover said as he pried his son's sweaty fingers off the gun. The middle-aged man bent over and broke into harsh sobs.

At that moment, one of the police officers walked into the lighted circle and, meeting no resistance, handcuffed Henry Brookover behind his back. The second officer grabbed for teen-aged Kyle who took off—darting like a rabbit across the moonlit lawn. The officer dashed after him, caught him by the shoulder and pulled him down. He fought like a wildcat, biting, scratching and slugging. Ultimately, he was pushed down prone on his stomach. The officer handcuffed him behind his back and hauled him to his feet. Kyle stopped struggling, but was shaking convulsively.

The officers began leading the two men away. It seemed to be over, but then the mother grabbed *Wednesday's Child* from Grampa Brookover's hands and held it aloft. She was silhouetted against the firelight and her eyes caught the red glow of the blaze, making her look demonic. Her bright hair flared in the wind. She bared her teeth as she stepped toward the fire, raising the painting in the air directly above the flames.

"No, no, no!" Billy Jo shrieked just as her dark-clad cat burglar boy-friend came out of nowhere and tackled the woman. The mother lost her grip on the painting and for just a moment, it seemed suspended in space before it settled—catty-corner atop the flames.

Only the frame on the painting caught fire before Mark grabbed hold of it, burning his hands and screaming in pain. The child's mother grabbed the other side of the painting, trying desperately to wrestle it back into the fire. She and Mark grappled for the painting in the cold dark night.

IN THE MIDST OF THE CHAOS, BILLY JO FELT THE WORLD go completely quiet. The child had just seen her father and brother taken away by the officers. Her mother was screaming, but little Jamie was wide-eyed and completely silent. She must have been terrified for months about her illness and the curse. The strands of the case that had seemed like disconnected wisps all summer long came together in a sudden connection. There was only one thing that made sense in this situation. Billy Jo knelt by the wheelchair and asked, "Jamie, are you adopted?"

The little girl nodded.

"Then the doctors are going to save your life," Billy Jo said calmly. "The curse only applies to the Brookovers who are related by blood. It can't hurt you."

"For sure?" Jamie asked hopefully. Her eyes were wide.

"For sure," Billy Jo said and placed her hand gently on the child's little shoulder.

Mark dragged the still-struggling Brookover mother over to Billy Jo standing beside the wheelchair. "Mrs. Brookover, you haven't committed a single crime. Go back into the house with your daughter, now," he said firmly.

"Because she was adopted, the curse can't touch your daughter," Billy Jo said. She hoped she was getting through to the woman who turned toward her. "The curse only applies to the Brookover blood."

Calling to Kyle's teen-aged girlfriend, she said, "Brittaney, come here. I need your help. Please take Jamie back into the house." A weeping Brittaney stumbled forward, grabbed the handles of the wheelchair and started pushing it across the dark lawn.

"Mom," Jamie wailed and held up a tiny white hand.

"The curse can't hurt her? Are you certain?" Mrs. Brookover asked. She was still breathing hard, but seemed to have regained some level of control again.

"Yes, the curse only applies to the Brookover blood," Billy Jo said again.

The woman nodded, walked toward her child and took Jamie's small white hand in hers.

Billy Jo took a deep breath. It was over. She looked for *Wednesday's Child* and saw it lying on the grass. Grampa Brookover leaned down, picked it up and handed it to her.

"It's yours now," he said and smiled.

The frame of *Wednesday's Child* was still smoldering, and Billy Jo blew on it to extinguish the embers. On the other side of the fire pit, Dory picked up *Children by the Lakeshore*.

In the sudden quiet, they could hear a conversation between the cops and two dark-coated men who had just arrived. Wayne and PD walked into the lighted circle.

"You two are about a day late and a dollar short," Dory said sarcastically. "I'm feeling a bit dizzy," she said and grabbed for the back of an Adirondack chair to balance herself. "But, I am really, really relieved to see you two. Think I'll just take a seat for a moment." She sat down abruptly in a lawn chair.

Billy Jo looked at *Wednesday's Child* in the moonlight. The waves in the painting rolled, cresting over and over as the children played. *Children by the Lakeshore* would have to be returned to Mrs. Poitou at the History Society, but for that single moment in the century since it was painted, *Wednesday's Child* belonged to her alone. She had saved it. Pride rose in her soul.

Billy Jo turned toward PD. "It took me over a month, but the paintings case has finally been solved," she said with a pleased smile.

"Took longer than we both thought, but you stuck with it right to the end. I'm proud of you," he told her.

"I need my hand bandaged, but what should we do with the paintings now?" Mark asked. It seemed such a trivial question after the night they'd had, that Wayne and PD couldn't help but laugh.

# THIRTY-EIGHT

I T WAS A COOL EVENING IN SEPTEMBER, the Saturday of Labor Day
weekend, when the bride, her maid of honor, Channing, (Lucy's
nurse from the ER) and Billy Jo arrived at the Episcopal Church. The
two women in the bridal party, both dressed in green scrubs, carried
long white boxes tied with pink ribbons in which reposed their gowns.
Billy Jo wore a pale lavender dress with a handkerchief hem and an off-
the-shoulder neckline. Dory had insisted on her buying breast-lifting
tape. Although the tape was itchy and uncomfortable, Billy Jo could tell
it made her look good, especially in profile. Mark had whistled when
she appeared.

"Is it just you and your Maid of Honor in the wedding party?" she
asked Lucy as the three woman entered the church and walked down the
corridor to the changing room for brides.

"It's me, Wayne, PD, and Channing. Plus, Liam and Mark are ush-
ering," Lucy said as she opened a door with an arched top. They walked
into the oak-paneled room and set the white boxes down atop a glass-
topped credenza. Lucy untied the pink ribbon and removed the lid
of the box looking down at her wedding gown. As she and Channing
removed their scrubs, Billy Jo lifted Lucy's full-length ivory satin gown
and laid it across her outstretched arms. When the bride was ready,
she helped her step into the dress. Channing pulled her apricot satin
bridesmaid's gown on over her head and sat down in a chair to put on
her shoes.

"You look like a goddess," Billy Jo said, gazing at Lucy standing in
front of a large mirror. "Did you manage to get the Arboretum for the
reception?"

"We did. They closed everything down for us and set up an open bar, a dance floor, a string-trio which will be playing classical music and of course enough tables for our dinner guests," she said.

"The weather forecast is for high winds tonight. Hundreds of the yellow and red leaves of autumn will be swirling in the air. The only thing in the forest tonight will be the glowing transparent cube and you and Wayne dancing. It's going to be perfect," Billy Jo said.

"What are the guys doing?" Channing asked. Looking in the mirror, she pulled out a curling iron from her make-up bag and re-touched her bangs. They were, of course, dyed to match her apricot gown.

"Probably changing into their tuxes in the groom's room," Billy Jo said.

"When are the flowers arriving?"

"Shortly. The florist is bringing my bouquet and yours too, Channing. Then she is going to the groom's changing room to give Wayne, PD and the ushers their boutonnieres. Wayne insisted on having a smaller bouquet made, it's a little replica of mine. He didn't tell me why, just asked me to trust him," Lucy said, looking bemused.

At that moment, there was a crisp knock on the door and Billy Jo said, "Come in." The door opened and Dory (elegantly dressed in floor length rose velvet, her hair adorned with diamond hairclips) entered the room. Behind her was a terribly thin young woman wearing a tea-length peach gown. The florist followed them inside, juggling a stack of white boxes containing the flowers.

Lucy's eyes went wide, and she stepped forward, "Anne, my little sister, is it really you?" Sudden tears sprang into her eyes, and she wiped them away causing significant damage to her make-up.

Anne nodded, breathing shakily and the two sisters embraced, hugging each other and crying. Their reunion lasted quite a while. Lucy didn't seem capable of letting go of her sister. She kept touching her sister's face, her shoulders and holding her hands.

"How can this be? How did this happen?" she asked, brushing her eyes with her hands.

"Your husband-to-be found Anne about a month ago and she's been in rehab since. I called your bridal shop, and they made her dress," Dory said. "Pretty neat surprise, huh? Your sister's the one who gets the extra bouquet and I think you best reapply your make-up."

Lucy sat down breathlessly at the small, mirrored vanity. Her hands trembled as she reached for her make-up bag. "I'm so thrilled you are here, Anne. You can't imagine how much I've missed you. How are you feeling?" she asked.

"Clean as a whistle," Anne said, although her voice quavered a bit as she reached for the bouquet Wayne had ordered.

"You're staying with us from now on," Lucy said in a fierce voice. Her hair had originally been coiled in an elaborate twist at the back of her head, but some tendrils had escaped during their embrace.

She started pinning them back in place before Dory said, "Leave it as is. You look just perfect. Let me take a look at your mascara, though. It's run a little. Hold still and I'll reapply."

Lucy did so and then pulled on long ivory gloves that covered her arms to the elbow. Billy Jo handed her a bouquet of white Calla lilies and trailing fragrant stephanotis.

"Lower your head and I'll attach your veil," Dory said. A little satin band clipped the veil above Lucy's French twist. The veil's rolled edging just kissed her shoulders.

"Aren't you going to cover your face with the veil?" Dory asked.

"You're kidding right? That's for young virgin brides," Lucy grinned.

"Where are your shoes?"

"I have them," Billy Jo said and set the shoebox on the floor. "Do you want me to put them on for you? I don't want you to mess up your hair or flowers."

"I'll do it," Anne said and knelt at her lovely sister's feet, helping her into a pair of low-heeled satin slippers. Then she tilted her head. "I can hear the music starting," she said.

"Who's giving you away?" Billy Jo asked as the group left the room.

"Nobody. I'm giving myself to Wayne today," she said and followed her attendants down the stone-flagged hall with a joyous smile on her face.

WAYNE AND PD WERE IN THE GROOM'S DRESSING ROOM with Ryan and Liam. They were already in their tuxes and putting on their boutonnieres.

"What's happened to the paintings since the night they were recovered?" PD asked.

"Captain Schlachter took *Children at the Lakeside* to the Historical Society the morning after the raid. Billy Jo brought *Wednesday's Child* back here and as you know, she's since had it restored. It was damaged slightly from the fire, but it's now with Mrs. Walcott. Billy Jo and Mark presented her with the finished provenance," Wayne said.

"Are the Brookovers going to do jail time?" PD asked.

"Despite my heated protests, Billy Jo dropped all the charges against Kyle. When our tender-hearted compatriot learned the boy's motivation was to save his little sister's life, she decided not to pursue legal action. And since *Children at the Lakeshore* was returned undamaged to the History Society, Kyle only got 30 days in juvie," Wayne said.

"What about Kyle's father?" PD whispered. "Will he do time?"

"There's some question now as to whether it was the father or the grandfather who was the mastermind of the operation. It seems likely that it was Grampa Brookover who started it. The theft was probably his idea originally, but then Henry got on board full-bore. Currently they are both in custody," Wayne said.

"Henry Brookover better get his share of jail time. He shot Dory six times!" PD said.

"I'm sure he will. Let's go guys. I can hear the music starting," Wayne said.

"What about engaging that rehab nurse, Debbie, to stay with Lucy's sister while you're on your honeymoon? Did you get that done?" PD whispered, and Wayne nodded.

"Couple other things I forgot to tell you," Wayne said as he and PD walked down the side aisle toward the front of the church. "The charge against Topper Gaines was changed from voluntary to involuntary manslaughter. Since there's no basis for a conspiracy charge with involuntary manslaughter, Steve's case got tossed out and he was released. Then, because Camille knew Abigail planned to give some money to Steve and wanted to honor her wishes, she got her friend Hayley, who's a social worker, to get Steve's mother into a Medicaid-supported dementia facility. She also gave him the insurance money from Abigail's totaled vehicle and he bought a car with it. He has transportation now and can visit his mother."

AS THE GROOM AND HIS BEST MAN WALKED DOWN A SIDE AISLE of the church and reached their positions in front of the altar, the ushers, Liam and Mark, walked toward the back of the church and began seating the attendees. The Episcopal Reverend Father who was conducting the service entered the area. He was dressed in a full-length white cassock decorated with gold embroidery. Greeting both men, he double-checked the names of the bride and groom, asking if they should be referred to as Doctor and Detective.

"No. Today we are just Wayne and Lucy," the bridegroom said.

"But soon to be Mrs. & Mrs. Nichols," the Reverend said smiling. He turned back to a table behind the altar to check that the glass communion set, wine and bread were ready.

Wayne looked out at the church pews that were rapidly being filled with their guests. Sheriff Bradley and his wife Mae were seated on either side of Ben's young son, Matthew. Ben and Mae were each holding one of their twin babies in their laps. Deputy George and his wife were sitting with the Sheriff's office manager, Mrs. Coffin and Detective Rob. Mae's parents, Mr. and Mrs. December, were in the pew with Mae's sister, July and her family. Dory and her boyfriend Al, looking very spruce in white tie and tails, were seated together. Mark escorted Billy Jo to a pew. She was accompanied by the elderly William Dorne, the Docent from the Art Museum, elegantly attired in an old-fashioned tux. She had asked if he could attend the wedding so she could tell him the whole story of the paintings. Lucy had said it was fine.

Further back in the sanctuary, Wayne spotted Cara Summerfield. She was sitting with Tracey Dimond who held baby Danny in her lap. Wade Marston, Cara's high school sweetheart, was sitting with them. Cara's husband, Grant, trailed the group and slipped into their pew. Looking further back, Wayne saw Lexie Lovell and her young husband who were seated with her little brother, Teddy. Poppy Delaney and Gramma Lovell were there, too.

Wayne smiled to himself seeing all the people he knew and had come to love in Rosedale. When he was in law enforcement, he'd grown close to the employees who worked in the sheriff's office, but all the rest of the congregation were Rosedale Investigations clients he'd met due to his new job. He'd missed out on a family as a child, but now it seemed, he finally had one. And they were there to celebrate his wedding to Lucy. He blinked and brushed a hand across his eyelids, deeply moved.

After Mark seated late-comers Sylvia Walcott and her grandmother, and Liam escorted Camille Raines to her pew, (she waved at Wayne) the two young men walked to the back of the church.

The Reverend nodded and the organist began to play, "The Bridal Chorus," as Mark took the hand of a quaking Anne Ingram, placed it gallantly atop his bent arm and walked her slowly down the aisle toward the altar. Channing then took Liam's arm confidently, smiled up at him and followed them.

Lucy stood quite alone at the back of the long candle-lit aisle. The previous afternoon, she'd asked Wayne to spend the night with PD out at his cabin. He teased her about being superstitious, saying it was an old wives tale that bridegrooms weren't supposed to see their brides before they saw her dressed in her wedding gown, but he'd done as she wished. He hadn't seen her since.

Her long satin dress echoed the shape of the elegant Calla lilies she held in her gloved hands. The strapless gown was enhanced by a pearl necklace she had inherited from her mother and her grandmother's pear-drop pearl earrings. Her slender shoulders and lovely face rose above the tight satin bodice.

As the organist began the allegro segment of the music, the movement that signals the bride to begin her walk down the aisle, the congregation rose. Lucy adjusted her veil and raised one hand to touch a curl that had come forward to cup her glowing face.

Looking at her, Wayne felt a sudden intense thrill run through his entire body. Her long, slender neck, her face and coiled hair filled him with delight. He knew the shape of her body as well as he knew his knew his own; the set of her chin, the shine of her hair, her brilliant smile. A rush of memory brought him back to their first date.

*He remembered everything about that day, the time of the year, the leaves falling slowly in the still air, the sounds of kids playing, the tumble of the water over rocks in the glossy river and Lucy's happy smile.* The memory swept through his mind as he thought about all of the aspects of his bride's character—her competence as a physician, her gentleness with her elderly patients, her delight with children, coupled with her mostly-hidden but sweet vulnerabilities.

"I love you, sweetheart," he whispered and although she couldn't possibly have heard him, his bride raised her smiling face to his.

Then Lucy gathered a fold of her gown in her left hand, and holding her bouquet in her right hand, began to walk down the aisle. In the dim light of the candles in the church, her smile was the brightest thing in the world.

*I no longer have a wish list,* Wayne thought. *All my dreams are coming true today.*

L YNDA FARQUHAR IS THE CO-AUTHOR of the successful seven-book Mae December mystery series which she wrote with her daughter, Lisa (penname Lia Farrell). Those books feature Mae December who runs a dog-boarding kennel and solves mysteries with handsome sheriff Ben Bradley.

*In the Frame* is the third book in her current PI mystery series titled Rosedale Investigations which includes *The Blind Switch* and *The Blind Split*. She's also written a memoir entitled *The Cottonwoods*. All were written under penname Lyn Farrell.

Lyn is a master gardener and an art sleuth always on the lookout for her famous grandfather's paintings. She's also a "dog mom" for Dezi, a Cavalier Spaniel who is jealous of her cell phone and tries everything he can to distract her from writing. She has two biological daughters, six step-kids and twelve grandchildren. She is a retired professor emerita from Michigan State University where she worked for the College of Human Medicine for 35 years.

www.ingramcontent.com/pod-product-compliance
Lightning Source LLC
Chambersburg PA
CBHW011516100726
47899CB00010BD/3397

* 9 7 8 1 6 8 4 9 2 0 3 7 2 *